D0965817

Also by Jamel Brinkley

A Lucky Man

WITNESS

WITNESS

——STORIES——

Jamel Brinkley

Farrar, Straus and Giroux
New York

Farrar, Straus and Giroux
120 Broadway, New York 10271

Library of Congress Cataloging-in-Publication Data
Names: Brinkley, Jamel, author.
Title: Witness : stories / Jamel Brinkley.
Description: First edition. | New York : Farrar, Straus and Giroux, 2023.
Identifiers: LCCN 2023002252 | ISBN 9780374607036 (hardcover)
Subjects: LCGFT: Short stories.
Classification: LCC PS3602.R53183 W58 2023 | DDC 813/.6—
dc23/eng/20230123
LC record available at https://lccn.loc.gov/2023002252

Designed by Patrice Sheridan

Our books may be purchased in bulk for promotional, educational, or business
use. Please contact your local bookseller or the Macmillan Corporate and
Premium Sales Department at 1-800-221-7945, extension 5442, or by email at
MacmillanSpecialMarkets@macmillan.com.

www.fsgbooks.com
www.twitter.com/fsgbooks • www.facebook.com/fsgbooks

1   3   5   7   9   10   8   6   4   2

For my mother and my brother

I was to discover that the line which separates a witness from an actor is a very thin line indeed; nevertheless, the line is real.

—JAMES BALDWIN

The most important thing about people is the difficulty they have in identifying and acting upon what's right. The world is full of illusion. We carry nemesis inside us, but we are not excused.

—ROBERT STONE

Be an eyewitness to this too . . .

—GINA BERRIAULT

CONTENTS

WITNESS

BLESSED DELIVERANCE

Who knew that old-ass Headass was capable of even greater feats of headassery? Our little crew had become accustomed long ago to his foolishness, the imbecilic way he walked around Bed-Stuy with his lips swelled up, duh-duh, all the various look-at-me antics. We were bored with him, he was dull, the five of us paid him no mind. He might as well have been a fire hydrant. It had ceased to affect us when he interrupted our hangs in the park by barking out one of his nonsensical jokes, every punch line a non sequitur, or by unzipping his dusty jeans and pulling forth from the opening, inch by inch, the ashiness of his dick. By the time we started high school, his pratfalls on the basketball court while a couple of us tried to hoop were no longer amusing—we just dribbled around him and told him to go bother people his own age—and when he would dig in the trash for scraps of pizza or the half-eaten remains of fried-hard chicken wings, clowning wasn't worth it anymore, it was no longer worth the breath for one of us to say to another, *hey bitch, hey motherfucker, hey, peep it, there he goes again, you see him right, look, there he is, there goes your father.*

Truth be told, we didn't even know Headass was still around.

Word was he'd been framed for armed robbery or some such and was doing a bid. Others said he'd been tracked down by a very distant relative and was living in Louisiana among his people, if it's possible for near strangers to be your people. The most dubious and therefore most prevalent rumor contained some version of him plummeting tragically into the East River from the hive of coffin-size, bike chain–bound plywood shanties that sheltered the homeless just below the upper deck of the Manhattan Bridge. What had actually happened, we eventually found out, was a police raid of an abandoned building on Lefferts, a former hotel where Headass, among others, had been squatting. Nothing had changed about the status of the building—it hadn't been sold to some developer, at least not yet—but for whatever reason (we knew the reason) certain cruelties of the law were now being strictly enforced.

By the time senior year rolled around, however, it didn't really matter what had happened. The five of us weren't thinking about Headass at all. Other things were on our minds. College, for instance, was becoming an exciting prospect, even though we were each interested in different ones, and regardless of the fact that the guidance counselor had cast a puckered frown at our lists of schools, striking out the Harvards and Yales, and the Howards and Spelmans too, meanwhile telling us through his teeth that despite our grades and vocabularies and test scores we shouldn't get our hopes too high. Our parents all seemed to be going through it too, some losing their jobs, some suffering the very first symptoms of what would be fateful illnesses, some separating divorcing reuniting testing new loves, and though we hardly talked much to one another about these things in any explicit way, there was an awareness among us of a common feeling, disgust but also bafflement that we had so little sense of who our mothers and fathers really were, and that despite our trepidation about growing dull with age, life apparently would never stop with the excitement, leaping from the gray shadows of alleyways to jump you, knocking you to the ground and seriously kicking your ass. We weren't old yet, however. Far from it. Which meant that our bodies, unbeleaguered, and intact as far as we knew, weren't dull at all, they were fascinating. Which meant that we could do whatever, or whoever, we wanted with them, and who and what we wanted to do could change from week to week or day to day or moment to precious moment, in such a sudden and all-consuming way that each new desire was, in essence, the first ever desire, with every one prior to it cast instantly into a pitch-darkness as formless and empty as the original canvas of the earth. Much of what we (a few of us, at least) wanted to do was sex. For the most part we (a few of us) hooked up, or approached doing so, with those outside of our crew, but since the summer we (again, a few of us) had also developed new and irresistible interests in one another. The fact that we were friends, that we had grown up together since we were little boys and girls, didn't make these particular desires strange, it made them strong. Even though some awkwardness ensued, some friction, there had always been trust among us, you see, and with trust comes the gift of an ample room, or better yet, an open field, like the ones in the Botanic Garden or in Prospect Park where on warm days, when things seemed simpler, we used to lavish time, each field providing a volume of space in which to flex and stretch ourselves freely, to play, to recognize that our bodies absolutely belonged there, among all the other fragrant and colorful organisms surrounding us.

One afternoon, during a balmy October weekend, the five of us assembled for the first time since school had started up again and took a walk, something we used to do frequently. Call it an act of nostalgia. We stopped outside of the new store just across from the street of brownstones that always placed decently well in the annual Greenest Block in Brooklyn contest, and stood as one, peering in through the clouded windows. A sign said the store was open, but it truly looked nowhere near ready to welcome customers yet. Inside, among towers of large, haphazardly stacked boxes, were intricate arrangements of junk, each of which was surrounded by four low unattached grids of metal wire leaning precariously against one another. A strong sneeze could have sent them all clattering to the floor. Each arrangement contained variations of the same stuff: plastic bins, downy cushions, blankets, bowls, and pellets of dirt. A trio of white people—two women and a man, all wearing tan aprons—moved around slowly within the delicate maze of cardboard and metal, carrying large bags of what appeared to be desiccated grass. As they began to toss the twirling grasses here and there, everything around their feet twitched into motion, the entire floor leaped to life. The cushions weren't cushions at all, we saw, but living things, animals— rabbits—grouped inside of rickety makeshift cages.

We stared as we realized how many there were. About twenty cages, each housing two or three rabbits, so maybe fifty in total. Most of them were hopping around or furiously nibbling, but some settled quickly back into absolute stillness. There was something striking about these in particular, the assurance of their repose, the serene confidence that everything they wanted would eventually and inevitably arrive.

In response to all of this, we slipped easily into our trademark goofiness and banter. Riffing on our old script felt like a form of solace. When Walidah, incredulous, expressed her opinion that the animals were too large to be rabbits, that the somber droop of their ears meant they were something else entirely, Roni told her to shut up. "We all know your ideas about the world still come from cartoons," she teased.

"They *are* plump, whatever they are," Antonio said, putting his arm around Cherise. He eyed her with the overwrought expression of hunger he had developed during the summer. "You should find out what they eat," he added. "We can put you on their diet."

Cherise, who had always been self-conscious about how narrow she was, watched with a slight frown as the animals ate. She seemed uncertain whether Antonio's words amounted to criticism or encouragement. "Guess they do look happy," she said finally, and then slipped the pleasing fat of her bottom lip into her mouth to suppress a smile.

"They are indeed rabbits," a man's voice announced, "but actually there are guinea pigs and chinchillas too." The voice sounded peculiar, like something massive pressed densely small, both loud and restrained at the same time. The white man with the apron was peeking his head out of the open door. "Come on in, kids," he said. "Let's introduce you to them."

Shrugs. When we followed him inside, the two women were cheesing maniacally at us, and for reasons we couldn't discern they kept nodding their heads. As we separated and looked around, the man explained that the place was actually a rescue, and then he began rattling off the names of the animals ("That's Oreo, that's Marshmallow, Sasha's over there, and that's Balthazar . . ."), but he spoke too quickly for us to keep up. He had a pronounced underbite and a highly suspect chin beard that might as well have been a glued-on strap of mangled pelt. His face and skull

were captivating, to be honest, but it was in our best interest—in
the best interest of *us*—to focus on what made his features hilar-
ious, to imagine his onrush of words as, say, a waterfall flowing
over the jagged precipice of his bottom teeth. After naming all
the animals for us, he mentioned, almost as an afterthought, that
his own name was Cyan. He neglected to introduce the women.

"They eat grass? Dogs shit on grass."

"Technically it's hay," Cyan said, pointing a finger upward.
"But they can't subsist on hay alone. It doesn't provide all the
nutrients." He then offered us an opportunity to feed the animals
some lettuce.

"So you can really get thick like that by eating lettuce and
hay?" Antonio asked.

Cyan gave a heh-heh laugh, false and uncomprehending but
good-natured, and then called toward the back of the store for
someone named Reginald. In a moment, this Reginald walked
in, except Reginald wasn't Reginald. Reginald was Headass. He
stood there, looking even taller and lankier than usual, though
a bit more youthful, with a semblance of a healthful glow. He
was also wearing an apron, and against his chest he held a clear
plastic bin filled with wet, brilliantly green leaves. His pants
and kicks were clean—well, clean for Headass, anyway, meaning they weren't filthy—and his matted hair was parted oddly on
one side. The part itself, which revealed his pale skin in a broad
strip, glistened with some kind of grease. We gaped at the sight
of him, he yawned at the sight of us. Then, in a snap, a crooked
grin stretched the left side of his face, like the banner of some new
country tautened by a sudden wind.

"Y'all hired Headass?"

Cyan pursed his lips and then gave his heh-heh laugh again.
"It was always our intention to engage people from the commu-

nity," he said in his funny voice, with enough brightness to blind us. "Reginald here was the perfect person to help us out."

The sound of that name had the effect of a magic word, activating Headass again. He stepped forward, but instead of distributing the food among the animals in any way that would have made sense, he set the bin down on the floor, grabbed a handful of the greens, and stepped over the tremulous perimeter of a cage, entering it with two easy strides. He lowered himself until he was sitting cross-legged with the cage's three rabbits, who, after a moment of wariness and agitation, reacted surprisingly well to him. Headass slowly lifted one of the rabbits, a portly auburn-colored one with flecks of black, and set it onto his lap. With evident pleasure, he began feeding it the edge of a leaf of lettuce.

"It appears that Reginald and dear Chicory have made a love connection," one of the women said.

Headass was imitating the rabbit now, with rapid, pulsing movements of his nostrils and mouth, as though he were eating too. His fingers slowly stroked the air just above the fur, never touching it. The gesture made you feel the animal's heat. When one of us started laughing, a moment passed before we could all figure out why, but when we did, the laughter became reassuringly infectious. The pellets scattered there in the cage with Headass—scattered in all the cages—weren't made of dirt. He was sitting gleefully in a pile of the rabbits' droppings.

We left the rescue and walked shoulder to shoulder to shoulder and so on, incandescent with jokes and laughter, five lit bulbs on a string. It may be ridiculous, but seeing Headass, genuinely taking notice of him, really witnessing him rooted there in that playpen of dung, seemed to bind us in a way we hadn't been bound in months, at least since the end of junior year. We walked and without speaking we agreed on which direction to turn on which corner, we came to an immediate consensus about where (the pizza parlor) and what (a pepperoni pie) to eat for lunch, and as we ate we expressed one enthusiastic opinion about the new album everyone was talking about, which had been released without warning at midnight. We quickly agreed on which song was the best, possessed of the most fire, and after lunch when we played it aloud on one of our phones, we stopped walking and claimed a little pocket of Marcus Garvey Boulevard, making it gorgeous as hell with our singing and our shouts and the perfectly synchronized dance steps we devised right there on the spot. Even the two of us boys who had grown increasingly shy about that kind of display, especially in the last few months, were completely into it for a minute, gleefully popping our butts along with the girls until it became suddenly too awkward, and when our little performance was done we all leaned into one another and cackled in a spirit of gratified exhaustion, without a trace of cynicism, irony, or embarrassment.

As we resumed our walk, one word seemed to come to all of our minds at the same time: *Reginald*. Why were those white people referring to Headass as *Reginald*? we screamed, which sent us into more fits of laughter. And then—again, all at the same time, it seemed—we invoked Toby for Kunta Kinte, SoHa for lower Harlem, DoBro for downtown Brooklyn, all the examples we could think of that illustrated the ways they claimed the right to name and rename whoever and whatever they pleased. We agreed without debate, without an utterance of doubt, that Reginald could not under any circumstance be his government name, but we did not speak of the fact that we too had named him—we had done it ourselves, or our uncles and older cousins who had grown up with him and gone to school with him and were also, sometimes, a part of *us*, had done it—and so it was easy to avoid that particular complication since he had always, as far as we knew, answered to Headass, and, after all, it was a different thing entirely to speak of what we, whoever *we* comprised at a given moment, decided to call ourselves. We avoided the complications of that too, the idea that Headass was also, sometimes, in a peculiar way, a part of us, because in that moment all that really mattered was the beautiful hazy dream of we-the-five restored to harmony.

But then, when it was suggested that we go over to Antonio's apartment, which is exactly what we would have done before, back when things were normal, he hesitated. In the span of a silence like that you could hear the sound of the breeze plucking, stalk from stem, a yellowing leaf away from its branch. Antonio looked down at his hands as they gripped the sides of his jeans. He told us we shouldn't come over today. It was messy. Things were still weird at home. He said lately his mother had been feeling even worse, and he started to say something more, anxious to offer additional excuses, as if he needed them, but instead let it trail away. "Yeah," he added uselessly after another heavy pause, rubbing the splendid bulb of his nose. Cherise cleared her throat and said she had to go too. Then the two of them said hasty goodbyes and walked off as if holding hands, going in a direction where neither of them lived.

"So," Roni said to Walidah, "what was it you were gonna show me? One of your cartoons . . . ?"

Walidah nodded, her eyes shrouded beneath their lids. "Yeah, that's right . . ." Then the girls, who had developed a new and hard-won intimacy, left together too, a careful distance maintained between them, together but apart, and just like that, with inexplicable ease, our reunion, our alliance, was again, however lovely the bond, broken.

Two weeks later, though, our dormant group text lit up with a message from Cherise, telling us all to come by the animal rescue again to see what was happening. She was already there, a second message said. So was Antonio.

Walidah and Roni were the last to arrive, but they made it in time to see some of the spectacle. Headass was stalking back and forth outside of the rescue, wearing a bulky costume. The intention was probably to attract people who were, or could be, lovers of the Leporidae, but he was playing it all wrong. From where we stood along the curb, the fur was convincing enough, smooth as though someone had carefully combed down all the fibers, and aside from a smudge here and there it gleamed a solid silvery-white. But below at the feet and up by his hands, which were raised, fingers rigid and spread as in the posture of a demon giving chase, the color graded into the hideous fleshy pink of skinned game. As Headass moved his feet and hands mechanically up and down, he seemed to carve the air with the costume's pointed yellow nails. For some reason, he was also wearing a stiff plaid vest, which jumped on his body like an ill-fitting shell. But the strangest thing, the thing we couldn't stop whispering to one another about, was the way Headass's face peeked out of the creature's open mouth, as though he was being swallowed or bizarrely birthed. The costume gave him a frightening crown of sharp buckteeth that were the same awful yellow as the nails. Up top, the eyes were garish rings shaded pale blue and salmon. If it wasn't for the ears, which were as languid as those of the real rabbits inside, it would have been reasonable to think Headass was pretending to be a rat with albinism.

Behind him, Cyan stood in the doorway of the rescue, leaning within the threshold and chewing loose fistfuls of peanuts. He must have heard us asking one another about the sound Headass was making. "Little-known fact," he called, "but rabbits have the ability to purr, just like our feline friends. It's much cooler though. You know why? Rabbits do it with their teeth."

Headass wasn't doing anything with his teeth, and the noise he was making didn't sound one bit like purring. It was more like a drawn-out, melancholic moan. He was hardly stopping long enough to breathe.

Cyan wiped his hands on the front of his pants and came over to us. Specks of papery brown skin from the peanuts had become stuck in his beard. "This was Reginald's idea, you know. So we let him choose whichever costume he wanted. It's maybe not what we would have gone with but there's definitely something to it."

Maybe Cyan wasn't all bad, for an invader.

"It was cool of y'all to hire a homeless dude."

Cyan seemed taken aback by the comment. He said, "Well, technically . . . he's a volunteer."

"Wait, you don't pay him?"

He listened to Headass moan and nodded regretfully. "If only we could."

"Do you feed him?"

Cyan balked. "*Feed* him? Well, there's always lots of left-over romaine, not to mention—let's see—bok choy, watercress, kohlrabi . . ."

Maybe not.

We watched Headass stop, spin on his heels, and start again in the opposite direction.

"There haven't been as many adoptions as we might have liked," Cyan said to us, changing the subject. The two white women who worked there were the only people inside. "Not a single one so far, in fact. But folks seem curious, that's for sure. They slow down when they pass by. They peek in. Building interest is always step numero uno."

"You can't really expect there to be a lot of rabbit adoptions in the hood," Roni said, with a razor in her voice.

"Why not?" he replied. "History tells us that rabbits appeal to people from all walks of life. Certain rodents too, studies have shown. Besides, this isn't really *the hood* anymore, is it?"

Cyan was right about that last part, though he spoke as if he had absolutely nothing to do with it. His comment made us stare first at him and then around at the drivers parading by in their eco-friendly cars and the cyclists who actually wore helmets and biking shorts, pumping their nickel-bright knees, assaulting us with their show of law-abiding goodness and safety. But all of that was oppressively dull—we knew it too well—so we didn't comment on it. What was interesting to us were the people and places that were gone. When Cyan went back inside, and as Headass continued his marching and moaning, we found ourselves scrutinizing the rescue itself. What exactly *had* been there before? Any one of us could have gone in and asked Cyan or the rescue ladies about it, but none of us wanted to. There was nothing appealing about the possibility of acquiring the information from them, from some records they had dug up as part of a business plan. It would have been that merely. Information, data. Looking it up with a phone would have felt similarly cheap. The thing was to remember, to use our minds and their keen branching tails, to recollect via the spark of the scintillating connections we could make on our own. But once the topic was broached and we discussed it among ourselves, no one could conjure up the answer. For a long time, before the opening of the rescue, the space had been empty, with a sign in the clouded window that read COMMERCIAL SPACE FOR RENT.

All of a sudden Headass pivoted and walked briskly toward us, as if all his back and forth had just been a way of winding himself up. He stood directly in front of us and peered down into our faces, fully inhabiting his bestial role. The teeth of his costume pressed pinholes into his worried brow.

"What's up, Headass."

He shook his head.

We glanced at one another. He had always answered to Headass. After a second refusal, it seemed worth it to try the only other thing we knew: "What's up . . . *Reginald*?"

He shook his head again, even more emphatically this time. Then he took a deep breath through his mouth, pressed his lips together, and moaned. We all laughed, but it was thin laughter, tentative, nervous. He took another deep breath and then moaned again, with even more force and resonance. We didn't hide our bewilderment. Headass could talk, we knew, but he was refusing to use his words. He did it again: deep breath, tensed mouth, long plangent moan. Then he pointed one of his frightful nails at us. He nodded briskly and the ears of the monstrous rabbit flopped. The sickly eyes on top of his head seemed to look down at us too, his multiplied vision holding us in place. Then, one by one, we came to understand. What started with the incredulous stares of the other four became, gradually, through a process of reluctant submission, our unanimous choral moaning in response to his call. He moaned and then we moaned—Antonio did it so loudly you could feel the vibrations of his chest—and for a while it went on like that, antiphonal, until finally all six of us made the sound together.

After that, satisfied perhaps, Headass turned and went into the rescue. Before we left, we took another look through the window. The towers of cardboard boxes were gone, but the rest of the interior looked as it had before, just as perfunctory and helter-skelter, still unsure of its purpose. Headass stood at the same cage he'd sat in two weeks ago, the claws of his costume curled into the gaps between the metal, staring raptly at one of the creatures within.

We didn't get very far together after that. It seemed to take a colossal effort just to make it to the corner. What we (some of us) had felt coerced into doing by Headass had cast us into a net from which we (some of us) were eager to escape. The excuses all came so quickly. Antonio's mother was still sick, he said; Cherise had chores to do, she said; Walidah and Roni wanted to put in some extra time studying for an upcoming exam, they said. And then they all left, and the street that would one day win the honor of Greenest Block in Brooklyn was, at least for the immediate interval, also without question the loneliest.

The next time we went to the rescue was about a week later, on a day that could have been special but, other than being the chilliest of the season thus far, was depressingly ordinary. After the interminable hours at school we simply found ourselves going in the same direction at the same time, so we just gave in to the accident of being together. It would have taken too much effort and consideration to do otherwise. The conversation, if you could call it that, was halting and slight, much more feeble than small talk because we were the ones having it, because it was us. Our hands stayed balled in our pockets, our chins tucked into our scarves.

"It's brick outside today."

"It was brick *inside* today. How you gonna make kids come to a school with no heat."

"Write this long-ass essay, but you gotta do it with mittens on."

"It's fucked-up."

"Yeah, it's fucked-up."

"It's brick as hell out today."

"For real."

Cyan was in front of the rescue, sweeping abscised leaves into a pile. He greeted us warily, without a word, barely raising his hand to wave. His mouth dropped open, and the heft of his jaw turned this expression into a shock of surrender. There was none of the outsize enthusiasm with which he had previously announced himself. For a while we watched him work, listened to the swish of the broom and the rasp of the leaves.

Finally, it was asked: "Where's Headass?"

Cyan stopped sweeping. "Why didn't anyone tell us he was troubled?"

"Troubled?"

He lowered his voice. "Mentally disturbed."

"Wasn't it obvious?"

"We thought he was a little eccentric, quirky maybe, but generally fine, totally within the range of our expectations. You guys could have said something."

"Why do you think we'd do that? Why would we tell you anything about him?"

"Is there a good reason why you wouldn't?" Cyan said. Since

none of us could muster a response, he continued: "Anyway, it doesn't matter. Please don't mention him to us anymore. From now on, consider Reginald persona non grata here."

"But what happened?"

His face became strained and then relaxed into a grimace. "There are things called zoning ordinances, okay? There are *rules* that have to be followed. And your friend, he put us in violation. If we hadn't found him by chance the other night, there could have been serious consequences. He was staying here, sleeping here behind our backs, agitating the animals when we weren't around. He totally and completely abused our kindness."

"Where is he now?"

Cyan looked genuinely aggrieved by the question. "Who knows! And more importantly, who cares?" he said. "As long as it's far away from us." Then he began to sweep again, fitfully, extending the bristles uncomfortably close to our feet. None of us moved though. We just stared holes into his head. But even this communal act of aggression couldn't hold us together for very long.

"Man, fuck this place," Antonio said. "We out."

"Wait, we don't have to let this mess up our day. What should we get into now? Where should we go? Don't you guys want to do anything?"

His eyes got dull. He exhaled loudly. "The day was already messed up. It's been a dumpster fire since the second the fucking alarm went off," he said. "There's not a damn thing we can do about it. There's nowhere to go but home."

And there they were again all of a sudden, the realigned configurations unmistakably visible. Antonio and Cherise, Walidah and Roni, the lovers and the confidants, each pact sealed with palpably forced devotion. Cyan watched as we separated, two by two by one, and went every which way. At one point he yelled something to us that had the striking ring of optimism, but we weren't close enough to hear it.

Later on, at home, Dad was waiting. "Happy birthday," he said. He held a brown paper bag, crisply folded and sealed with a square of tape. It was obvious that there was a book inside. "Couldn't get you what you really wanted this year—you know how it is—but next year, next year . . . Anyway, it may not look like much but betcha you'll like it."

"Thanks, Dad."

"'Preciate you, son," he said. "Lord knows what it would be like without you. Without the rock. Sturdy and steady, no matter what."

"Dad, you know that place that opened up a little while ago, the animal rescue?"

"Animal rescue?"

"Yeah, with all the rabbits and stuff."

"Oh, that place. Talk about a sore thumb. What of it?"

"Do you remember what it used to be?"

He made himself look thoughtful, one of his playful displays of effort. Anyone who really knew him knew that his chief affliction was an inability to ever forget. After hamming it up this way for a while, he snapped his fingers. "It used to be a church. One of those storefronts, you know."

"That's right . . ."

"The Cathedral of Blessed Deliverance. That's what it was called."

"For real?"

"Lying is dying," he said. "You'd walk by on service days and the singing that came out of there was good enough to bring you to your knees. That one's gone, but there are still plenty of them around. More than ever, it seems. That's where we live: Cathedral City." He handed over the paper bag. "Now come on and open your present. And guess what your dad's gonna whip up to eat tonight? Your favorite."

Not long after dinner, Dad started crying in his room again. Usually his weeping was legible, and easily classified. There had been a taxonomy of his tears. The sounds of angry heaving meant his attempts at getting a second job had resulted in some new humiliation. Pathetic quavering meant he wished Mom would change her mind and come back to us. And so on. But the sound he was making now, which came directly through the poster of Sun Ra on the wall, was some kind of hybrid. Usually you can't decide what you want to be sad about. Usually you don't get to decide. Sometimes it all hits you at once. Sometimes you don't even know what all is hitting you.

Better to let people be when they get that way, though. Earlier that summer, Antonio made a similar horrible sound when he found out exactly how ill his mother was, and how much time he was likely to have left with her. Who knows what else he was figuring out, what else was baffling him. When you hear someone you love make a sound like that, the problem isn't that you don't know how to respond, it's that you lose all your reserve, the discipline and self-restraint that were actually keeping everything intact. So you take liberties. You close the door to your friend's room and begin gathering the dented soda cans and empty water bottles, arranging them in rows on his desk. You pick up every loose bit of soiled, funky clothing from the floor and the chair and drop them into the hamper in his closet. You stack the crusted cereal bowls on top of the smeared plates and neatly arrange all the used spoons and forks. With nothing but the palm of your hand, you wipe away the dust on the screen of his TV. You completely understand the power possessed by the illusion of order, so you clarify the shapes and lines of his room. When he makes the horrible sound again, you sit on the bed where he's crumpled into a heap. You clear your palms of dust and lay your body down beside his. You put your arm around him and pull him close and hold fast, your chest knocking against his back. When he turns toward your body and its offering, you kiss along a meridian of his face, first on his eye, then down beneath his cheekbone, then lightly on the leftmost edge of his mouth. You say that you're sorry, but he doesn't understand what you mean. Or maybe he doesn't want to. He decides you're requesting forgiveness for what you've just done, and he refuses to grant it.

So, no matter how horrible the sound, it's best to stay very quiet and avoid calling any attention to yourself. It's best to do absolutely nothing, but if you must do something, scroll through the selection of old photos saved on your phone. Read the first few pages of your new book. Lie there gazing at the poster of Sun Ra on your wall and think about the perfect silence of outer space. Attempt to go away and get lost. Try, as a means of control, to obliterate yourself without violence. Try to endure the long waking hours and then slip unnoticed into sleep.

Nearly three more weeks passed without the crew spending any time together. The calendar on the refrigerator at home said so. Otherwise, how could you tell? The air outside felt the same as it had the previous month, with a single exception, that one notably raw day, and people had yet to bring out their thickest gloves and heaviest coats. We did see one another at school or on the street, two or three of us at a time, in passing, but never all five. And the way we interacted during those random encounters, with shrugging superficiality, seemed to acknowledge that this was it, this was what life did, plain and simple, nothing profound so maybe don't worry too much. It pulled bodies apart.

But one morning brought us all back together in a way worth remembering. It was early on the Friday before Thanksgiving. The sun hadn't risen very far in the sky and it would be painfully early when it fell. Bed-Stuy wasn't fully awake yet. People were on their way to school or work, walking listlessly, sinking down to the subway, or languishing on corners while waiting for the arrival of the bus.

Near the corner of Halsey Street, a chubby stray cat leaped out from behind a tree and made an odd purring sound. It was obvious, however, on second glance, that it wasn't a cat. It was a rabbit of course. It looked like one from the rescue, the one they called Balthazar. The rabbit jumped again, and it seemed to move in reaction to something. In a moment a sound, a distant clanging, came within earshot.

Following the sound that day would, if you didn't know better, give the impression that our little slice of Bed-Stuy was like some town out in the Midwest, teeming with wild rabbits. On just the next couple of blocks more than a dozen of them, barely moving, became visible. There was something funny, uncontrollably funny, about the sight of them, as though they too were participating in the city's early-morning torpor.

It didn't take too long to find the source of the clanging. Out on MacDonough, close to the open door of the unlit rescue, Headass stood with a large metal spoon in one hand and an empty pot in the other. Among the people who had gathered there, Antonio and Cherise, Roni and Walidah, standing together-apart in their pairs. As Headass continued to bang the spoon against the pot, more loudly and rapidly, some people in the forming crowd began to warn him. Others were cheering him on. More rabbits came into view, as though drawn by the noise, while others hopped or lumbered away.

Over the next few minutes, the crowd grew and the cheers intensified, punctuated with random shouts of "Yeah!" and "That's right!" but also "Be careful!" and "Don't get got!" It wasn't clear what the crowd, as a collective, was articulating exactly. Everyone seemed to be smoldering in their own private fire. The warnings were easier to understand than the cheers, but it all made sense somehow. It made sense that it didn't make sense, and when the five of us exchanged glances and nods, perhaps granting one another permission to join in on the shouting, it felt good. We-the-five weren't a thing anymore, and we wouldn't be ever again, but for a little while, as long as Headass kept up the intensity of his racket, we could be part of another thing, a large and incoherent body that had plenty to say and no need or desire to justify itself.

Such things tend not to last, however, and sooner than we might have expected, it was done. Without warning, Headass stopped. Truth be told, he may have just gotten bored. He looked at the pot and spoon in his hands like they no longer held any interest at all. After he dropped them on the ground, the crowd started to disperse. People had to go back to their lives. Cherise and Antonio, Roni and Walidah too, they left. They went in the direction of school as if the routine of things had never been in question. They kept walking until they were gone.

"Headass, you should go too. It's not safe for you to be here."

But he paid the concern no mind. Instead, he crept over to a car parked directly in front of the rescue and ducked behind it, disappearing completely for a moment. When he rose into view again, one of the rabbits he had emancipated, a dark one, was nestled in his arms. Grinning, he approached with it. The rabbit struggled a bit, flailing its little limbs, but then it relaxed as he got close. Headass didn't smell so good. With great care, he extended his arms, offering the animal for affection. He seemed so proud as he held it out. Its nose fluttered.

Its fur was even softer than expected, the warmth of its body an astonishment. It was the same rabbit from that first day, the one he had sat with in the cage, obsessed. "This is Chicory, isn't it?" The words came automatically, blurted at the exact moment of remembrance. But he shook his head and responded, "No, no," his voice richer and more sonorous than it had ever seemed before. He smiled broadly and said the animal's name, pronouncing the word slowly, savoring each of the syllables, sharing the true name he had given it out of love.

Then he told me his name. Then I told him mine.

THE LET-OUT

The woman came out of the museum and navigated the masses
in the plaza. No matter which way she moved or how often men
tried to get her attention, her gaze remained soft, completely
nonchalant as she surveyed the crowd. Every first Saturday of
the month, the museum offered free admission as well as lectures,
performances, films, and a dance party, a popular program of
events attended by thousands. Aside from the leering Romeos
and the stunning head-turners, there were also white people, elderly people, families burdened by their children. The woman
cut through them all with unperturbed elegance, or they moved
their bodies to make way for hers, or it seemed that they did.
The gold and emerald colors she wore leaped out, the lit glass
of the museum's pavilion glowing behind her. One guy stepped
away from his friends and into her path, but she dodged him
effortlessly, her floral sundress fluttering, her purse bouncing
against her thigh. He reached for her wrist, but with no effort
at all her arm slipped away, escaping that too, and he turned to
watch as a breeze pulled her dress against the shape of her body.
The woman's mellow beauty—and the tranquility and charm of

her rejection—left his eyes full of bitter longing. Then her gaze abruptly sharpened. Whatever she had caught sight of made her halt, and caused her expression to become puzzled. She shook her head, the movement like a tremor had run through her, as though a notion had charged into her mind only to collapse seconds later under the weight of uncertainty. But all of a sudden she started walking again, with more quickness and purpose. Her steps were bringing her in the direction she was looking, and it became clear, despite every self-abnegating doubt, that she was walking toward me.

I felt as giddy as a little boy. I looked to my left as though my friend were standing there, but he hadn't trusted the prospects at a museum, so it was an exchange of glances with no one. The woman was dark, deliciously stout, her strong legs probably twice as thick as mine. Though I felt self-conscious in my basketball shorts and my father's hand-me-down Globetrotters T-shirt, I stood tall and puffed out my chest, relaxed my face until it felt like a placid mask. The woman glided past a few more people and walked right up to me, holding her purse in one hand and a pack of cigarettes in the other. She wore jewelry everywhere. Bracelets, necklaces, rings. Her short curly hair was styled somewhere between a pixie and a bob. The heat of her sweating body was very close, and her scent was like a complex of spices and honeyed smoke. Through fake eyelashes she stared boldly up into my face, as though expecting me to spread my arms for a hug.

"I have the worst timing!" she announced. "Can you believe it?" She took out a cigarette but then, looking at all the people surrounding us, put it back and placed the handsome red package into her crocheted purse. She was much smaller than I had imagined and appeared to be around my mother's age, in her forties, maybe even fifties. From her appearance and enunciation, it was clear right away that she was the bougie type; she had the strange transatlantic accent of the Black intelligentsia. When she caught me observing her, she looked away coyly and then sighed. "Polka! Why would they play polka? What makes anyone think people want to dance to such ridiculous music?"

Before I had time to think, I did a few half steps and jumps in response. My long legs and feet became a blur. I had taken some lessons my first year of college, one of my many attempts to meet people. If you gave it a chance, I told her, polka was actually pretty fun.

"Then you should be inside cutting a rug," she said, clearly amused.

"Why be in there when there's so much to look at out here, right where I'm standing?" My voice shook as I spoke, but she laughed and touched my arm, and I felt proud.

"Oh, is that what you're doing here all by yourself? Looking?" Her gaze, lingering on my face even more, seemed to be posing additional questions. "Well, at least the exhibits are high quality," she said. "I actually came yesterday to see them, but by the time I got here the museum was already closed."

"Bad timing," I said.

"The *worst* timing. But today here I am! I made it, and let me tell you something, I can't stop thinking about the photographs. Exceptional. What did you think?"

"I thought they were exceptional," I told her, which was a lie. I hadn't seen the photography. I hadn't gone inside the museum at all. Only one thing had brought me all the way down to Brooklyn that night: the let-out. It didn't matter to me what music was playing. The true dance was the shadow dance, or the dance that follows the dance, and it was here, where a circle of boys who dared to be daring raised their arms and voices in collective awe of girls

taking pictures of themselves in various poses, their bodies vague
silhouettes against the pavilion's shining glass. Here where every
blissful perspiring body was spent, which is to say less guarded,
which is to say carefree, which meant a heightened chance for
possibility. Here where there was an openness to the haphazard
and the serendipitous, where it seemed feasible to make contact.

"You haven't told me your name," she said. When I told her
what it was, she closed her eyes and nodded, gave a little hum of
pleasure. Then she shared her name, which was Ramona, and
looked at her watch. "There's still over an hour before it closes,"
she said. "Come on. Show me some more of that fancy footwork,
prove me wrong." Then she raised her arm and waited.

She wanted me to take it, I realized, and this, despite my
highest hopes, was a complete surprise. What in the world was
happening? For my friend the explanation would have been
simple. I could hear his whispering voice now: "Cougar, a *cougar*
stalketh." He'd joke that way whenever we saw a woman of a
certain age acknowledge the force of her sexuality. But women
like that never actually spoke to us; we were never their prey.
Besides, the quality of Ramona's attention seemed different from
that. For one thing, *she* (a woman) had noticed *me*, which hardly
ever happened. I was not the kind to be noticed. It felt thrilling to
be picked out from the background, to step forward rather than
recede.

Up to now, every let-out had gone full tilt down the road to
disaster. Just last week my friend and I, each home from college
for the summer, had gone to a Manhattan nightclub together,
which was what we usually did; I had never gone to a let-out
alone. We arrived at close to four in the morning, when things
started winding down and the people in the club were beginning
to leave. After a few false starts, my friend took the lead and we

approached a group of women wearing short-shorts. They looked exhausted as they emerged, with bleary eyes and sweat-ruined hair, but after my friend's come-ons they had no problem summoning the energy to tell us off. "Little boys, why don't you go home to your mamas!" one said. "Get your broke asses out of my face!" said another. Week after week that summer, we had accumulated these stinging rejections, but they were predictable, reliable, and, frankly, accurate. It was true that we were young—a year too young to even get into the club—and broke—too broke to afford the cover anyway. What's fair is fair. I took some solace in being judged on the merits. And I had read my mother's self-help books many times: "Success is the sum of small efforts, repeated day in and day out." At some point things would be different.

I hooked my arm into Ramona's, but she wouldn't move until I moved first. We walked through the growing crowd like that, arm in arm toward the museum like two smitten lovers on a date. She swaggered against me, bumping me with the swell of her flesh, the swing in her hips even more emphatic than when she had first approached. People went out of their way to look at her, but she ignored them. Instead, she kept glancing up at me. As we pushed through the revolving doors and went inside, the odor of spice and smoke was heavy in her hair, overwhelming in fact, and I had to fight off a strange wave of nausea as it rose from the top of her head.

We threaded our way through the people in the pavilion, past a line of wide brick pillars, and into the lobby of the museum. The faint sound of the band grew louder and led us to the party upstairs. The acoustics were awful but that wasn't a deterrent. The spacious court, surrounded by sleek ivory archways, was filled with people, but in stark contrast to the scene on the plaza, almost everyone here was white. High above us rose a ceiling with a broad skylight. From its center hung an enormous brass chandelier, like a watch suspended from a chain. But the very best feature was the floor, made of terrazzo and paneled glass. As I showed Ramona a few simple steps, we both kept looking down. From certain angles there appeared to be another floor underneath this floor, made of the exact same materials. Was it an optical illusion, or was it real? I couldn't tell, but at some point the question ceased to matter. The important fact was that I was dancing with a woman, this woman, on sheets of glass layered beautifully by a subtle magic.

Ramona rolled her eyes and complained playfully about the music, but she never stopped moving. She did so with agility and grace, no surprise given the way she walked. Once she got the basic steps down, I taught her a variation of side steps, which she picked up quickly. With the same dreamy expression from before, she looked up into my face and said, "Okay, I'm ready. Let's dance."

I wasn't sure what she meant. Ready for what? Weren't we already dancing? But then she took my right hand and placed it low on her back, where the cut of her dress exposed her flesh. She held onto my shoulder and our free hands came together. At first she took control—interlocking our fingers and drawing us unusually close—but then she relinquished it. She waited again for me to lead, and I became eager to do so, to prove to myself that I could. As we danced, the scent from her hair was so full in my nostrils I could taste it.

"I haven't danced like this in so long," Ramona said after a while.

"I thought you'd never danced to polka before."

"To live music, I mean," she said. "I mean in the arms of a man."

I smiled. "One of my first memories," I told her, "is of my mom and dad dancing in our living room."

"So he's the person who taught you how to lead."

I laughed, thinking of the rare times my father would try, without success, to coax my mother into a bit of romance. "Oh, I don't think it's a *real* memory," I explained. "I'm pretty sure I made it up. I used to do that kind of thing a lot when I was young."

Ramona leaned away to look at me, her expression bemused, but then she gave a little squeal of delight. "Well," she said, "certain lessons just don't need to be taught. It's biology. It's in the blood."

We fell silent for a while and varied our steps. I kept wondering about the position of my hand on her back, which should have been higher, near or at her shoulder blade. The spot I touched, wettish with perspiration, felt hot, or the flesh of my own hand did. Every muscle she had seemed to be connected to that spot. Whenever any of my fingers pressed against her, it felt as if I was sending out vibrations she could detect. Some part of her body would tense up, alert, like a spider listening to the strong silks of its web. The space between us widened a little, and she would close her eyes from time to time, smiling pleasantly. At one point she began to get carried away and seemed to go someplace else. She shimmied her shoulders, shifted her rib cage from side to side and exaggerated the motion of her hips and hams, as if dancing to Cuban salsa. Her movements compelled me to imitate them. My shoulders and hips followed hers. I shook my ass as if I had just discovered its existence. The feeling was strange, and the way we were moving must have looked strange too; the eyes of other people were on us, staring with bewilderment and in some cases even something like anger, as though we were stealing from them, or as though we were an infection or a stain, threatening to spread. Their looks didn't bother me though. Wherever Ramona was going I wanted to go too.

We kept dancing until there was a break in the music. Ramona clapped wildly during the applause between songs, which was when I noticed a wedding band among her many rings. I stared blankly at it as the music started up again.

She looked at the wedding band too and then at all the jewelry on her fingers, before drawing her hands up slowly to her necklaces. "To tell you the truth," she said, "that ring is by far the most boring thing I'm wearing. It tells you the very least about me." Then she added, "Don't worry. My husband is all the way on the other side of the country. And he doesn't really give a damn what I do. He certainly doesn't care if I dance with another man."

She seemed to be going out of her way to refer to me that way, as a man. With or without her husband's approval, it seemed obvious that Ramona was looking for some excitement. I watched her head tip left and right to the music as she scanned the court. The more I thought about it, the more curious I became about her relationship with her husband, but any concern I had about somehow violating her marriage was draining steadily away. I was simply too curious about where things could go.

"I want to see the photography again," she announced. "I leave tomorrow so I won't have another chance. Let's go back. We still have time. You can show me the one that was your favorite."

We linked arms again, but then she slid hers down and took hold of my hand. Our fingers were interlocked for a second time,

and when her thumb started skimming across mine a current ran
through my body. Everyone was looking at us as we left the party,
which was a new experience for me. I had never been that kind
of person before.

Ramona and I ended up riding the elevator with two well-
dressed middle-aged white women. They were discussing the
latest horrors in the local news—a girl shot to death in Queens,
families being displaced in Brooklyn—but with a kind of theatrical dismay. Then, as they became aware of Ramona, they got
quiet and frowned. For some reason, the raw fact of her was too
much for them to bear. Under the elevator's fluorescent lights, her
abundance of jewelry, her brightly painted nails, and her dark
sticky caterpillar lashes could have made her seem tawdry, but I
felt protective and proud of her. The two women made no effort to
hide their disapproval of her, and of us holding hands. Scowling
at them, I put some bass in my voice and said, "Is there a problem
here?" The women simpered at me but neither said a word in
response, and when the door opened they rushed off the elevator.
Ramona and I got off too and walked in the opposite direction,
toward the galleries.

"I see you've got a little bit of a temper," she said.

"I get it from my mother," I admitted. You could sense the
pulse of my mother's temper always, but it almost never flared. It
seemed to be held in check by what I could only understand as her
modest expectations regarding life. A few early memories cast her
as a laughing woman, but it seemed likely that they were also inven-
tions, nothing more than wishful make-believe. "Definitely from
my mother," I said, "or at least that's what my father likes to say."

"And you think he's the gentle one?"

I wondered for a moment if Ramona was thinking about her

own marriage, her own husband. "Is gentle the same thing as quiet?" I asked. "No, I don't think so."

"Well, you seem gentle *and* quiet, like a hunter in a forest, so it must be your daddy you take after for sure."

"I don't think so," I repeated.

"I bet people say you look like him."

"Like who?"

"Your father." Her eyes darted up at me and she studied me for a moment. "What's wrong?"

"Nothing," I said. "It just feels like I'm talking to someone who's been secretly watching me my whole life."

Ramona looked down, her lashes fallen low over her eyes. "When I first saw you," she said, "I couldn't believe it. It felt like 1989 all over again. What I mean is, I knew him. He and I were friends then. Back in the day," she added with a hint of irony. "I should have told you immediately, but then I wasn't sure. You actually don't resemble him as much as I thought."

"I don't understand," I told her.

"Your father," she said. "He used to be my friend. But that was a long time ago."

The sensation of holding Ramona's hand immediately lost all of its allure. I was a little boy being escorted across a busy street.

"How could you have been friends?" I asked. "You're from the other side of the country."

"I live there now, in California, but I'm from here. I grew up in the Bronx."

"Just like my father . . ."

"I was running up and down the Grand Concourse when I was just a fresh little thing in pigtails. But tell me, how's Lawrence doing these days?"

My hand pulled reflexively away from hers. It was disturbing to hear his name—his given, proper name—in Ramona's mouth. No one called him Lawrence, not even my mother. Even worse, the question seemed to invite a comparison I was unable to make. I could tell her he was better or worse now, but better or worse than what? My father's involvement in my life had been suspended in the late eighties, at the very end of the decade. I was only five then, and, aside from the things I fabricated for my own peace of mind, I hadn't yet formed many memories that would endure. What I remember most from those years aren't images or events, but sensations, feelings of anger, aggression, and obstinacy, a soup of emotion in which I was constantly simmering. Like the sulky child I was said to have been, facing a question I didn't want to answer, I kept my mouth closed and shrugged stiffly in response.

Ramona and I were rambling through the galleries. We paused here and there to look at some of the photographs, but they made no impression on me. Not many other people were around, mostly elderly couples or solitary eccentrics who stood much too close to the art. Ramona stopped to stare at a large-scale photograph frenzied with garish streaks of yellow and crimson paint, and I stood beside her.

"You have his mind, don't you?" she said. "It feels like you do. Does he still tell those incredible stories?"

She was talking about my father again. "Are you sure you two were friends?" I asked. "It sounds to me like you've got him confused with somebody else. The man I know barely says a word."

"Is that right? Things change, I suppose. Just tell me, please, that Lawrence isn't balding."

This was what people of a certain age did, I knew. They obsessively asked about those who had once been a part of their lives. I'd seen it at reunions and other family functions, and it was

obvious that the obsession was about something beyond satisfy-
ing one's own curiosity; it had more to do with taking measure of
the self. But I was still annoyed that Ramona was talking so much
about my father. It made me think I had to contend with him, or
with some implausibly wonderful version of him that was shielded
in the armor of the past. A new edge came into my feelings about
Ramona too. She seemed to know my father better than I ever
could, and that, on some level, also made her a rival.

"Actually, he's been growing this preposterous afro," I told her.
"Stop!"

"No lie," I said. "And the facial hair . . . It's like he stepped
out of a time machine. I told him that 1972 called and wanted
its muttonchops back. It's too embarrassing. I keep thinking, this
man can't possibly be my father."

"Well, you do have his hands," she said, assuring me. "And
you're tall and thin, just like he is."

"Way taller than him now," I said. "He's only—what?—fifty,
but he's already starting to shrink. And forget thin—he's got an
old-man belly. I swear to God he's ready for the retirement home."

"Well, let's see, you're younger than he was when I knew
him," she said. "Maybe he was just as tall when he was your age
and he's been getting smaller and smaller ever since. Maybe when
his mama birthed him he was a giant."

She began laughing hard at her own joke, which made me
wonder for the first time if she might be a little nuts, but I quickly
put that thought away. I made a futile attempt to picture my father as a giant. He had always seemed small to me, diminished,
even when he returned to our family and I myself was no bigger
than a twig. Both of my parents seemed especially diminished
to me now, and this quality they shared was a central reason I

was convinced, despite any troubles they may have had, that they were 100 percent right for each other.

After her laughter subsided, Ramona studied me again quietly. The intensity of her gaze made me feel like the subject of one of the surrounding photographs, as if I were also on display. All I needed was a frame around my neck and a place on the wall.

"So," she asked, "did Lawrence ever find someone else?"

"Someone else?"

Her hands came together in front of her stomach, her fingers forming a barrier between us, a flimsy pulpit she stood behind. "When things didn't work out with your mother," she said slowly, with a bit of condescension, "wasn't there a divorce?"

A childish urge rose in me then, an impulse to take a swipe at the place where her fingertips met, to blast her little pulpit into pieces. "Where are you getting that from?" I asked. "You're way off. They *are* together."

She considered this for a moment, and I did too. What I had said was the truth, but the strain in my voice had made it sound much more like a lie. All things considered, maybe it was both. The family was intact, yes, but we hardly talked to one another. My parents were frequently apart because my father traveled for work. The only thing they did together, which I sometimes did with them when I was home, was watch stupid sitcoms or reality shows while shoveling dinner into their faces. Other than the TV itself, all you would hear was chewing and scraping. Those awful sounds had driven me to leave that very night and take the subway alone to Brooklyn, but I knew our family ritual was absolutely necessary. The feeling at home was this: *any* attempt at conversation could lead to *too much* conversation, and too much conversation could be deadly. The source of our strength

was a strict and tacit agreement to preserve and cherish, at all
costs, the simplicity of things. So much is made about the impor-
tance of achieving depth in human interactions, but what about
the delicate surface, what about the skin?

"They got back together . . ." Ramona said finally. "That's
wonderful. It is." But the expression on her face didn't match the
brightness of her tone. Her jaw shifted from side to side and her
tongue leaped around in her mouth. It was as though she was deciding whether she liked the flavor of a drink she had never tasted
before. "He found his way back to her. That really is something
else . . ."

"What do you know about my mother anyway?" The sense
that Ramona disapproved of her was overwhelming.

"As far as I can tell," she said, "I don't know a thing." Then,
with an abrupt turn, she walked toward the next room of the gallery. Two small children with their faces painted like kittens separated and darted around her in order to avoid a collision. A guard
eyed the girl and boy warily before announcing that the museum
would be closing in half an hour. I considered going immediately,
just leaving without saying goodbye, recrossing that impatient
street on my own. But I needed to know more about this myste-
rious man, *Lawrence*. And I needed to understand what Ramona
wanted with me, the way she looked at me. The contours and ends
of her desire.

In the next room, filled with black-and-white photographs,
Ramona and I maintained a distance. As she walked around, I let
my eyes run over the main label introducing the work. The artist
was known for the images she took with her wide-angle lens, and
for her method of taking them, which emphasized quickness and
spontaneity, and, above all, her subjects' total lack of awareness
of her presence. The photos were mostly taken of people in New

York. Before I could finish reading the label, Ramona's scent made me look up. There she was, smiling next to me. She seemed to have reset herself.

"You were supposed to show me your favorite," she said. There was a hint of flirtation in her voice again, a hint that something exciting, even forbidden, could still happen. "So which one is it?"

"I don't know yet," I told her. I had forgotten about my earlier lie. "It's like you said, they're all exceptional."

But she insisted, with a flutter of her false eyelashes.

So we went around together and I pretended to reconsider the art. After a minute or two, I chose the most blatantly sexual photograph in the room. A man and a woman embraced—in Central Park, according to the label—as he pressed her back against the trunk of a tree. Both of them were very attractive. One of her legs was lifted and curled around him, and his hand was halfway up her short pleated skirt.

Ramona hummed. She examined every part of the photograph for an absurdly long time. I didn't understand what she was looking for. When she finally spoke, she asked me to explain why I liked it so much.

"What do you mean *why*?" I said.

"I mean, what does it make you think? How does it make you feel? Why do you think the photographer took it? What does it communicate to you?"

Her questions annoyed me. She was playing dumb by playing smart. The reason I chose the photograph should have been obvious, and more than sufficient. There was no need to explain. If the script of the evening was what I thought it was, she should have simply taken her cue.

"I don't know, I just think it's hot," I said. "Don't you?"

"To tell you the truth, I don't think it's very interesting at all," she said. "Here, let me show you *my* favorite."

The photograph she liked, on an adjacent wall, also featured a couple, a man and a woman, though they were dull by comparison. They were walking down a street, neither one looking at nor touching the other, both in the middle of long, perfectly synced strides. Other than the harmony of their steps, there wasn't a single remarkable thing about them.

"This might sound like total nonsense," Ramona said, staring at the photo, "but do you ever think that something can happen in your life that stops time dead in its tracks?" Her question was accompanied by a heat that seemed to radiate from her head, and I became aware again of her scent. "Here's what I mean. It's like whatever future you could have had, all that *newness* waiting out there to introduce itself to you, it just vanishes, it gets cut off entirely. Then the only options you're left with, the only ones you can even imagine, are the ones you've already had." Her tongue and jaw became active again before she continued. "Tell me, why do you think your parents got back together?"

I took another look at the photo, as if the answer to her question might have been hidden in it. I thought of her husband. The guard announced that the museum would close in fifteen minutes.

"They realized they were still in love," I said.

"Is that what you really think?"

"What else could it be?"

"Have *you* ever been in love?"

"Not yet."

She laughed dryly. "That's mighty optimistic of you. I've been in love, in that deep bone-marrow love, only one time. That's it. After you experience the real thing once, you assume it will happen again. But what if it doesn't?"

"I don't know what you're talking about," I told her.

Ramona frowned and kept staring straight ahead. "No, I suppose you don't."

"This one wasn't taken in New York," she said, pointing. "See?"

I took another look. There on the sidewalk, underneath shadows cast by the couple's legs, and washed out by the brightness of the sun, were a few stars from the Hollywood Walk of Fame. I had missed the stars before, and the shadows and the sunlight too. The photograph seemed to fill with details now, buzzing with them.

"Have you ever been out there, to Los Angeles?" she asked. "When people manage to escape New York, that's often where they end up. Or at least I did, for a little while. It's beautiful in all the ways you'd expect—the palm trees, the weather. Goddamn, that weather! There's the smog of course, but you can bank on it being bright and seventy-five almost every day."

She got quiet for a moment, but I didn't say anything. I just watched her.

"On the flip side, the sameness of it can work your nerves. I guess it's not *actually* the same, but time gets funky, like you're stuck in a loop, or in a simulation of life instead of the real thing. I didn't feel like that, not at first. But some people do right away." She raised a finger to her eye and touched the tips of her long lashes. "Like your father. Lawrence never liked it that much."

It was becoming clearer now, what she was suggesting.

"He was there too," she said, "when I was."

I responded as I often did, especially when I was younger, with a sort of willful, innocent denial. At home I was allowed to sit in my innocence, the way a neglected infant is left sitting in a soiled diaper, but I hoped now that it might force Ramona's hand. "Is that where the two of you met?" I asked foolishly.

She shook her head, and the motion wiped away the wry smile that was forming on her face. "It had already started, the situation between us. Your father and I, we ran away to Los Angeles, together. When I went there, I went with him." She closed her eyes, and I could see them rolling beneath the lids.

One of the things that my family declined to talk about—perhaps the source of all the other things—was that span of time in the past. I'd had vague memories of asking to see my father, and of my mother looking down at me kindly and saying that I couldn't, that he was too far away. Or maybe as usual I had invented this, especially the comforting tone of the response. What I really recalled was the feeling of his absence, that near-boiling sensation that had defined my early childhood. Afterward, the sensation abated but it never went away; when my father returned, he stepped into the absence he'd left but he was no longer equipped to fill it. The thought of this made the feeling blaze within me now, and even more acutely.

"I knew about you," Ramona said. Her eyes were still closed. "He would tell me about you, back when everything between us seemed to be fine. I wanted to meet you. I was even willing to . . ." She shook her head. "But then things stopped being fine. And then your father left. And then there I was, alone in paradise."

I looked at Ramona—her hair, her face, her body—and imagined her as a younger woman. I imagined his hands touching her. I looked again at her jewelry and wondered if anything she was wearing had been a gift given by him. I scrutinized her with something like disgust, but I couldn't help comparing her, favorably, to my mother, who was a slight, unadorned woman, the color of stale coffee with too much cream. Other memories, whether real or false, came to me then. Ramona's odor, the odor of spice and smoke, wafted back through the opened vents of the years and into the furnace of the past. Through my father's hair, along the sleeves and collars of his shirts. I saw my mother when she was young, with only me (and herself) to care for, the odor clogging her nose and her throat as she held my small hands and whispered useless consolations.

"Can you see it?" Ramona asked.

"See what?" I said, and I could hear the soak of petulance in my voice.

"We would walk down this street together, this exact street. Hollywood and Vine. Can you see it? We were beautiful, inarguable. People would look at us and smile. They would turn their heads to watch."

"What is *wrong* with you?" I said.

Ramona opened her eyes and looked at me like I was the one who had asked something insane. "One day," she said, "you'll want someone to give you the nod. You'll want somebody to remember the person you were when you were happy."

I wanted to tell her that this wasn't true, that in my family we never asked each other to remember anything. But I also wanted to protect my family from her. I refused to reveal anything else about us.

"What are you doing?" Ramona asked, staring wildly at me. Her eyelashes were black clots.

"Nothing," I replied, but it was an obvious lie. I licked the salty wetness from the corners of my mouth and wiped my cheeks before pinching my lips together in shame.

I looked away, toward the tick of the guard's shoes as he approached us. He stopped and announced, in a lower voice than before, that the museum was now closing. Together, Ramona and I slowly retraced our steps through the galleries, one person who had dreamed up life's memories and another who had actually lived them, but neither of us could be corroborated, so both of us slumped along in postures of defeat. I wanted to turn away and leave her on the spot, this woman from my father's past, but I remained by her side. After all, she was part of my past too, and my mother's. She belonged to us, and that belonging was irrevocable, even if no one at home, including me, would ever speak her name.

In the lobby, we joined a larger group of chattering people from the dance party and went with them past the redbrick pillars and then out through the heavy revolving doors. She took the pack of cigarettes from her purse and didn't wait. Her lighter sparked and she cupped her hand, obscuring her face for a moment that stretched into forever as she exhaled smoke and then began walking ahead, alone, through the crowd. We parted without either of us saying another word. I didn't move. The doors churned at my back. The voice of a woman, emerging from the dimming lights of the museum, said excuse me, and someone else demanded I get out of the way so people could go home. But what was the point of going home? Someone who knew me was out there, I imagined, someone I knew who would find me among all the shadows drifting along the plaza. So I waited, I stood in place.

COMFORT

It is May. Or it is June or July—or August. Or maybe it isn't summer at all, Simone's most hated time of year. Maybe it's simply that the days feel long and that they scald, the sensation of being baked in an oven. The brief peace promised by the night cracks like a pane of opaque glass, shattered by her thoughts and her dreams, crushed as though within the tightness of her chest. She sleeps, at most, for an hour at a time. Maybe the joint she smoked earlier makes her anxious that she's being watched or has heard a strange sound. The remedies she insists on using for her insomnia fail again and all at once. The lavender oil dabbed onto her wrists and temples prickles and raises bumps on her skin. The melatonin gives her headaches—or maybe, she can admit with some shame, she's had a few too many glasses of white wine. The silk of her eye mask causes her to sweat and in the total darkness she panics, so she takes it off. What is that sound? There's a man sleeping next to her—as there often is, especially since she lost her job—but he is silent. Sometimes when she expects to see a man next to her, there isn't one, and she wonders how she made it from the couch to the bed. Tonight she ignores the man. She listens. Her empty stomach contracts and burbles. Her mouth tastes like vomit. She gets up, goes to the living room to retrieve her phone, and comes back. Throughout the night, she can't help picking it up from the nightstand and staring at the screen.

Whenever she puts the phone down, she imagines. Sometimes, if she's able to manage some sleep, she dreams. Later, during the day, she won't be able to tell the difference, but she often sees James Brown there in her room. The singer is wearing tight slacks and a newsboy cap, but he is her father and she is a little girl. He begins to dance, calling out the names of his steps to her as he does them. The funky chicken. The mashed potato. The camel walk. The robot. The soul train. He grunts and goads himself on, his shoes tapping and shuffling along her hardwood floor. At one point, during the mashed potato, he drops to his knees with a thump and bounces immediately, incredibly, back up to his feet. The sound frightens Simone. She dislikes all the grunting and goading and tapping and shuffling, even though he smiles throughout the performance. All he wants to do is entertain her, reassure her. When he's done, he notices that she's afraid. His smile becomes strange, a rictus, scaring her even more. Through his teeth he says he'll come back to her later, soon. Then he leaves, but not through the bedroom door. He makes his way out through the back window, which doesn't open.

The yard behind her street-level apartment has seen better days. The lawn furniture is speckled with dirt and rust. Weeds fill the openings of the chain-link fence, like scrawls of crayon made by a child. On the other side of the apartment, through the living room windows, past the bins for trash and recycling, is a street on the edge of Bed-Stuy infamous for its potholes, but the neglect of the street will surely cease as the gentrifying neighborhood continues to fall.

It is June or July or August, or maybe it isn't, but the sun rises, or seems to, much too early, always sooner than Simone expects, lighting the peach-colored facade of her building and heating the pocked concrete of the stoop. She used to love sitting out there with her older brother, Marcus. They would talk about a time when neither of them would be living check to check, when they would save enough money to buy an apartment, or even a town house, on a street she could clearly imagine, one that didn't require the presence of white people to address the problem of holes. With the settlement of the civil lawsuit, Simone and her parents can actually purchase some property now, but the idea of doing so seems impossible, like eating a bowl of ash. Holding on to the money feels like one way of coping with loss; trading it all away for something else feels like a loss twice over.

The alarm on the man's phone shrills through Simone's teeth. She sits bolt upright, leaping too quickly into waking life, with far too much violence. She was able to achieve only the shallows of sleep. The waking feels like another shattering, of glass she vaguely sensed but couldn't perceive. Her head throbs. She doesn't recall which of her three men is beside her. He wasn't roused at all earlier when her stomach growled or when she went to the bathroom to throw up, and his alarm doesn't affect him now. She goes to the other side of the bed, silences his phone, and walks over to the window. She peeks through the blinds instead of permitting the full flood of day. The state of things in the backyard—the weeds, the filth, the rough patchy grass, the dead leaves from autumn—makes her think again, as she has on other mornings, that today will be the day she cleans it. The landlady kept quiet about it for a while, but lately she's been reminding Simone that caring for the yard, in exchange for reduced rent, is a condition of her lease. "You still have to mind your responsibilities," she says.

The man is naked on top of the sheets, his shoulders and arms muscular, his midsection round, his legs skinny, his toes oddly long. Simone remembers drinking with him in the living room, and while the rest of the night is fuzzy, she remembers a few other things too. He complained playfully when she put her panties back on—"Stay ready for round two," he said, drunk and drowsy, throwing his arm over her and pulling her close—but she's never liked being naked in bed with a man after fucking him.

She wonders again about Officer Brody's wife, the quality of sleep she gets lying next to her husband. "Bet she sleeps just fine," Simone's father said one day. "We know that bastard husband of hers don't give a shit, and I guarantee she don't either." Her father is probably right. Simone knows better than to assume the virtue of white women. Her father always made sure she and Marcus read the right histories. Her mother always made sure she used her eyes—though she was careful to warn that, like anything else, they can be taken away from you, snatched right out of the sockets. Regardless of what her father says, Simone can't help imagining it, the appalling intimacy of sharing a bed with a man like that. Opening your eyes in the morning and watching his vulnerable sleeping body, a body that has shown the horrible cruelty it is capable of when awake.

Kelvin is the man in Simone's bed, but she has him saved in her phone, and in her mind, as Bamboo, the name of a Caribbean restaurant in Flatbush. He approached her there while she was out with her best friend, during a time when going out with a friend still felt like an easy thing to do. There are varieties of numbness. "Might as well get you some Bamboo," Dana said that night, followed by a burst of her high, teasing laughter. Whenever Simone decides to send a text message and invite him over, she says the same words to herself: "Might as well get you some Bamboo." He's currently her favorite among her men, but now, if it's time for anything, it's time for him to go. When she shakes him, he stirs and mutters something about watching cartoons, like a little boy remembering the happiness of Saturday mornings. She tells herself that he's still her favorite, and keeps shaking him until he wakes.

Bamboo will leave with hardly any fuss but a lot of care. He offers to make breakfast before he goes. "With what?" "I can go out and get some stuff. No? Well, let's go to the diner then—my treat." Simone rejects this idea and a few others before seeing him out. She tidies the apartment, but only a little. She clears the bottles of chardonnay and whiskey from the coffee table, washes the tumblers and wineglasses in the sink. After that, as on other days, she feels suddenly exhausted and tells herself she's done enough. She sits on the couch with her phone. There's an unsent text message she must have written last night, to Dana: *Where are you? This son of a bitch over here again grinning like an idiot like his only word is yes*

Why would she write a thing like that? She hasn't had a single negative thought about Bamboo. She enjoys his smiling face, which looks as though it should have dimples but doesn't, and she likes that his appearance suggests strength. She enjoys the ease of him, his willingness to come over whenever she asks him to, his compliance when she wants to be left alone. She likes that he doesn't insist too strongly on going out, or on talking about her troubles. She likes that he doesn't cling to any expectations, that he shows no disappointment or bitterness on the nights they simply drink together before she sends him away. When she fills in the gaps of certain nights, creating the story she tells Dana in her mind, it's Bamboo that she imagines lifting her like a bag of bones from the cushions of the couch and carrying her in his arms so she can sleep in her bed. She imagines this, or sometimes dreams it, though who can tell the difference? The message she wrote makes no sense. She deletes it and finds herself giving Dana a call.

"Are you up?" Simone asks.

"Am *I* up? You know Dana gets that worm. Question is, what did you get?"

Simone hears her own laughter as if it came from someone else's coarse, cracked throat.

"You sound terrible, which means it must have been good enough to holler. Come on, you hermity bitch. Let's meet up and get some brunch. You can tell me all about your life of sin."

"Brunch? What day is it?"

"*What day is it?* Oh girl, somebody knocked you into next week! For real though, let's hang. I feel like I haven't seen you in forever and a day. Maybe we can get some of the crew together."

"I wish I could," Simone says, "but what I really need to do is clean this yard."

"You still haven't done that?"

"I know, I know," Simone says. "Today's the day though."

"Just do it tomorrow."

"I can't think about tomorrow. Today's the only thing that makes sense."

"Why don't you let me come by and help?"

"No need to have you stuck in my mess too. I promise we'll see each other soon."

Dana exhales loudly. "Are you sure you're okay, Simone?"

"Nobody can really be *sure* they're okay." It's what her brother used to say. Marcus had an interest in diseases, in troubles that could elude the eye. Unlike most other men she knew, he never hesitated to go to the doctor when he was sick, and he never missed an annual checkup. Sometimes he fantasized out loud about becoming a doctor himself. "Don't worry about me," she says. "Really, I mean it."

By the time they get off the phone it's late morning. Simone feels guilty when she does this, reaching out to Dana only to immediately withdraw. She stays on the couch for a while, her head still throbbing. The throw pillows smell like Bamboo, like the viscous body oil he uses on his skin, the old-school sweetness of Egyptian Musk. Sometimes the pillows have a different scent, but her men never seem to notice the traces left by the others. Men hardly notice things like that, but Marcus would have and he would have made fun of her for it. He used to sleep on the couch all the time, crashing there after he and Simone spent evenings together talking, getting drunk or high, watching movies or listening to music. He couldn't believe that she paid so much rent even with the arrangement with the yard, but he loved her apartment. He said he felt at peace there, that it was his sanctuary, even if the couch was uncomfortable and sleeping there tortured your back. He paid much less for his place, but it was tiny, in a noisy complex, and because his neighbors attracted mice, Marcus had them too.

On a day like this, Officer Brody's wife might take her time fixing breakfast for her husband and their two young children. Simone figures that he isn't the type of man who cooks. The smell of fresh coffee and scrambled eggs, of fried sausage and buttered toast—pancakes with blueberries and cream for the boy and girl—rouses Officer Brody from bed. He comes into the kitchen, taps his fist against his son's, and frets the edges of the girl's freshly trimmed hair. He presses himself against his wife's back, and she tells him to be careful, hot stove. In response his hand furtively caresses her thigh, in a way the children can't detect.

Or maybe the Brodys are the kind of parents who don't hide such desires for the sake of the children.

In any case, Officer Brody loves his wife, and she loves him too. Unconditionally. Simone knows this. Before storming out of criminal court with her parents, she took a few moments to stare at the wife, at her dyed-brown hair gathered into a professorial bun, her modest glasses nearly an exact replica of her husband's. She observed the way the wife tearfully hugged Officer Brody, the purity of the expression on her face, not even a glimmer of doubt regarding her husband's honor. Or if she did doubt it, even if she doubted it a great deal, she didn't care. That's what the clarity of her tears and the spasms of her embrace said: *I don't care what you might have done to that man and to his family. I don't care about the story—the only story—that makes any sense. All that matters is this. They say you're not guilty, so you aren't. You're coming home.* Simone saw it in the courtroom that day, and has seen it in the photographs she's looked at over and over since. The wife's hair is naturally red, and like her husband she doesn't actually wear glasses. Other than that, the photographs don't show anything different. Officer Brody's wife loves him. She loves his attention and his devotion to their children. It's easy for Simone to imagine him as a wonderful husband and father during that time; and maybe he still is, however long later, the best man he has ever been in his life, committed to the role, identifying completely with the idea of his innocence.

Simone stares at the remainder of the joint she smoked yesterday before Bamboo came over and then with him after he arrived. She lights it and smokes. Once she's high again, she's forced to acknowledge the grip of her hunger. The kitchen linoleum feels sticky under her feet. In the refrigerator, all she has is a carton of spoiled eggs, a sprouting onion, a bag of wrinkled mushrooms, half a bar of salted chocolate, vinegar, ketchup, and a nearly empty bottle of white wine. She snaps off a square of the dark chocolate and eats it. In the living room, her phone rings, the soft tinkling of bells, a sound that is hardly there. Simone gets to the phone in time to answer, but she doesn't. Instead, she silences it and tells herself she'll return the call later. She already knows what her mother will say, that Simone should come back to church or go to the church's support group, or that she should contact that therapist, a Black woman recommended to her a long time ago. Or she might quote some verses of scripture, from Luke or from Matthew.

In the afternoon, Simone changes her clothes and, with a tremendous effort, goes outside for groceries. The weather is bright but very breezy. She's unsure if it's warmer or cooler than it's supposed to be. At any rate, she isn't properly dressed for the day. Her head heats up in the loose knit of her hat, her bare legs become stippled with gooseflesh. The sun pummels the back of her neck and the breeze relentlessly threatens her skirt.

Simone spends a lot of time walking along the alleys of the supermarket, staring at the signs. The traffic of customers makes her think of thoroughfares. The arrangement of products doesn't make any sense, and she finds the sheer number of them overwhelming. Her headache has gotten worse. For a while she stands helplessly in front of the insane variety of canned beans. In the produce section she picks up a red apple and sets it back down. She apologizes to an older woman for being in the way, then picks up a pale green apple and sets it back down. Finally, she manages to hold on to a bunch of unripe bananas, cradling it like a baby in the crook of her arm as she rushes to the cashier. After waiting in line, she tries to pay with the credit card her father has authorized her to use, but the fruit alone doesn't cost enough to make the transaction. She grabs several things from the display by the register, an assortment of mints and candies, and adds them to the bananas so she can use the card. No one stares at Simone or talks to her the way they used to, back when Marcus and Officer Brody were in the news, but she is acutely aware of herself. As the man at the register bags her items, she thinks about how ridiculous she's being, even finding it all kind of funny, but she refuses to laugh. She presses her lips together. Unlocking her face just a little would mean losing all control of it.

With her bag in hand she turns the corner onto her block, but sees, from across the street, someone who looks like Dana approaching her building. Her hair is different, longer, but it's definitely Dana, her small mahogany-colored face, her forehead, as usual, shiny with oil. And who else has that sprightly, syncopated walk? She strides through the gate to the brownstone, around to the side of the stoop, and directly to the door of Simone's ground-floor apartment. Simone retreats around the corner and leans back against the wall of a building. A flash of childhood memory—playing hide-and-seek with Marcus—flickers like an old snapshot twisting in the breeze. There seemed to be an agreement between them, that he would always find her. Heart racing and pounding, she would scramble to hide, brushing against the surfaces and edges of the neighborhood as she ran, marking herself with dirt, breaking open the scabs on her elbows and knees. She hid and was uneasy as she anticipated the moment when he would leap out and find her, but she was also terrified that the moment would never come. Her phone buzzes and she checks it. There are two text messages from Bamboo. *Did you eat*, he asks. *Just checking on you.* Simone puts the phone away without answering. She wants nothing more now than to be at home again, but what if Dana has decided to wait there for her? A man walking by gives a friendly nod and says, "How you doing, sis?" Simone doesn't respond. She goes back in the direction of the supermarket. Better to keep moving if she doesn't want to be found.

Officer Brody and his family don't live in the city anymore. After an administrative leave and a dismissal he's a different kind of officer now, no longer police. Simone knows where they live. She's found the exact location on an online map. She's looked at photos of it, street views and aerial views. She knows what it looks like in the morning, what it looks like at night. When the maples are full and green, when all their branches are clean and snows cover the ground. For Officer Brody's wife, it might be the fulfillment of an old-fashioned dream, a life of safety and peace away from the city. Or maybe she's bored out of her mind in the suburbs, maybe she despises it there. Simone admits that it's entirely possible the woman feels that way. Entirely possible that she hates what her family's life has become. But even if she hates it, she has it. The life of her family is intact.

Simone walks with her arms against her hips, pinning down the sides of her skirt. Once again, she's caught in a congestion of people. The sounds of their amusements and disappointments, which she'd rather not hear, reach out to her. The buzzing of her phone adds to the noise. Her head continues to throb; it gives off a sickening incandescence. She wanders around until she finds herself in front of a liquor store. She should go in, just to get more wine. Inside, as she hands over her father's credit card, she points to the bottles lined behind the counter and asks for a fifth of whiskey too.

She knows Officer Brody's new job title, community service officer, a joke her father has remained addicted to telling. "Isn't it funny?" he says, expecting her or her mother to echo his acid laughter. If they don't laugh with him right away, he keeps repeating the title of the job and asking again if it isn't funny. He sometimes says, "God most certainly must be a racist. Who knew that the motherfucking lord of racists would have his throne way up there in the sky."

When Simone gets back to her block, she doesn't see Dana anywhere. She opens the gate, ignores the mailbox as she usually does, and takes out her keys. But just before she gets to her door, someone calls her name, a voice from above. A greenish face, so pale it's almost white, peers down at her from the top of the stoop.

"My eyes ain't as good as they used to be," the face says, "but they're good enough for me to see you haven't done a solitary thing with that forest out in the yard yet." It's Simone's landlady. She's wearing a mask of cosmetic clay, still drying on her skin.

"I'm gonna do it today, Ms. Norman."

"That's what you said the other day."

"No, really—"

"And the day before that, and the day before that."

A fragment of laughter slips from Simone's mouth.

"Maybe I'm a little country, but I'm not a buffoon. At this rate, you're gonna be saying *today* till kingdom come. Do you even know what the word means?"

"I'm sorry . . ."

"Have you found another job yet?"

"I've heard about some things."

"You're too old to have your daddy sending your rent checks for you."

"I have a few leads," Simone says. Her shoulders are so tense they begin to tremble.

Ms. Norman's expression relaxes and she faces the line of the street. Then she comes down from the top of the stoop. She ends up standing too close to Simone, which is something she always

does to people. The still-drying mask emphasizes the creases running across her forehead. The late-afternoon sun picks out bits of
copper in her eyes. She lets out a breath and arranges her mouth
into a smile.

"Ms. Norman, you don't need to say anything. You've been
so understanding . . ."

"Let me just say this—"

"I'm all right, really."

"—let me just say this, and you listen good, okay? Look, I
know you been having a hard time, all right? I know it. But it's
been four years since it happened . . ."

Four entire years? That can't be true, Simone thinks, but it
also feels like the truest thing she's ever heard. Part of her is surprised that Ms. Norman didn't say ten years, or twenty.

"So what you need to remember is this. Grief is a journey,
and time heals all wounds. But you have to let it do its work.
That's the important thing. Time heals all wounds!"

Simone stares into the two wide circles outlined by the clay,
up at the faint brows and back down into the copper-flecked eyes
themselves. She opens her mouth to say something, but closes it.
She gathers both of her bags in one hand and slaps Ms. Norman
with the other. The mask cracks open at the older woman's cheek.
Bits of it flake off into the breeze's current. "I'm sorry," Simone
says. Her voice is trembling. She mumbles another apology and
then excuses herself, rushing to slide her key into the lock. She
lurches through the door and shuts it behind her.

Simone's arms begin to spasm. She drops the bag of fruit and
candy on the floor but manages to hang on to the bottles. She
goes to the couch and sits down to calm herself. She listens for
yelling or a knock on the door. She looks around at each of her
belongings, which may not have a right to be there anymore. The

impulse she had outside, the surprising urge for violence, is still with her. It reminds her of something, the weird feeling Marcus said overcame him at times in museums. Surrounded by things he was forbidden to touch, he felt he couldn't fully trust his own body. He would stand at a distance and hug himself, checking the desire he had to tear the canvases from the walls. In response to the wild craving that made her hit Ms. Norman, and in fear of it, Simone's body shakes all over.

Instinctively, she takes out her phone. There are missed calls from Dana and more messages from Bamboo: *Text me back, okay? I'm worried about you. Let me know if you need anything.* "Don't worry, baby," Simone says aloud. "Time heals all wounds." She laughs the way her father does, two low rueful grunts, brutal sounds she takes some pleasure in making. The phone lights up and vibrates. It's Ms. Norman, but Simone sends the call directly to voice mail. She sets the phone aside and brings the bag of alcohol into the kitchen. The cork from the chardonnay bottle slips out without a sound. The first buttery sips of the wine make Simone so happy she finds herself clenching her fist.

She opens the door to the backyard and brings her wine outside. No one is in the adjoining yards. The sky already seems less bright than it did when she was talking to Ms. Norman. The breeze continues to blow. She takes hold of the fence and inhales the stench of the swaying weeds, observing the toothlike patterns at the base of each leaf. The tall weeds seem to have punched through the dirt and the crevices of stone. They've been growing untended for so long. She has no desire to deal with them. She's never had the desire to do so—the truth is, she's hardly ever dealt with them herself. It was typically Marcus who pulled the weeds. He even claimed to enjoy the chore.

Simone studies the metal chairs and sits in one of them. The rust will probably stain her clothes. She looks up when she detects movement at Ms. Norman's windows. No one is there, but the image of the woman's shocked face shedding its mask remains, exhausting Simone down to her marrow. She stands again and pours some of the wine on the weeds, as if to water them. Then she throws her glass against the building and watches as it explodes. What was left of the wine streaks slowly down the wall next to her bedroom window. Back inside, she fills another glass and returns to the couch.

Drinking usually made Marcus want to dance. At some point he would set down his drink and say, "Oh, I'm feeling *right*." He'd tell her to turn up the music she had picked for him—he loved hip-hop, funk, and soul. At some point he would stand and start to move, alternating between seriousness and self-mockery. "Watch out, ladies," he would say, holding the hips of an imaginary woman while he rocked his own side to side, forward and back, around and around. Simone would laugh and call him a fool. "Marcus, you're a fool," she says now. She can almost see her brother there, dancing in front of her, hyping himself up and grinning from ear to ear. "I'm about to make you an auntie, Si Si," he'd say. "What you want, a niece or a nephew? I got enough juice for twins." He'd carry on this way, like some sort of real-deal playboy, even though he rarely went out or tried to meet women. He would say he wanted to get himself together first, get a better job, a better place to live, figure out which version of himself he really wanted to become.

Simone takes the bananas out of their bag and snaps one away from the bunch. She looks at how green it is. Bamboo would have gotten ones that are ripe. Marcus once showed her an easier way to open a banana, the way monkeys prefer to do it, ignoring the stem at the top and pinching the nub on the bottom instead

to cleanly split the peel. "Animals just live better lives," he liked to
say. "I mean, fish breathe *underwater*. Think about that. Have
you ever really thought about that? Cows have four stomachs. Do
you know what I could do with *four* stomachs? Nobody would ever
mess with me. I'd be a mammoth. I'd be the most powerful man
in the world." Simone listens to the memory and laughs. "Marcus, why you so stupid?" She opens the banana the way he taught
her and takes a bite, but the flesh is starchy and firm, without the
slightest hint of sweetness. The hunk of barely chewed fruit sits
on her tongue for a while before she forces herself to swallow it.
"You're the one who should have four stomachs though," Marcus
said. "You need to eat more, Si Si. Men like a girl with some meat.
You can't be backing it up on 'em if all you have back there is your
tailbone. You gonna maim somebody." She replied by telling him
that men liked her just fine, which continues to be true. Bamboo
never makes a secret of his love for her body. Recently, however, or
maybe it was a while ago—it was so hard to tell—the last time she
saw her parents, her mother did say it looked like she was losing
weight. Simone didn't have a response for that.

The transition to evening is strange, a darkening that almost never fails to dim her mood as well. Her headache has
subsided, or she has grown used to it now. She opens her laptop
and looks again at the photos and videos, even though she knows
she shouldn't. The faces without glasses. The thick red hair that
the daughter has too. Bamboo sends another text but she doesn't
reply. Simone's mother calls again but Simone doesn't answer.
Unsatisfied by the wine, she starts feeding her hungers with whiskey. She feels some guilt about not texting back or taking the call.
When she gets the notification of a voice mail, she listens to it and
is surprised to hear her father's voice rather than her mother's.
The two of them were separated for a while, before Marcus died,

when he acted as if he was the man of the family, and it's still strange to think of them together again, even using each other's phones. Her father sounds exhausted: ". . . just wanted to make sure you're all right, baby girl. Call us back when you get this so old folks don't worry. Don't have me *and* your mama out here bald-headed. Let us know if you need anything, okay? Miss you, love you . . ." Before the voice mail ends, her mother says something indiscernible in the background, maybe the beginning of a question. Simone refills her whiskey glass. She eats some of the candy from the supermarket bag.

Officer Brody's story, or the story he was directed to tell, is quite literally impossible, though Simone can't help giving it the time of day, once again thinking of it, picking it apart. How is it that a man can hide a gun on his body that three police searches can't find? How is it that a man can shoot himself in the head with his hands cuffed behind his back in a patrol car? How is it that a man—a man like her brother—a man like Marcus—can be judged guilty of taking his own life? Simone wonders if Officer Brody's wife ever asks him those questions. Maybe when they are alone in bed after their children are asleep. Maybe when they get drunk together and her vision is less clear and the alcohol has unbound her tongue.

But Marcus would laugh at this kind of thinking. Simone can almost see him, laughing disgustedly in her living room. "You're right, Marcus," she tells him—she already knows what he would say. "Why do you think *those* people, of *all* people, are gonna ask questions? People don't ask questions they don't want to know the answers to, people like that least of all." "You're right, you're right," she replies. She goes to take a sip of her drink but is surprised to find the glass empty again. She reaches for the bottle, tips it, and watches the liquid pour.

She hates imagining it but she always does, wondering if there was something she could have done to prevent it, Marcus cuffed in the back of that car, unable to convince Officer Brody that he isn't who the police say he is, unable to articulate the thought that even the man they think he is wouldn't deserve such treatment. It's frightening, unbearable. She can almost see him, there in her apartment, grimacing at the image that once again locks into her mind. She can see him, even more plainly, upset at her now, angry at the thoughts prompted by the image of him shackled in the car. The thoughts she knows are wrong but thinks anyway: *Could he be guilty, somehow, of taking his own life? Even if he isn't guilty, did he ever want to take it? Was there ever any evidence, in what he did or said, of his wanting to take it? Was he in trouble? Did he need my help? Why didn't he ask for it? Why should he need to ask?*

And then, as always after these questions, even after she denies them, Simone can't see him anymore, not at all, no matter how hard she tries. He's gone. She takes another drink and then picks up the last of the joint from yesterday, little more than a roach now. She smokes it until the heat burns her lips. When it's done, the evening is too. She grabs her phone, thinking to call Dana back, or her parents, or even her landlady, but she can't. She scrolls through her contacts, her eyes catching on Marcus's name, and then on the names of her men. She considers sending a message to one of them, maybe a different man than yesterday's. But she likes how it was yesterday. She brings the glass to her lips again, savoring the strength of the liquor in her mouth. "Ms. Norman, forgive me for my sins," she says. "I don't know what came over me. Forgive me for my transgressions. I promise, I swear on his grave, that I'll clean the goddamn yard tomorrow." Or the today after today, she thinks, but for now . . . "Might as well get you some Bamboo," she says to herself, and to the living room,

which seems emptier than usual, wheeling a bit in her vision before it rights itself. For a moment, with some stability restored,
embarrassment and shame overcome her, an awareness of some
kind of complicity, and then, in response to that, a brief flare of
anger. Then she types a message on her phone, as she has done
many times before, with no hint of ambiguity or guile, an invitation: *Where are you? I need you*

When he returns, he notices that the door to the apartment is
unlocked, as it often is. She forgets. He sees the white plastic bag
from the supermarket, the black one from the liquor store. He
suppresses any desire to tease her about the unripened fruit. In
fact, he has no desire to tease or scold her at all. He chuckles with
deeply pleasurable satisfaction at the way she peeled the banana,
but the sound doesn't seem to disturb her. He shakes his head at
the candy wrappers scattered on the coffee table. He watches her
phone, with its unsent message, slip from her dangling hand and
fall to the floor. She looks so unwell lying there on the flattened
cushions, so frail, but he still believes in her, in the idea that one
day it won't be like this anymore. He wishes he could make her
eat more, or drink less, but he can't. He does just one thing before
he leaves, the only thing he can on nights like this, when he finds
her passed out alone on that backbreaking couch. He offers her a
chance at a decent night of sleep, a chance that she will hurt a little less when she awakens. A comfort. With uncanny tenderness,
he lifts her into his arms and brings her to her bed.

ARROWS

———————————

Helena Porter kept her room the way she said all bedrooms should be kept. Like a lady's armpit: neat, bare, and inodorous, not accessible to the eyes of enemies or strangers. This had little to do with propriety, however. A private room kept with this kind of bodily sanctity could, my mother believed, shelter her impatient, fumbling heart. She thought of these qualities, impatience and gracelessness, as particular to the hearts of ladies, to their outwardly refined yet inwardly childlike insistence on handling flames, the flames of longing or of love. According to the terms of her personal lexicon, a woman was a lady only if she was fascinating and ungovernable, and my mother considered herself nothing if not a lady. This was true before the accident, which happened when she was on her way back from one of her dalliances. And it was true, I'm sure, in the moments after the terrible collision, as she sat crushed and semiconscious in the driver's seat. It was true even now that she was dead.

There she was, the ghost that was my mother, sitting hunched over on the left side of her bed. When I reminded her that I was taking Pops up to Hillside the next day, she raised her immaculate face up at me and ruefully shook her head. "So you're really going to take my man away." She spoke in the usual tone of her mothering. Uninvolved and opinionated. Then she went back to what she was doing, attending to her toes, brightening the nails with the same chalky hue of white that dominated her walls and linens. The room had looked that way for almost fifteen years, ever since Pops had gone fully blind, when what had been their room became hers.

"Is it really happening so soon?" she said, keeping a careful eye on her toe work. "I don't remember it being so soon. You sure are in a rush to get rid of him. My man . . ."

"It's a good place," I said, frowning at her endearments. "They specialize in folks with Pops's condition."

"I specialized in other people's mess too," Helena replied. Then she had the nerve to say, "It's called being part of a family. It's just what you do. You find ways to live with inconvenience." At the open window the curtain slowly undulated, reminding me of a queen waving her square of lace. The clean musk pulled from the earth by the morning's rain began to fill the room. Helena stood and admired her wriggling toes. Against her hips she smoothed a slip that was a bit unseemly for a woman of her apparent age. She beheld her splayed fingers, which looked like stems pushing snowy buds out from their tips. Then she shook her head again. "A home. Like white folks do."

"This isn't 1957," I told her. "With the costs of his care and all, and the mortgage, it's what makes sense. It's what he needs."

"Oh, it's about *his* needs? *He* needs it? Hmph." Helena went over and looked at herself in the mirror. I couldn't be sure what she perceived there, if she saw herself in the exact way she appeared to me. She fussed with her hair a little and then performed the delicate magic that is a lady's application of makeup, attending to her face with the softness of brushes and powders. She reminded me of myself, of the way I could be sometimes, which is to say good-for-nothing. I too could find some minuscule thing to pour all of my attentions into. I thought of it as a strategy of self-preservation, but maybe it was simply a strategy of avoidance, one passed on to me through the blood.

"I'm still selling the house," I said.

"The house we scrimped and saved to raise you in."

"I'm grown now, and I have every right to sell it, and that's exactly what I'm going to do."

"I noticed. Hardly recognized the rest of the place."

"People are gonna start coming to look at it next week."

Just then a car's horn sounded outside, two short beeps followed by a much longer one.

"Ah, I'd recognize it anywhere, that peevish sound. It's so distinct, you know." Then, as if Tabitha and I hadn't separated, bitterly, long before the fatal accident, Helena added, "Maybe it's your lily princess putting all these notions in your head, hm?"

She turned to consider me, obviously amused with herself, and obviously pleased with the way she looked. Her hair was lovely, arranged in a row of impeccable curls around the long grace of her neck. Set in the room's field of white, she reminded me of those old photos of her that Pops used to pull out and brag on, asking how a man wouldn't want to just sop her up with the proverbial biscuit. Plenty of men had wanted to, in fact, and by her consent, and by his, a fair number of them had. It seemed, too, that the activity was ongoing, though I couldn't say if her gentleman callers now were also of the spectral variety or if she was still somehow carrying on with the living.

"Anyway, my dear, don't explain what I already know," she said, "just to make yourself feel better. Explain what I *don't* know, which is what in the world it has to do with me." When I failed to reply, she slid into her dress and stepped up into her shoes. "Since you're here, you might as well make yourself useful." Then she turned around. As I zipped up her dress I could feel, with certainty and solidity, only the fabric of the dress and the tab of the metal slider. Her flesh, of course, was something slightly beyond, just past the threshold of whatever divided us, little more than a heated compression of air. This task was familiar to me, one I had seen executed many times, feeling anger and shame as I watched. With inexplicable pleasure Pops would be the one completing her ensemble, like the final tuck and seal of a gift, even though he knew the nature of what he was doing, that the gift would soon be unwrapped by another. Then the cruel ritual would continue. She would kiss him on the cheek, she would leave, and she would return hours later, directly to her lady's chamber.

"You could go with him," I told her now. "To the home."

A smile grew hideously on her face. "The bottom line is this, son. Yes, you have the license to do whatever you want with the house, even if that means taking my man away from me, but I am not giving up my room."

The car blared again outside, an extravagant, drawn-out wail of impatience. The image of Tabitha leaning on the horn from the passenger seat was crystal clear in my mind.

"Your lily princess has summoned you," Helena teased. "So it looks like you have to go. More importantly, so do I. Please tell my grandbaby that he's loved."

"But we're not done here," I said.

"Oh, we are."

"So you want me to sell a haunted house."

"Don't act brand-new, my dear. It would be far from the first time," she said. "What old house *isn't* haunted?"

"The dead shouldn't be so selfish."

"Well," she dared to reply, "neither should the living."

I passed over the creaky floorboards in the hallway and through the uncanny scene downstairs, where my father sat with his headphones on, morosely listening to oldies on the radio. When I stepped outside I stood there for a few moments to relish the early-evening breeze, purposely delaying my approach to the car. As I reached the curb, Zahir bounced out and stood on my right foot, hid his face in my thigh. He looked up and grinned anxiously when I greeted him, showing me his mouthful of Chiclet teeth, then smushed his face back into my leg. I peeked into the car, past Tabitha, and said a hearty hello to Dennis, her current lover, who as expected was at the wheel, kneading the leather with his bulbous thumbs. He didn't even bother to look at me. His aviator glasses barely concealed the sore expression on his face, his lips and forehead fretted with a million lines. He was twenty-seven years older than Tabitha and seemed to me like an irrepressible pervert. The kind of dirty old rich white man who would squeeze her behind for kicks while she was sick as a dog in bed, never missing any opportunity to stake his claim. Whenever I saw him, I couldn't help but think that a man like this had always been her ultimate goal. Her marriage to me had probably just been one extended bout of slumming.

Tabitha slowly opened the passenger-side door, using the weight of it to nudge me away. Before stepping out of the car, she looked warily at the house, which she'd had a bad feeling about since the death of my mother, even though I had never said anything to her about the haunting or about my family's true history. She bent back into the vehicle to grab Zahir's backpack and then stiff-armed it into my chest.

"No need for the elaborate procedure," I said. "You could have just handed it to me from the car."

"Don't start with me, Hasan. I got out to say a proper good-bye to my son."

But nothing could convince me she wasn't showing off her outfit, a crop top and little shorts that weren't suitable for the weather. She clearly wanted me to see. She wanted to flirt Dennis's behind around, to demonstrate the meat on her bones. More fleshy, more classically curvaceous than I'd ever seen her, she even flaunted a pleasing little round of striped belly. I had no idea her body could assume such a shape, or that she would ever permit it to, especially in light of her crusade to eradicate every ounce of her baby weight, and then some. Hunting for a flaw, I fixed on the enormous sun visor she wore, which I instantly decided was the tell, the garment that identified her as a trophy and a simpleton. From somewhere within the shadows of the ridiculous hat, Tabitha informed me that she'd already fed Zahir his dinner.

"Why'd you do that?" I said. "I was planning to whip up one of his favorites tonight."

"Oh, you finally learned how to boil water? How wonderful." She tilted her head up at me and flashed a dishonest smile. In just a few weeks, her face had become prettier, more sensuous. Her hair, cinched into a high ponytail, looked and smelled freshly washed. "We'll get the boy on Sunday evening, around seven," she told me, and then added, "in *Brooklyn*, okay? None of your"— her hand twirled on her wrist as she searched for the words— "elaborate excuses this time. I don't want to hear any song and dance." Dennis was driving them out to his place in Amagansett for a getaway. They were irked that they had to come all the way up to Westchester to drop Zahir off. I was irked that she'd insisted on leaving him with me now, given everything I was dealing with, but it was in fact my turn with our son. The last few times it had been my turn I'd ended up being too busy.

I placed a proprietary hand on the boy's head. "Say bye to Mommy, Zaza," I told him.

Instead, he opted for chaos, crumpling to the ground and snickering wetly, with one hand still on my leg and the other around his mother's ankle. "I don't know why you're looking at *me* so desperately," Tabitha said. This time her smile was true. "Can't you handle it? He's not a baby anymore. You always said you looked forward to this. What did you call it? *The fun phase.* Well, he's in a phase all right, so have fun." Then she crouched down and took his face in her hands. "Bye, son," she said. "Have lots and lots and lots of fun," and then she gave him a lingering kiss on the forehead. With that she was back in the car with her porcine retiree and the lovers were on their way.

She often called Zahir *son* or referred to him as *the boy*—which even Helena said was harmless enough—but Tabitha was obviously trying to avoid saying his name, which she obviously hated. I had insisted on *Zahir*, a name I'd loved ever since I read the Borges story in college. And it was Arabic, like my own name. It gave me a kind of decisive claim on him, which his appearance unfortunately did not. The shape of his face was similar to mine and his hair was curly, though not kinky, but otherwise, in every other way, he looked exactly like Tabitha.

"You wanna see Pop-Pop?" I asked Zahir.

At the mention of his grandfather, he got up from the ground and danced in place, shaking his hands high above his head. There was an incredible affection between them. I followed him into the front yard, where he loved to spend time. I watched him pause to play among the daffodils, which he handled with unusual delicacy. I crouched beside him and offered a piggyback

ride. He continued to nudge the blooms with a finger before finally acknowledging me. After securing him, I found myself
staring at the house, attempting to see the place as a potential
buyer might. From here, and in the waning daylight, it looked
just fine, somewhat beaten by weather and time, but nothing, not
even the corner of windows that belonged to Helena's room, appeared obviously out of joint. "What are you waiting for, Baba?"
Zahir asked. His heart fluttered against my shoulder blade. For
some reason, the question and the sensation induced a feeling of
loneliness.

Zahir and I came into the living room as Pops was in the midst
of a loud fit of cursing, making the noises that would probably
survive him. "What the hell!" he bellowed, rubbing the side of
his knee. "Nothing's the way it was. How the fuck am I supposed
to live here another goddamn minute without breaking my goddamn neck?"

I set Zahir down so he could go to appease his beloved grandfather, but he was totally at a loss. He just stared at the old man
and then began looking around with a more general bemuse-
ment. As he did so, he kept absentmindedly pinching the flesh of
my hip with his surprisingly strong hands. I would lightly slap his
hand away, but each time it would come up again to pincer me.
He hadn't been to the house in a good while, but his memories
of it were apparently intact—and what he was seeing now clearly
violated them. I went over and pushed the coffee table back to its
new place, flush against the wall. To open up the room, a professional stager had displaced it there just that afternoon, one of
the final touches of over a week of painstaking rearrangements.
Staged homes apparently sold faster and for better prices than
homes in their naturally occupied state. The stager had said it was

important to showcase the house free of any stubborn emotional connections that were particular to our family. She'd respectfully advised, for instance, that we move the etched black-and-gold urn where Helena's ashes were kept from its place above the faux fireplace. "Selling, not dwelling" was her company's guiding principle, according to which she'd made every room alien for us, but easily navigable for any forthcoming strangers. Every room, of course, but my mother's. I knew well enough to stop her when she tried.

With his long, knurled fingers Pops reached to make sure his lounge chair was still there (it wasn't), and then he reached (more successfully) for the sofa, which the stager had cheerfully said was only "slightly off" before adjusting it by an infinitesimal degree. After stiffly lowering himself onto the cushions and irritably tossing aside two rented throw pillows, Pops exhaled and said, "Now, where's my grandson?" At this, Zahir snapped out of his reverie and charged over. The two of them whipped each other into a frenzy, my son shrieking and my father playfully growling. When the pandemonium finally subsided, Pops began his inspection, touching Zahir's hands and arms and face, taking measure of his height, commenting favorably on any changes, real or invented. This was their ceremony. "You're getting so big and strong," Pops would say, and Zahir would respond with pride and delight. "But maybe you're getting *too* big, hm? Too big for the adventures of Zaza the Bear?" When Zahir suffered enough of this teasing, and protested enough to satisfy his Pop-Pop, the time for stories would begin. The words came easily to my father. I had hardly known it before my son was born, or maybe I had forgotten it, but my father was a great storyteller. Yes, I had forgotten it. He loved to regale his friends with legends about Helena and her beauty. As I watched him now, and listened to him improvise another tale, it occurred to me that there must have been a time when he sat me by his side and told me stories. But the very thought of this was much too maudlin to entertain. I left them to their fun and went into the kitchen, but I could still hear the hum of his voice, could follow the tale's turns and reversals just from the tonal drifts of his murmuring. Maybe that would be it, the form of his haunting, disembodied threads of narrative floating faintly, like gossamer on the air.

Ghosts have been in my family for generations, but the ones on my father's side tended to be of the flimsier sort, available more to the ears than to the eyes of the living. His grandmother left behind her Sunday-afternoon humming, for example, and his disabled uncle persisted in the heavy step and drag, step and drag, along the length of his porch. My mother, on the other hand, had the telltale visibility and near-corporeality of many of the ghosts on her half of the family. This quality made it difficult for living witnesses to keep the necessary boundary, to distinguish between traces of things and the things themselves. You could treat the ghosts of my father's people like an overheard phrase of a familiar tune, taking notice of it and perhaps, for better or for worse, remembering, but only for a moment. With a ghost like my mother, however, you had to be careful. Before you knew it, that quivering body would firm into a pillar, around which your entire life, here and hereafter, would everlastingly revolve.

It was no surprise to me that Zahir, growing boy that he was, said he was hungry again. Instead of cooking, I ordered chicken lo mein and shrimp fried rice. The three of us ate the food heartily, though it felt somewhat illicit to make use of the staged table. Its central purpose now was to ratify the room surrounding it, to be inoffensive enough that one could easily imagine replacing it

with something better. Still, we ate on it, Zahir dirtying it with
sauce and stray grains I told myself I'd clean up later. We were
three generations of eventual ghosts enjoying a carnal pleasure
at what was a Last Supper of a kind, and my father was all too
happy to play, in the cheapest possible sense, the role of martyr.
He ate with a slow intensity, as though he didn't have any teeth,
with his mouth scrunched and lips protruding. These exaggera-
tions and made-up ailments were nothing new. When I was ten,
he accidentally cut his finger on a knife while making one of his
inedible meals and then tried to force-feed me a fatty slab of steak,
groaning the entire time as if he needed his entire arm in a sling.
He turned my reluctance to eat that cheap hunk of meat into
some kind of personal attack on him, an ungrateful son's insur-
gence against his dutiful, sacrificing father. After his tirade, he
left me by myself, maybe to search for that sling, and I stuffed the
remainder of the meat into paper towels, ending up with a pulpy
ball of grease that I threw away. Later that night he found the
discarded food and beat me with a cracked leather belt, swinging
it with his left hand. More than once he struck me hard with the
heavy buckle.

When he began to lose his sight, he also started to limp for no
evident reason. He didn't limp anymore, but now, fully into his
blindness, he sometimes acted as if other senses had been stripped
from him as well. I reminded him what time we were leaving in
the morning for Hillside, and he nodded once. I reminded him
that we had to be there before noon. He gave me another nod.
This was his mute self. Zahir forgot his appetite and began to
watch us with interest.

"It's the best thing, Pops," I said. "I can't come up here every
damn day, every damn weekend."

"Say what now?" he said, afflicted by sudden deafness. He

leaned in toward me with his mouth poked out and his wiry mustache pressed to his nostrils.

"Gotta live my life, Pops. And you need to get out of here. They'll take care of you."

"They who?"

"*People*," I said, as if that explained everything.

He took a big mouthful of lo mein and leaned back in his seat. He chewed with his lips as far away from his face as possible, and the noodles danced loosely as they slid into his hole. Oil spattered his mustache, the scruff on his chin and cheeks. He may as well have been a child grunting in a high chair.

"I'll pack the last of your stuff tonight," I said.

"Thank you, son, for taking such good care of me. I can't wait to go to the home." The oil practically dripped from his words.

"Pop-Pop *is* home," Zahir said.

My father raised his eyebrows but didn't speak.

"Well, Pop-Pop's moving," I said.

"Like when me and Mommy moved," he asserted.

"Kind of. You remember that?"

"No, I don't remember." And then he was quiet for a while.

Something came to mind then, my theory about how a ghost begins. The idea had a hoodoo grandiosity that did not come naturally to me, but I had to exceed my own limitations to come to any kind of understanding. I called my idea *the arrow of time*. Some people live with an almost appalling optimism, a sense that every next meal, every next sip of wine, every next tryst will be better than the last until the day they die. And if it wasn't—oh well—then the next one would be. Such people tolerate the past, give it their merest acknowledgment, the way you might quickly raise and lower your head to a passing stranger. Other people, people who tend to become ghosts, are different. They're the ones who turn around to face the past, and they get impaled by the arrow. Stuck on something that happened to them, or on an obsession, they're the ones who can't accept people's inevitably forward movement through the entanglements of time.

"So who's moving with him?" Zahir demanded suddenly. "Are *you* moving with him?"

"Pop-Pop is a grown-up," I said, and kept going despite my immediate regret. "He doesn't need anyone else to go with him."

Zahir's puzzled expression turned more severe. It looked like he was about to cry. "*Why* are you moving?" he asked his grandfather. "Can I see you at your new house?"

My father chewed his food with considerable focus, still deaf and mute, prolonging his dumb show of ignorance.

"You can see him as much as you want," I said. "The home isn't far."

But that was no consolation. Zahir flung himself from his chair and had an uncontrollable fit on the floor. Not that I tried to control him. I just watched it happen. Ugliness was the theme of his outburst. I was ugly. Pops's "new house" was ugly, and because he didn't recognize it, so too was the current one. Even the food he had just greedily consumed was ugly. Maybe, I thought, this was what would make him turn around and get stuck by the arrow. It seemed possible that his ghost would start today, at once, a tiny vapor inside him flaring up and pulsing alongside his quickened heart. Maybe he would haunt this house too, like my mother, refusing to leave the place where, perhaps, his purest happiness resided. And where it was taken away from him. His ghost would arrive here to find my father's ghost too. And perhaps mine, though I'd often felt trapped in moments further back in time. Briefly, the image of our ghostly reunion had a certain appeal. With Helena upstairs, coming and going as she pleased, the three of us would be fixed inescapably in the amber of this scene, at the model dinner table of the model dining room of our imperfect model home.

Zahir eventually calmed himself, with a tremendous effort that had a somnolent effect. I laid him down in the third bedroom upstairs, the one I used when I couldn't avoid sleeping over, and then went into my father's room, which had been my childhood bedroom, to put the last of his things in boxes. Pops stayed downstairs to smoke a small joint and listen to the final innings of the Mets game.

I sat on his bed and began the task. Pops had said there were just odds and ends left to pack, but what I found there couldn't be called miscellany. The items were mostly iterations of the same thing, a collection of framed photographs of my mother. The first few were mostly familiar to me, but then there came many, more than two dozen of them, that I'd never encountered before. For a long time one in particular held my attention.

It was a picture of Helena, Pops, and me, a close-up shot of our faces. They were holding me up between them, and I couldn't have been any older than Zahir was now. Pops's large eyes, which even then must have been faulty, were nevertheless, even in this still, quick with bits of life. Helena was like another woman, not just in terms of age—though there was a freshness to her beauty, recalling a young Vonetta McGee—but also as if the force that animated her, her element, were entirely different. Later in her life, and in her afterlife, she was white-hot fire, or she was air. In this picture she was water. Her hair, which was braided and beaded, looked as though it held drops of wetness, and whenever she wished to, or so the cant of her head suggested, she could flick them into our faces.

As the lamplight played over the surface of the frame in my shaky hands, I began to notice how heavily smudged it was. I looked more closely and saw that the glass was filthy with fingerprints. I examined the other photographs again, removing them from the box I had placed them in, and was astonished by how obsessively traces of touch filled the planes. My father must have groped them all with a manic frequency, and with a maniac's compulsion to undergo an experience in its cosmic entirety. But I didn't understand why. His eyes were essentially useless, and there were no textures for his fingertips to decipher. I was so absorbed in this mystery that one of the house's typical eruptions, a creaking noise in the hallway, startled me and my knee whacked one of the frames from the bed to the floor. Helena had probably just returned from her affair. I leaned over to retrieve the photograph, which was the one of the three of us. The glass still held together, but now it was filigreed, an intricate web spread across our faces.

When I was a boy, before I knew much of anything about the history of our family, my father had been so cruel to me, so bullying and manipulative, so weepy and seething and lashing, that it was easy to think of him, without any ambivalence whatsoever, not in terms of a ghost, but as a demon. His marriage to my mother, however, had always been impossible to fathom. Neither of them had ever spoken to me about it. *Stay out of grown folks' business*, my father liked to say. Seemingly from the start, their relationship had been a peculiar one, twisted and knotted by their various arrangements, and contorted by their circumstances, but it had never been sundered. My father, demon that he was, had actually been fairly successful by human standards. He had married the woman of his dreams, and had done what was required to stay with her, and his love for her had never ceased.

Instinctively, I picked up my phone. I had the urge to talk to someone—about this, and about everything that was on my mind. I pulled up my modest list of contacts and scrolled through but none of them meant anything. It was just a roster of connections that had been lost. I didn't have anyone to talk to, so I just stared at the screen. Eventually, I noticed the blurred reflection of a single swimming eye, like a fish twitching in the murk. When the glass of the phone went black and depthless it threw my entire exhausted face back at me, with only slightly more clarified gloom. I lay back on my father's bed within the walls of my old room, where he had most frequently beaten me when I was a child. I let my head fall to the side so I could look out the window. An old feeling returned. The desperation to escape this house and be done with it forever. I rested the idle phone along my temple and my cheek.

It was late on a Friday, so if she—tonight my intimate was a she, and her name, so it came to me, was Esther—if she answered her phone it would sound in the background like she was out at a party or a bar. Esther would tell me to hold on for a second. When her voice returned, the background would be quieter, aside from the intermittent shrieking of passersby and the occasional shush of car tires on the damp city streets. She'd probably be searching through her bag for a lighter and her cigarettes, which she called her *blues*. She would address me sweetly: *Hey stranger.* I would say I was thinking about my mother, and she would make some joke in reply, something like, *Never call a girl to tell her you're thinking about some other girl.* Then, knowing—as they all did—where this call was going, Esther would exhale smoke and remark on something irrelevant and disarming and mock-poetical, like the night sky, or on the moon in particular, and then, committing to this deviation, digging in her heels, she'd quote some obscure line of verse. "*The*

moon was a ghostly galleon tossed upon cloudy seas . . ." She would tell
me to look at the moon now and how beautiful it was. Though
the blinds were raised, the moon wasn't visible from where I lay,
but I would agree nonetheless. She and I agreed, of course, about
what we found beautiful. She would narrate at length some fable
about the moon's formation, and despite the pleasure of her voice
I would get irritated finally and tell her I had called to talk about
something real. Knowing everything—as all my intimates did—
she would say that was funny coming from me, the boy whose an-
cestry was intangible, a genealogy of ghosts. I would ask her what
she thought the qualities of my own ghost would be. She would
say I might be the first person in history who would shatter into
ghostliness, producing not one but many. I would ask why, and
she would say, *You're full of arrows, Hasan, you just can't let anything go.*
And then there would be an awful gap of silence filled only by the
occasional splash of the city's noise. She would say she needed to
get off the phone, and I would tell her to wait, that I had more to
say, that there was more I wanted to tell her, and she would end
the call by saying that I always had words, words upon words, an
infinite abundance of words, but would I ever be able to say one
true thing that could save me.

Another noise, a sharp rapping on the door, made me startle.
When I opened it, Zahir was standing there in the dim glow of
the hallway's night-light, his face waxy and tight with sleep, eyes
glued nearly shut. "I heard people talking, Baba," he said.

"Go back to bed," I told him. "Don't worry. That was just me."

I finally packed up the photographs, wrapping each frame in
newspaper and placing them all in the carefully padded box.
When I was done, I went downstairs to tell Pops he could come
up to sleep, but he wasn't there. Every source of light in the living

room had been turned on, and the room itself, burning under the scrutiny of all that illumination, was in complete disarray. Not only had the coffee table been knocked away from the wall again, the sofa with its pillows, the television stand, and the side tables had also been moved, making the center of the room impassable. The rug was bunched within the crammed furniture. The innocuous hotel-style art I had rented from the stager had been removed from the walls, and the enigmatic figurines and the scented candles and the artificial plants and the crystal vase that had been awaiting its future flowers were all tipped over onto their sides. It looked as though the house had been burglarized. I cautiously entered each of the other rooms—the kitchen and dining area, the downstairs bathroom. They hadn't been disturbed, but my father was nowhere to be found. When I returned to the living room, there was another distinct noise, the creaking of floorboards above me. Such a sound, in a house that gave off plenty of them, usually meant nothing, but I was jumpy, and suspicious now too, so I went back upstairs to investigate.

When I got to the top of the stairs, Zahir was out of bed again. He stood at the other end of the hallway this time, in front of Helena's room. He turned to me and the features of his face still appeared to be closed, like the folded petals of a tulip. "I hear people *talking*, Baba," he insisted sleepily, and then he reached for the doorknob. Just as he started to push into the room, I bolted across the hallway and grabbed him, lifting him into my arms. He hugged me tightly; tightly he wrapped his legs around my waist. As he began to tremble, weeping quietly over my shoulder, I held the back of his head. I didn't know why he was crying, and I got the sense that he didn't know either, that he was just reverting to the wordless instincts of a confounded baby. Or it was possible he had seen something. The door to Helena's room was only cracked open, and it probably hadn't been that way long enough for him to catch sight of anything. Still, he was right; there was noise coming from the room, though it seemed less to me like words than a throat-song of yearning.

When I stepped forward and pressed my eye to the crack it got quiet, an abrupt snuffing of the sound. The room was hazily lit, but it didn't take long to make out the dusky shape of my mother on the bed, facing the foot of it. I couldn't tell for sure but Helena appeared to be looking at me too. She tilted her head downward, and I realized she wasn't alone on the bed, and then it became clear she was astride him. I hadn't seen them together since before she died, and I hadn't seen them together in this room since she had claimed sole dominion over it. My base imagination of what they were doing quickly yielded to the much stranger actuality of what my eye perceived. He reached with the fingers of both hands, slowly up until they broke the permeable barrier of what would have been her rib cage, and sank into her. Then, after a moment of tremulous suspension, he drew the fingers out knuckle by knuckle, and with what felt to me like all the pleasure that can inhere in hesitation, he reached up and into her again, as if she was his own personal cloud.

I tore myself away from the door and carried my son downstairs to the ruins of the living room. I pulled the sofa back just far enough to gain access to it and then lay down with Zahir on my chest. It took him a while to find any comfort. He wasn't so much resting as he was wrestling, thrashing against me with his limbs. When his breathing steadied, I knew he had finally stopped crying, and when it relaxed and deepened, I knew he had finally fallen asleep. But I was unable to sleep. I felt stabbed all over by what I couldn't unsee. Bitterly, I also felt I was the only one there who hadn't been granted any exemption from time, the only one for whom the pressure of tomorrow would not even temporarily relent. So I just lay awake listening to the creaks and groans of the house until the sun began to rise.

As I put Pops's things in the car the next morning, I was surprised at the meagerness of his possessions. A couple of suitcases and a couple of boxes, that was all. As if he was heading off for two weeks of vacation instead of hauling away the equipment of an entire life. It was almost time to go, so I steeled myself for what felt like the first action that was truly irrevocable, the task of actually removing my father from our family house. When I closed the trunk, though, he was already emerging from the front door, led with great concern and patience by my son. Pops refused to let me help him get in, and Zahir tried to mimic this defiance as I secured him into the car seat in the back. Up in the house, at one of the windows to her room, Helena looked down at us. I couldn't see her expression, but I could clearly sense her frustration and her fortitude. She rattled the panes violently with both hands before she disappeared from view.

The drive was quiet aside from the low, indiscernible music coming from the radio. I wanted to say something, but I also didn't want to surrender the mercy of that silence. When we stopped at a traffic light, I studied Zahir's enigmatic expression in the rearview mirror. I was so transfixed, the car behind us had to honk to make me aware that the light was green. From that point on, I kept looking back at him. We ended up arriving at Hillside late, because of a detour, but in one piece, despite the difficulty I had keeping my eyes on the road.

The detour had come toward the end of the drive. I took an impromptu right turn and proceeded in that direction until we reached the parking lot of a train station by the lower Hudson.

Pops and Zahir were confused as I urged them out of the car. On the other side of the station, after you descend a long staircase to the platform for southbound trains, there was a place I knew, where you could have a special experience of the ever-changing river. I led my son and my father down to that place. From there, where today the river appeared swollen from the rain, we could taste the faint, bracing stench of the leaden water. We could feel on our skin the flexing of this arm of the sea and hear in the spring breezes the heavy admonition of its rush. This was a place where you had a chance to unburden yourself, where your concerns might be shaken off or transfigured, or washed away. We stood out there for a few minutes in sensory plentitude. Then Zahir took Pops by the hand to guide him down a few more steps and then forward, along the edge of the river's bank. I watched them walk parallel to the flow of the black Hudson as, for the moment, it roared south toward the harbor. In no time at all, much more quickly than you'd expect of a blind old man being tugged along by a fickle little boy, they opened a great deal of distance between us. As if they were frightened of me. As if they were taking flight.

SAHAR

Gloria had meant to talk to the delivery woman, to truly talk to her. She wanted to say more than just "Hello" and "Thank you," maybe introduce herself, though Sahar must have already known her name, at least for the moment, until the next person in her queue took hold of her mind. Gloria's lips went into motion, but the words came stripped of all sound. In response, Sahar smiled the way people do when they search for their friends in a room crowded with strangers, that pained but hopeful expression of discomfort soon to end. Then she handed over the food Gloria had ordered for dinner, gave a quick wave goodbye, and left the old woman standing there, on the threshold between her building and the full onset of spring. After a few cars and loose-limbed pedestrians ambled by, it occurred to Gloria that she should eat her food before it got cold. As expected, there was a handwritten note stapled to the top of the folded paper bag. Gloria shut the door and passed through the old lobby, ignoring the elevator that she hadn't taken in over a year, for the exercise, as well as the tarnished mirror above the table where parcels were left. She climbed the stairs to her floor, the sixth, studying the note

as she went. Each sentence was written in a different color and
the first was another inspirational quote by a celebrity. Maybe
Sahar had purchased a book of them, or maybe she jotted them
down randomly herself. This one in particular was attributed to
Superman, but it was obvious Sahar meant the actor who was
best known for playing that role. The rest of the note was similar
to the others, full of courteous exhortations. *Enjoy Your Meal! Be
Safe! May your Decisions reflect your Hopes, not your Fears!* As usual, she
had signed the note, *Your Courier.*

Whenever Gloria stepped into the apartment, a swell of
gratification washed over her. A new friend visiting for the first
time might have called the space small and the furniture old-
fashioned, but Gloria preferred to think of it as snug, decorated in
a classical style. It fit her as well as a cloche on Josephine Baker's
lovely head. In the brief time Gloria had been gone to pick up her
food, the sunflower in the window had burst, spilling its petals on
the floor beneath the sill. She swept them into her palm and put
them into a large mason jar where she also kept pennies, tangles
of ribbon, loose beads, and other pleasing slivers of color. She had
thought about keeping the notes there too, since she quite liked
the hue and quality of the paper, as if Sahar had chosen it with
care at a stationery store, but she would end up keeping them
between the pages of a volume of poetry by her favorite author.
Gloria didn't consider herself much of a writer, certainly not a
poet. But she took a lot of pride in being someone who read—her
husband, rest his soul, used to say she did so like a woman wild
with lust. In less guarded moments, she would confess that her
passionate commitment to reading had sometimes deluded her
into thinking she could one day craft a serious sentence or two
of her own.

The food from this particular restaurant wasn't as good as

she had hoped, which was a shame. Based on the enthusiastic reviews online, she'd been looking forward to trying the place, which had opened several months back. But the cubes of chicken were as dry as bones, the saffron rice made overly sweet with too many currants. The bread was supposed to be worthy of head-lines, but to Gloria it was more like yesterday's news. When she was younger she would have eaten every bite regardless, due to home training, but now, so close to retirement, she was becom-ing even less concerned with what was considered obligatory or proper. Maurice, her husband, used to say that when he finally retired, nobody would be able to tell him a thing. It saddened Gloria that he never made it to the phase of life she was about to enter. She was already experiencing hints of the feeling Maurice had alluded to, and she found that not giving a damn, even in very modest ways, was wonderful. It truly was something else. So not a word could be said to her, not even by her conscience, when she tossed the bad food in the trash.

It took her a while to realize she had thrown out Sahar's lat-est note along with the food. She fished it out of the garbage but it was badly soiled. She did the best she could to wipe it clean. As she looked at the note again, something, maybe that second glass of white wine she had decided to have with dinner, put her in a fanciful mood. The notion of writing a few words in reply to Sahar became interesting to her. As the darkness of the sky deepened, she sat beside the now-empty vase and did exactly that.

I'm sorry to say I didn't enjoy the meal you delivered today from that new restaurant, though I did like the other three you've brought me in the past month. Of course, the quality of the food from these various places doesn't have anything to do with you. You have been excellent, you should know, both prompt and cordial, and your notes have been a lovely, special touch. I've tried to show my awareness and appreciation of that when I tip. I worry when I see how low the default amount is on the app. I bet you come across a lot of cheapskates, rich ones probably, but I firmly believe that good work deserves recognition.

I suppose I think that way because of my own life of work. I've made up my mind to retire in one year—a year! can you believe it?—from a job I've had for nearly forty, in the field of hospitality. The room service staff of the Q Hotel. You probably know it. Perhaps you've made deliveries there. It isn't so far from where I live. Given how frequently I've seen you—I've never seen any other delivery person from the app more than once—maybe it isn't far from where you live either. Or maybe that doesn't have anything to do with anything. Sometimes I feel like I don't really know how the world works anymore. There are too many wires strewn about, it seems, and every one of them is invisible. But maybe it's better to be blissfully ignorant and avoid getting too tangled up.

When the weather is nice the way it has been lately, I often make my way to and from the hotel on foot. You probably know this, but the neighborhood it's in is called something else now, at least by the white people who moved in a minute ago to live the life of Riley, but we still consider it part of our own. It's a good time for me to be getting out of this line of work. I remember when I would bring fifty or sixty glasses of orange juice to people's rooms in a morning, but these days we're lucky if the number of breakfast orders reaches ten. You can imagine what that means for our tips. Some other hotels have gone ahead and eliminated room service entirely. Concierges, bellhops, and doormen too. I guess they figure there's no longer a need when there are tablets and rideshares, and when people like you can bring guests a meal from almost anywhere in the city. I know what this sounds like, but don't worry. I'll tell it to you like this, the way I used to tell Maurice (husband, he's dead): "It is your fault, but I don't blame you." It drove him a bit crazy whenever I told him that, but all it means is I understand how people get caught up in things that are much bigger than they are, things they really can't help.

Or here's what I mean. Last year we went on strike with our union, so there we were standing outside hollering and carrying on, singing our little songs, chanting our little chants. Meanwhile there's an unending stream of your people pouring into the Q, bags of food in hand. For all I know, you may have been one of them. Were you? Some of my colleagues— I think everyone who labors with others is a colleague—they got steaming mad as they watched the delivery people march in and out of the hotel lobby. I even got jostled a few times, but once I started throwing my elbows around, that calmed down quick. There was no legitimate reason to get upset. As if we didn't know how inadequately your people get paid. As if we couldn't imagine how your people must hope and pray never to fall seriously ill. And, I said to Apollo (doorman, prone to righteous anger), as if we didn't all have the same icons of convenience lined up neatly on our phones.

Well, here I am, running my mouth, when all I really meant to do was express my gratitude, in a fuller sense than merely sealing a transaction with a robotic word of thanks. Or by calculating 35 percent. It's strange that you've been my courier four times in such a short span, strange enough that in some way it must be meaningful, but I'm not so foolish as to think I'm the only customer of yours who receives notes. I don't believe I'm special. Everyone deserves good, thoughtful service—everyone decent, anyway—and it's clear that's what you take time and care to provide. I usually don't have trouble expressing myself in person—in my day, my girlfriends were always impressed by how boldly I made myself known, even to men, Maurice included—but with you I can barely get out two words. They stick in my throat. So I've decided, right this very moment I've decided, to hand this silly missive to you the next time we see each other, which, in light of how things have gone, I'm sure will be soon. I hope you read it. And if you do, I hope you won't think I'm loony tunes.

Retirement had been prominent in Gloria's mind for a long time, especially since Maurice's death four years earlier, but after mentioning it in writing she grew more obsessed with the idea. During the next few weeks it became ubiquitous in her thoughts, even at night, when it tore at the already delicate silks of her sleep. Expressing it once demanded further expression, she decided, so at the next available opportunity she officially informed her boss that she would retire the following April.

"That's marvelous, Gloria," her boss said. He removed his glasses to fix her with his clouded eyes and told her again how marvelous it was. "It's about time you put your feet up. You've been here even longer than I have."

"Much longer," Gloria said.

He laughed, but it sounded more like he was hawking something up. "Remind me. Are you the longest tenured?"

"Apollo and I may have started around the same time."

"But who was first?"

"I don't have any memories of being here before Apollo, and he would probably say the same about me."

"You've been a team player from the start, haven't you?"

"I wouldn't presume to say so," Gloria told him, "but I wouldn't deny it either."

He studied her and began plucking at his bottom lip. "I have to say that I'm, well, detecting something odd in your tone. And this isn't the first time. You've seemed kind of irritable lately, more than usual," he said. "I'm not the only one to have noticed it. There have been rumblings. Is there something going on?"

Gloria had heard this sort of thing before, often from men but especially from white people. "Perhaps certain people sometimes get the wrong impression from my face."

Her boss leaned back in his leather chair and grasped the lapels of his suit jacket. He had a wide jaw and his red scalp showed through his thistly salt-and-pepper hair. "You don't have to be that way, you know."

"I'm not sure I follow you, sir."

"Well, I've always found you . . . let's call it sphinxlike," he said. "Which I obviously don't mean as an insult. I understand that things were probably different back when you first started working here, but times have changed. Society has evolved. Nowadays people of all kinds, no matter how different, speak clearly and frankly with each other. You can speak frankly with me. You can be yourself."

"Of course I can, sir," Gloria said, rising from her seat. "Thank you."

For the rest of her shift, she wondered who had been reporting that she was irritable. The word bothered her, though she took pains not to show it. *Irritable.* It reminded her of other words, the ones that followed her husband around his entire career at the construction company, out in the field and then later during his years in the office. *Churlish. Surly.* Gloria's ear had immediately flagged their fraternal ugliness. *Angry. Irritable.* From Maurice, she had learned the fateful trap of such words, the cruel way they accused you again and again of being what you weren't until, almost inevitably, you were nettled into becoming that very thing. Who was calling her irritable? The more she thought about her current colleagues in room service, the more she accepted that it could have been almost any of them. They were all significantly younger than she was, newer generations of employees, and none of them showed much interest in getting to know her. In the past, there had been more collegiality, or what Gloria personally liked to think of as comradeship. People tended to look after one another. She remembered that whenever she came to work ill, others, the women especially, picked up the slack for her without a word of complaint, certainly without tattling, and she did the same for them. If you called out sick, or if a boss was aware that you weren't working at peak efficiency, there were sure to be penalties. You could lose wages, or worse.

Before she left the hotel for the day, she stopped to chat with Apollo out front. Spending some time with him usually made her feel good.

"What's shaking, Apollo?" she said. This was their customary way of greeting each other. "How's your mother doing?"

"What's shaking? Mama's ticker is still ticking," he said. "The Lord woke her up this morning so I'm happy to say she's still here, driving me crazy." Apollo alluded to his faith pretty often, but he wasn't pious. He spoke enough about other things, with just enough vulgarity, to let you know he was also a Saturday-night sinner, and completely unashamed of it.

"And how about you?"

"Always blessed. As a matter of fact, guess what happened today," he said.

"Not doing that. Just tell it."

"Go on. You'll never guess."

"You know I don't like that kind of game," Gloria said through pursed lips. "So you'd best spit it out already."

"Damn, girl. One of these days I *will* convince you to play with me."

"Is that right?"

"It's gonna happen."

"*Your* ticker wouldn't last two minutes, old man," she said. "Now come on and spill the beans."

Apollo's flirtatious grin devolved into a dutiful smile as he opened the door for a white couple entering the hotel. Then he tugged down his jacket and cinched up his tie, the meticulous adjustments his nimble fingers automatically made countless times per workday. "It was a rare and precious miracle," he told Gloria. "A visitation from the mists of the past. If I hadn't seen it with my own eyes, I wouldn't believe it."

"What on earth are you talking about?"

"A guest of the hotel—some kind of time traveler, I suspect, maybe even a pilgrim of some sort—came out here and—get this, girl—he asked me to hail a taxi for him! At first, I didn't know what he was talking about. Taxi? What's that? I don't speak none of the ancient languages. But then, after I figured out what the man meant, I looked at him sideways, 'cause it had to be some sort of practical joke. But he was dead serious, so I said okay and did it. I had to rely on muscle memory to do it, but I did it. And that's not even the real story. You're gonna think I'm making this up, but before he jumped into the yellow relic I managed to find for him, the man *tipped* me, Gloria."

"No he didn't."

"He tipped like he lost his damn mind. Put that paper right

into my hand. Ten dollars. Genuine legal tender, no lie. I honestly can't remember the last time that happened."

Apollo opened the door for a young Asian man coming out of the hotel. He looked to be the age of a college student and was casually dressed in jeans and a T-shirt, trailing his wheeled luggage behind him. He kept glancing down at his phone and then up at the street.

"I gotta admit, you were right," Gloria said. "I never would've guessed that."

"Well try this one. Guess who has extra money burning a hole in his pocket plus a burning desire to take a pretty girl to dinner." Apollo had always teased her this way, even when Maurice was alive. He seemed to understand how unlikely it was that anything would ever happen between them, and he seemed to be fine with that. Besides, he needed every dime he could get his hands on. His mother, in her early nineties now, was under his care.

"Let me give you some advice about pretty girls," Gloria began, but then something else caught her attention. A rideshare car arrived, and the driver got out and insisted on putting the luggage in the trunk even though the young man could have easily done it himself. The driver was telling him there were mints and bottles of water in the back seat if he wanted them.

"Cat got your tongue, huh?" Apollo said. "Stunned into silence."

"I'm sorry . . ."

"What you sorry for? Don't feel bad. This isn't the first time I've had that effect on a lady."

Gloria's gaze followed the car as it merged into traffic and slowly drove off.

"All jokes aside, you want to get some dinner later? You look like you could use some good food, and some good company."

"What's that supposed to mean?" Gloria said.

"I don't mean nothing by it, girl," Apollo said. "You've just seemed sad lately, that's all."

Gloria declined Apollo's dinner invitation kindly, without any of her usual sharpness or sly humor. When she got home she ordered food for herself, but the delivery person was a man, someone she'd never seen before. The food was baked fish, jollof rice, and vegetables from a Senegalese restaurant she trusted, but she ate it reluctantly, as if it wasn't delicious.

She had the next couple of days off and intended to use that time to relax, but each night, even though she went to bed early, she was unable to stay asleep. The night before she had to return to work, she got up and began to write by lamplight.

That was you the other afternoon, wasn't it, picking up that clueless-looking boy in front of the hotel. Not that I was surprised to see you doing that. It's no secret what life these days means for so many people, what it requires people to do. Full-time workers with benefits having to drive or deliver food to make ends meet. For all I know, you have half a dozen jobs—gigs, I mean—or even more. I hope it's not true though. I hope you're not caught up in the hustle. The unpredictability. What I mean is, I hope you're not running yourself ragged.

Did you notice me standing out there talking to that man who thinks he's handsome? (That was Apollo.) I have to ask. Did you notice me? I was worried that you did, for a half second at least, and purposely decided not to say anything. But you wouldn't do that, would you? I understand that time is of the essence, that you'd want to fit as many rides (or deliveries, for that matter) as you can into the shortest possible span of time. If you had seen who I was, though, you would have at least waved or said a quick hello. I guess a logical explanation might involve that odd phenomenon. You know the one. If you come to associate a person with one specific context, they become unrecognizable when you encounter them anywhere else. Your eye can take in all of the person's features but they don't mean anything, they don't organize themselves into something substantial enough to seize upon. The person, simply put, is out of place.

It did, after all, take a good while for me to accept without question that the young woman I saw the other day was in fact you.

I believe it was this phenomenon that saved me from being discovered the one time I stepped out on Maurice. Well, I was discovered, so I guess the word I mean is confronted. It was during the most difficult part of our marriage, when he was caught in that trap of being angry. Angry that the people he worked with had succeeded in making him angry. (I can explain this more when we finally speak.) You know the effect that anger can have on your ability to perceive, how it can blur the edges of your vision. It wasn't so much that he couldn't see me anymore during those difficult days, at least in the beginning. It was that he couldn't see the life we had so carefully built together. His anger came home from work with him, to the little town house we had worked so hard for, and it kept gnawing at the walls. What used to be a comfort and a shelter was becoming no more than a void. And he saw everything inside of that void with what Ms. G. Brooks (the great poet) called a "clear delirium." His inner eyes had lost all sense of proportion and scale, which meant that when he looked at me he was looking at a monster. I've never been vain, or not excessively so, but I couldn't stand being regarded as something grotesque. I'm not boasting when I say I think I'm rather pretty, even now. But I felt his fear and his disgust and his utter lack of desire for me, and I tried to be patient and understanding, but the heat of his anger wouldn't relent. If anything, it worsened. His sweet nothings were replaced by plain old nothing, just scorching hot air. He stopped talking to me. He stopped touching me too, even in bed, and when I touched him, when I took hold of his buttocks, or his thigh, or the lovely weight of his privates, he didn't respond. Whatever part I touched, he seemed to detach from himself, and I was left holding a bauble I might as well have found on the street, a toy that would keep the creature distracted while his essence—his wallowing, fuming, brooding nucleus—sank more deeply into the pillows.

So, as I said, I stepped out. I'm not proud of it. One day I told Maurice that I had to work a double shift, not that he cared enough to require an excuse, and I met up, just once, with an older man who had lived in the hotel for a while. He was a darling and (Maurice, cover your ears) a terrific lover. Most people you sleep with vanish into the mists, but a special few remain clear as day. He was staying near Grand Central then, and before we went to that apartment, we had drinks at a restaurant in the station. It's embarrassing now to think of our flagrancy. We sat where anyone passing by could see us, instead of wisely requesting a table or booth hidden in the back. There I was in this dress—and it was quite a dress, let me tell you, deliciously red—openly flirting with the man who would take it off, when my husband walks by carrying a shopping bag. He looks right at us, right at me—a sustained look, you understand, you could have counted each of those seconds out as slow as molasses and gotten to a considerable number—and then he keeps on walking without saying a word. It was like he didn't know who I was. Like I was neither his wife nor his newly created monster. I was somebody else. A salacious woman in an indecent dress, getting drunk with a darling loverman in Grand Central station. Do you get what I mean?

But of course he had seen me, and had recognized me—or eventually he did—as surely as I saw and recognized you outside of the hotel. He must have understood, for once, what I meant by fault without blame. He shed much of his anger after that, which was no great solace, because whatever's shed needs to be swept up, and guess who was responsible for that? He couldn't relinquish his anger just like that, you understand. He had to see it pass through my hands, he had to observe my willingness to hold it. He became slightly messier around the house, leaving just a little more for me to put in order. He started talking to me again, but almost never with any delicacy. His words were sharply edged obstacles I had to navigate. He began touching me again too, but he did so with less patience than he used to. It was exciting sometimes, passionate, but other times it felt like he just wanted to get it over with. At any rate, the terms of a bargain were slowly and wordlessly agreed upon, and we remained together, settled into an adequate happiness which was not without a low hum of tension that refused to fade until he died. I don't know if I would recommend it, staying in a marriage like that, but I don't know if I regret it either. Every once in a while, I would glance up from reading and catch him looking at me and there I was again, wearing that red dress. So to speak. In his eyes, anyway. Sometimes good would come from it. Sometimes he'd get evil. Sometimes nothing would happen at all. It all depended on the day. On whether he craved the red woman or detested her, on whether he was fascinated by her or cowed. In any case, it was fine, more than fine, because I knew that he knew that his power was no greater than mine.

There I go rambling on again. I'm sorry. I think all I wanted to say was that I feel glad to have caught a glimpse of you the other day. I don't know why exactly, but it was sad not to have seen you at all for so long. I won't tell you how many times I've ordered deliveries these past few weeks. It's embarrassing. Maybe I'm already saying too much. Well, no one ever said I was shy.

Gloria woke up the next morning buzzing with a peculiar sense of contentment, despite getting only a few hours of uninterrupted sleep. She felt expansive and beautiful and light. It was shaping up to be another sunny day, so she took an unhurried walk to the hotel and decided on the way that she would get another flower for her apartment after work.

When she arrived, a man she didn't know so well was at the door. Gloria went up to him and asked after Apollo.

"Oh, he'll be here later, probably by the time you leave. Had to take his mother to some appointments or something, so he asked if we could flip our shifts today."

"That's very nice of you."

"It's a snap to be nice when somebody makes it worth your while. He offered me ten bucks, but I told him I'd only do it for fifty. It's hard out here. You gotta drive a hard bargain. Plus, I'm not really a morning person, you know?"

Gloria's mood quickly deteriorated, even more so as she endured another slow day of room service. It felt to her like her colleagues were keeping their distance, and talking about her behind

her back. When she spoke to them, they responded tersely, and
with the sort of politeness that was clearly an affectation.

During lunch, while she sat alone eating her turkey and
cheese sandwich, she read a two-month-old newspaper someone had left in a pile. She had a curiosity about slightly outdated
accounts of then-current events. The question of what could be
captured and comprehended about the present in the midst of
its unfolding interested her. As she flipped the yellowing pages,
she was reminded of how cold and dry it had been in March, despite the unusual warmth of early winter. There was a picture of
the mayor and his wife wearing scarves and heavy coats as they
departed Gracie Mansion. One article covered the arrival of a
"polar vortex" that Gloria had no desire to recall. Another piece
reported on a slew of part-time workers who were laid off from
a warehouse in Chelsea. The warehouse belonged to a company
owned by a billionaire, but the workers were dismissed because
seasonal demand had died down. Before they were let go, many
of them, in terrible need of money, had suffered a late spike of
influenza, which had spread rampantly throughout the facility.
The article focused mostly on one man who had continued to
work while flu-ridden, Harold Anderson, just a year younger than
Gloria. There was a photograph of him with over a dozen others
whose names were only briefly mentioned, if at all. As Gloria
scanned the image of the laid-off workers, she kept returning to
the figures in the back whose faces were somewhat obscured, as
though they had been smudged by the swipe of a dirty thumb.
She stared at them until one of her young colleagues came in and
asked, in a passive-aggressive way, if she was still on her lunch
break. "Time to get back to it, huh?" Gloria said, rising at her
own pace. "Thank you for reminding me of my duty. I'm sure a
great many urgent tasks are waiting to be done."

The rest of her shift passed slowly, and it didn't help that she felt distressed by the conduct of her colleagues, the article about the warehouse workers, and the fifty dollars, even though each thing seemed somewhat trivial or irrelevant. It did make her smile, though, when she told herself that she would see Apollo soon. She wondered how his mother was doing. Then she remembered how, in the past, the women on the room service staff would secretly set aside leftover bananas, oranges, muffins, croissants, and cups of apple sauce for the bellhops and doormen to take home as care packages. Only mildly illicit. She decided she would do exactly that now. As she filled two bags for Apollo and his mother, she felt the old surreptitious thrill, but it wasn't the same. She was acting alone.

Apollo accepted the food with unrestrained surprise and appreciation. "Look at God!" he exclaimed. When Gloria asked after his mother, however, his shoulders slumped. "I know we kid about us being old heads and everything," he said, "but, girl, my mother is *old old*. Flesh wastes away, and that's a bitch. But we can't forsake those whose strength is gone."

That evening, Gloria got home and realized she had forgotten to buy a flower. She felt lethargic and lacked an appetite, so she decided not to cook dinner. She didn't order anything either. For almost an hour she tried to read poetry while sipping wine, and then, when her head got feathery soft, she took up her pen.

You've become an error in my life. You are no longer, ever, where I hope or expect you to be, but then, from time to time, you show up in the strangest places. I have no way of knowing for sure, but it's possible I saw you today in an old newspaper. A possible you from the recent past, I mean, which maybe isn't enough to make someone's hair stand on end—especially since the city is just a big old teeming grid of coincidence— but sufficient to lend you the air of an apparition. The idea of the dead persisting among us doesn't scare me. In fact, I have taken pleasure in the feeling that my husband has sometimes been here with me in this little apartment where I intend to spend the rest of my days. Still, the idea of the ghostly living, of living ghosts, strikes me now as frightening indeed. Because you're still alive, you can be hurt, you can suffer, but you're also forced into a condition of drifting, without hope of respite or satisfaction.

However, the person in the newspaper photo may not have been you. Perhaps it wasn't. Probably it wasn't.

I'm wondering now if you pray and, if so, to which manifestation of the higher power.

Personally, I'm not what you would call a praying woman, but it seems to me that life, on occasion, has a way of calling even the most closed and stubborn minds to at least consider the efficacy of prayer. For some reason, I've received such an invitation today. I really don't know why. Nothing has been upended, but I have a feeling of foreboding like you wouldn't believe. Whether it's about me, or about you, or about my friend (Apollo) and his mother, I can't tell. Maybe it's about all four of us. Maybe it's about every one of us.

Or maybe it's simply a sense of unease that I have because I've never expressed myself in this way before. I've always felt somewhat archaic, you see. No one, not even Maurice, has ever had much access to the truest language and content of my inner life. Before now, I've never had deep, forthright correspondence with anyone. I've never even kept a diary or a journal. A woman and her wall of books (and sometimes a flaming dress worth one's notice)—that's all I've ever been, really. I've long seen myself as a person who could maintain a rather unyielding barrier (that wall maybe?) against a world that seemed to have no place for all of me, and I suppose it's shocking to discover how permeable I actually am.

I think I'll pray tonight. In my own language, my own rhythms, no matter how chaotic and unsuitable they may be. You've given me the courage to do that. I have no doubt that if you were to read what I've written to you, you would hear me and understand me. One step of conviction can lead to another, and then more.

A lot has happened since I wrote to you yesterday. I'll get to that in a moment, but first I want to tell you that I've been reflecting on the meanings of your name, which I looked up today as soon as I got home. Well, I put my new sunflowers in water first. After the experience I had today, I splurged this time and bought two.

If the information I found is correct—and one day you'll have to tell me if it is—your name can mean moon (or, crescent moon) or dawn (or, the time just before dawn). It can also mean, somewhat oddly, both awakening and sleeplessness. Or vigil. What's to be done with all of that? The conclusion I've come to is to resist conclusion. Given how much things have shifted since our first encounter, there are all sorts of clever things I can do with any of those meanings, but all I would be doing is flattering myself, making it all about me. The thing I want to know is what it means to you. Maybe, my courier, to you it means absolutely nothing. Maybe it's simply your name.

The meaning of my own name is obvious, but all it is really is a pretty combination of sounds, which don't strike the ear so prettily when they come out of the wrong mouth. Today at work my boss called both me and Apollo into his office. He brought us in together, like some ludicrous justice of the peace, and then told us both to sit. Let me narrate the rest for you.

"Gloria," he said, wretchedly, "this isn't the first time I've had to talk to you about your attitude."

"My irritability, you mean," I said.

"Exactly that. And Apollo," he said, "you know that you're supposed to clear all shift changes through my office."

"But, sir. I just needed something done quick, and it used to be that—"

"I don't care what it used to be like, Apollo, in the old days. What I do care about is the ethics of how things are done now."

"The ethics?" I said.

He glared at me. "It's come to my attention that in addition to the bad attitude and the lack of communication with my office, there is also an even more serious problem of theft."

"Theft?" Apollo cried.

"Which is quite serious, I'm sure we can agree," our boss said. Then he sat up tall and added, "Let's not belabor this. I'm going to have to let you go. Both of you."

"You're firing us?" I asked, almost amused.

"You doing this because I took it upon myself to get my shift covered and because you want her to, what, smile more?" Apollo asked. "Because she gave me some bags of stuff y'all end up throwing in the trash anyway?"

"These violations are serious, quite serious."

"Damn it, man, why you doing this? How can you do this? She's damn near retired!"

"Be that as it may," he said, and then went on with some tortured, unmemorable nonsense—but it was the way he said

the words Gloria and Apollo (another name with grand signif-
icance) that communicated everything he thought about us,
everything he felt we were guilty of.

My tone may seem calm but, Sahar, no doubt you can see
by my handwriting that I'm shaking as I write this. I'm not
equipped to go without my usual income right now. I'll have
to find other work, at least for a year. This scares me so much,
given my age. But I'm even more worried about poor Apollo
and his mother. I saw how upset he was when we left that office. Then he rallied and made a great show of toughness,
cracking wise to show how much he could withstand. Sweet
man, he also tried to reassure me with an impassioned sermon
about the inherent value of the many years of experience that
"old heads" like us have to offer. We both laughed. I think you
know the kind of laughter I mean.

I've spent the last few weeks looking for work. No luck yet. Same
for dear Apollo. This morning, out of the blue, I called him and
suggested we go have lunch together. Neither of us had eaten
out or ordered delivery since we were let go. Apollo responded
to my invitation with a cartoonish sound and what I can only
imagine was a wide-eyed double take. He didn't even make any
of his "pretty girl" jokes. All he said was, "I would like that."

The restaurant was this vegan place he wanted to try because he was considering a switch to that diet for his mother.
I didn't care for the food, to be honest with you. The dish I
ordered ended up being some kind of beige concoction. At the
center of all the beige was a paste made of cashews, and the
slice of pie we foolishly ordered to share for dessert was basi-
cally a big old wedge of packed sand.

I'm getting ahead of myself though. When we sat down,

a lovely young woman came over and introduced herself as our server. My heart jumped. She was about your height and weight, with a similar build, and her skin was the same splendid shade of brown. For a second, before my eyes could blink and refresh themselves, I would have sworn she was you. I would have bet my life on it. But of course she wasn't you. And that's okay. I introduced myself and Apollo to her, and the three of us ended up having the most delightful conversation. I hope I get a chance to tell you about it. In the end, I insisted on paying, despite Apollo's protestations, and I made sure to leave a gratuity that the server would find honorable.

I really enjoyed myself, even though the menu was a catastrophe of bricks and muck. It was such a nice lunch. The server was nice, and Apollo is too. I won't be able to treat him to a meal at a restaurant again anytime soon, but maybe one day I can cook something for him. For him and his mother, I mean. I also won't be able to order any food deliveries for a while. And if I ever go anywhere again, I'll take the subway or the bus, or I'll walk on my own two feet. Show off my ankles and my calves. What I mean to say is, I'm not sure when I'll see you next. It may be a long time before I'm able to bear the cost of another attempt to hail you. But Sahar, my courier, my colleague, my comrade in the struggle of life in this country during this increasingly worrisome age, I'll keep writing to you until we get a chance to really meet again. I can't wait to hear what you have to say. Meanwhile, I hope you won't think I'm arrogant or presumptuous, but I've decided to keep my little letters to you in between the pages of the poems of Ms. G. Brooks. Soon it'll be difficult to fit the volume back into its place on my wall. I have quite a lot on my mind, which of course I already knew, but it turns out that I also have the words to say it.

BYSTANDER

Anita knew better than to confess. She also knew better than to deny. It was a question of power, she thought, of asserting her authority. So she tried her best to keep her mouth shut as she stood by the hearth-like heat of the stove. Normally she made the family meals in peace, without being accosted like this, left alone to work and muse in the kitchen, but behind her, beyond the curved shield of her back, her daughter, Dandy, kept going on with her loud complaints and paced here and there, impervious to the soothing alchemical fragrance of the cooking. Horace, dependable Horace, was also there, as a show of support for his wife, but Anita found his presence irksome as well. She settled her nerves by stirring the carefully measured blend of spices into the yellow curry she was making for dinner. It was important that she remain composed. No offense to Horace, but she was the adult here, which is to say she was the mother, so hers were the only accusations that really mattered in this house anyway. (It was just an apartment, as she well knew, but she called it a house in earnest.) If a child was going to behave recklessly on the internet, Anita reflected, as she tasted the yellow glaze of sauce on her cooking spoon, a mother had every right to know. Besides, she thought, while deciding instinctively on a bit more turmeric, how could a word like *spying* be meaningful when her daughter had been alive on this earth for barely sixteen years? That wasn't long enough to lay claim to any privacy at all.

Out of nowhere Anita said, "Plus you've never earned a solitary dime of your own." Random eruptions of thought into speech were often her habit. "Not one red cent," she continued. "You don't have an ounce of industry. When you were little, you didn't even want a lemonade stand."

"A lemonade stand?" Dandy cried. "Who do you think we are? *Where* do you think we are?"

"Not a real lemonade stand," Anita said, turning to the girl. "I'm obviously making a point."

Horace grunted in agreement. Meanwhile, Dandy primed her face for weeping, eyes squeezed nearly shut, mouth so deformed it seemed to be stretched apart by two hooked fingers. This wreck of a face only proved Anita's point, that her daughter was still an immature child, still—especially with her disastrous new haircut, a self-inflicted Caesar—the funny-looking baby she had been, maundering and defenseless, constantly bungling her way into some mess or another. Until she was ready to leave the house and make wise decisions, demonstrably capable of that colossal task—taking care of herself—she still needed to be watched.

"But what *is* your point? What are you even talking about?" Dandy blurted. She trembled in her unfashionably loose jeans and oversize T-shirt. Her sneakers squeaked raucously as she trampled the linoleum. "I never understand a word that comes out of your mouth."

Leaning against the counter, Horace didn't know what Anita was talking about either, judging from the expression on his inoffensively lopsided face. But after taking a noisy sip of his pre-dinner coffee, which he said roused his digestive juices, he seemed to remember the proper order of his allegiances. "Here's the long and the short of it," he said to their daughter. "You just can't be out here doing stuff like that."

"I didn't do anything!"

"Lower your voice," he told her. "You know exactly what you did. You made your little feelings as clear as day."

Dandy tore her gaze away from him. She kicked lightly at a paper bag of recyclables on the floor, rattling the bottles and cans. "Well, what reasonable person wouldn't?"

"And then," Anita added, "not even five minutes later, guess what, you somehow thought it would be a good idea to keep going, to escalate the situation." Dandy had informed her alarmingly high number of followers online that she despised the president. She said she wished she had enough money to have him assassinated. "Meanwhile, all there is in your pocket is lint. Meanwhile, you don't even have enough money to hire a flea."

"Why would I hire a flea? And why do you two keep *spying* on everything I do?"

There was that word again. Plus, to be accurate, Horace hadn't really been involved. As usual, he had little to do with Anita's decisions. She was the one who had tracked down the social media account in question, all on her own.

Ignoring her daughter's accusation again—*don't confess, don't deny*—Anita tried a variation of the speech she frequently gave. The mule of the world. Maybe Dandy would understand this time that her dual burdens, being Black and female, meant she had to be more careful and more intelligent than any other sort of person, more than her mind, the grossly unfinished mind of a teenager, could possibly imagine. The fact of the matter was, people like her got hurt, or even worse, just for walking down the wrong street at the wrong time, merely for having the audacity to exist. Anita concluded this particular version of her speech by saying gravely, "There are certain things you just can't do."

"That's your message to your daughter?" Dandy asked. "That's your great feminist slogan? *There are certain things you just can't do?*"

"I didn't say a word about feminism."

"Of course you didn't," Dandy said. "You would never."

Horace's attention was going serenely back and forth between mother and daughter, the same way it did when he watched television, following the graceful pendular motion of a basketball game.

"And why are you defending the president anyway?" Dandy continued. "Real talk: why defend *any* president—they're all war criminals—but especially this one. Why? Aside from being an idiot, a cheat, a sociopath, and a liar, he's also, let's see, racist, sexist, xenophobic, ecocidal . . ."

Horace, obviously pleased to have the opportunity to dole out some sweeping fatherly wisdom, replied that life itself was all of those things too.

Dandy rolled her eyes. An insipid gesture, so conventionally and disappointingly adolescent.

"I can't worry about the White House," Anita said, turning back to the stove. "My job, my God-given vocation, is to worry myself—to death, if need be—about *my* house. I don't care very much who the president is. I care very much who *my daughter* is."

Horace hushed Dandy before she could talk back again, so Anita gave him a little smile. Horace. He had begun to lose even his very modest good looks, which in the past might have made you take notice the fourth or fifth time your eyes passed over him, but his sturdy reliability was only deepening. For a woman like Anita, he was merely reasonable as a husband but ideal as the father of her child. Helping her manage the turmoil of mothering, he was a nearly perfect adjunct.

"I saw all those awful responses to what you posted," Anita said. How long would it take to unsee them, she wondered, all that terrifying abuse hurled at her daughter, all those strangers calling her a "bald monkey" and a "little nigger bitch," their Jim Crow–inspired warnings promising harm and even death. Dandy had gone so far as to reply to some people, daring them to act on their threats. She, a not-yet-grown Black girl, seemed to be saying, over and over again, *go ahead, hurt me*, rejecting safety and security, which to Anita was a kind of insanity. Practically immoral.

"I'm not worried about bots and trolls," Dandy said.

"Well, your mother *is* worried about them, and the elves and the goblins too, okay? We're both worried," Horace said. "And it's not just that. I don't think that hard head of yours allows you to understand how serious this is. This isn't make-believe. My buddy at work, he told me this white guy in Idaho or wherever-the-heck did the same thing you did, the exact same thing, and guess what, the Secret Service came after him. *The Secret Service*, Dandy, came after *a white man*. This isn't a fucking game."

Anita raised her eyebrows. She disapproved of swearing in general but Horace tended to use it judiciously, with fatherly sternness only when he seemed to think she needed that kind of support. He had figured out quickly that she didn't even like the play of profanity in the bedroom. Anita made a constant effort to keep her own imprecations tightly shelled within her skull.

"Here's what's going to happen," she said now. "Before you go to sleep tonight, you and I are going to delete your social media. Every single account, you hear me? I will sit there with my eyes wide open and watch you do it. I won't even blink until it's done. Then you'll hand that phone over to me and I'll hold on to it until I'm good and ready to give it back."

Before Dandy could protest, the rice cooker beeped out a tinny version of "Twinkle, Twinkle, Little Star." Everyone listened quietly, almost respectfully; for some reason the device's little tune was sacrosanct. When it finished, Anita talked over Dandy, telling her to make herself useful and fluff the rice. When Dandy refused, Horace slammed his mug down.

"Do what your mother says," he told Dandy, but she just slipped her thumbs into her pockets and glared at him. "Go set the table too while you're at it," he said. "And fix your face so we can have a nice dinner."

"I'm not hungry," she insisted. "I had plenty of food for lunch. But I guess you already know that too."

"Just go sit at the goddamn table," Horace said through his teeth.

Dandy seemed on the verge of an all-out tantrum now, but apparently she had enough good sense not to go that far. She breathed sharply in and out before storming to the table crammed between the couch and the wall in the living room, then dropped with exaggerated heaviness into a chair, Anita's chair. She crossed her arms and pouted. Anita turned and opened the lid of the cooker, releasing a puff of vaguely popcorn-scented steam. She gazed at the hot smooth cake of rice for a moment before carving into it with the edge of the paddle. It bothered her when Dandy behaved like this, staging her irresistible attraction to lawlessness.

On top of being irritating, it also made Anita herself feel diminished. She had conditioned her daughter to be much better, starting when the girl was only a fetus. Anita had done all she could to make sure her womb was a conservatory of stimulation and nourishment.

But when Dandy was driven out of the lush uterine bath and, a little later, placed clean and snug in Anita's arms, she was disappointing. Ugly as sin, first of all, and the intoxicating new-baby smell Anita had been anticipating ended up being little more than the mellow funk of a cheese. Horace reminded her that most newborns are funny-looking, but as weeks and months passed, the ugliness remained. Dandy wasn't ugly now, thank goodness, but she wasn't beautiful either. She looked fine, fine enough anyway, though there was a maddening suggestion of a mustache above her lip, and even worse than this persistent shadow was the tarnishing effect of her new haircut. It was decisions like the unflattering hair and the lunatic declarations about the president, the latest of her daughter's many acts of defiance, that gave Anita the sensation of dwindling. Things like the casual lies the girl often told—maybe she thinks lying is acceptable if you don't happen to be the president—and the dismissive attitude she'd developed toward her education. Or the nightmare back in middle school, when she'd gone so far as to send a topless photo of herself to some boy she liked. Or, during her first year at the all-girls high school, her sudden willful refusal to eat lunch in the cafeteria, despite already being quite thin. Anita had devoted most of her thoughts and actions during the last decade and a half to raising the most extraordinary and inviolable person, but Dandy seemed committed to being as foolhardy as possible. There was still time, however, still time to get her on the right track. Two years of high school remained and, though she hadn't told anyone yet, Anita was already set on having Dandy attend college here in the city while continuing to live at the house. And if even more time than that was required, so be it.

Horace had taken care of the utensils, the paper towels, and the serving bowl of salad. After Anita fixed each plate of bright curry and rice, with painterly care and attention, he brought it to the table. When she began rinsing the last of the dishes she had used for cooking, he told her to hurry before her food got cold, but there was one more thing to do. Whole milk, honey, avocado, almond and cashew powders, protein powder, and two cracked eggs, all blended together briskly with a spoon. For over a year, she had been forcing Dandy to drink this concoction twice a day, at breakfast and dinner, to counter the campaign of weight loss and malnutrition the girl had begun. Anita gave the drink to her daughter and then came to a tactical decision that made sense in her own mind. She sat not in Dandy's usual chair, but instead in the fourth one, the seat they kept for a guest, though there hardly ever was one.

Horace ate with gusto, Anita slowly and self-critically, and Dandy not at all. She just poked at a smothered wedge of sweet potato with her fork. By sitting there, in the wrong seat, at what Anita thought of as the head of their perfectly square table, Dandy drew more attention to herself. Through the still-open curtains of the living room window, the last of the day's late-winter sun touched her differently, her face half hidden in a razor slant of shadow. Anita took a close look at her. Who was she anyway, underneath that barbarian self she insisted on presenting to the world? The worry had been that the girl would be unreachable, as if Dandy was from the far-off future and Anita the distant past, as if, then, the instability of the anxious present prevented it from working reliably as a bridge. But the frightening thing about her, and maybe about all children, was that she seemed to exist in a state of temporal confusion, inhabiting various eras at once. Dandy's preternatural ease with technology, for instance, which far outstripped Anita's respectable competence, made her seem like an impossibility. And what was that music she listened to? What did all those acronyms she used mean? There were so many acronyms, so much pulverizing of language into the tiniest of particles. So many irritating bits of noise. On the other hand, Dandy had her great-grandmother's eyes, but in a way that was almost absolute, meaning that beyond the resemblance of shape and the same dark brown, amber-specked hue there was the sensibility to which those eyes were wired, that old dignified woman's weary impatience with the state of the world as it had been back then, and the simmering disappointment she'd surely have now, if she could see how little things had changed or how, in some ways, they had gotten worse. And Dandy, who could often seem subliterate, would occasionally surprise you by using words like *nincompoop* and, yes, *busybody*, which were outmoded, weren't they? The girl was an ancestor and an evolvement all at once.

"Why are you staring at me?" Dandy muttered from across the table.

Anita forced a smile, stiffly false, onto her face. "I'm wondering why, instead of eating your food, you're just messing with it like you're a toddler."

Dandy lifted the fork but there was no food on it. She peeked her tongue out and tasted the dots of sauce on the points of the tines. "Happy now?"

"To tell you the truth," Anita said, "I could be much happier. Why don't you just eat your food?"

"I told you I wasn't hungry."

"Well then, at least have your drink."

They both looked at the beverage, mud green with yellow slivers of yolk.

"You know I hate this," Dandy said.

"If you ate the way a growing child is supposed to, you wouldn't have to drink it."

The girl started to say something but flung her hand up to her chest instead. A shade of color drained from her face, and her gaze seemed to direct itself inward.

"Dandy?" Horace asked.

"What is it?" Anita asked. "What's wrong?"

Her expression remained vacant and somewhat alarmed for a few more moments, and then she was back from wherever she had gone. She settled comfortably into her usual state of annoyance. "Oh nothing," she said, "except that this shit you keep making me drink gives me diarrhea. Just looking at it right now is making me gassy."

"Watch your mouth," Anita said. "Why do you have to be so vulgar?"

"The thought of having to drink this sewage again makes me want to throw up. It's *vile*."

"Don't talk to your mother like that," Horace said.

"She asked a question, I answered it."

"Look," Horace said, "you're gonna swallow every drop of that stuff *and* you're gonna eat every grain of this food your mother took the time and care to make for you. From scratch. Why? Because she loves you."

Dandy glared at him again and then picked up the drink. It slid into her mouth slowly, like sludge, until there was nothing left in the glass but a skim of grit and froth.

"Now go on and eat your food too," Horace said. "I want to see you clean that plate."

"It's okay, it's okay. She's not hungry," Anita said, rigidly smiling again. Horace was doing too much. "So," she said to the girl, "this lunch you had at school today. I would like to hear more details about this enormous lunch. I'm so curious. Why don't you tell us all about it?"

Dandy looked up from her plate and glared. "Why don't *you* . . ." She went on to say something so shocking to her mother that it struck like the first blow in an ambush. Anita flinched. Her ears rang. Then Dandy tore from the table with her hand at her chest again and closed herself in her room.

Horace jumped up. "That child must be out of her mind," he said.

"It's okay . . ." Anita said.

"Okay? How is it okay?" Horace asked as he lowered himself into his seat again. "If I even *thought* about talking that way to my parents, they would have slapped the black off of me."

Anita had never liked that phrase, which Horace nevertheless persisted in using. Even now as she tilted her head way back to conceal her eyes from him, she couldn't help but see the scenario played out literally, like a projection on the ceiling. Horace as a child shrinking from his mother. She had been the one more likely to beat him. But it wasn't the fearsome maternal largeness itself that Anita objected to. The central problem, which Anita decided was one of character, and which prevented her from ever wanting to become close to Horace's mother, was the artlessness of the woman's domination.

Then Anita saw herself opening Dandy's door (the lock had been removed) and striking her and then what? The girl's skin peeling off like a layer of cheap paint? Would her entire phenotype change or only her skin? Would her nose split in the middle to reveal a thinner, pointier one? Or would she just become a faint echo of herself, a pallid, ghostly twin? Every possibility was a horror show, but Anita kept seeing more and more of them. Entering the room, hitting Dandy as hard as she could, and then something momentous happening. Her daughter immediately changing. In one vision, whatever defect the girl had that allowed her to speak to her mother that way, the way the crustiest foul-mouthed strangers spoke to women on the street, was impercep-tibly but instantly corrected. Other corrections and realignments followed, each as relentless as a wish. ". . . and do you have any idea how much it wounds a mother when she's unable to feed her own child?" she said to her daughter, before slapping her again.

A hand squeezed her arm on the table. "Of course I do," Horace said tentatively. His hazy reflection appeared beside hers in the glass of the now-darkened window. When she looked di-rectly at him, confused for a moment, his forehead was wrinkled in concern. "Are you okay, baby? You're trembling."

Anita wiped her face dry with her free arm. "A cup of sliced peaches," she said.

"What?"

"*That's* what she had for lunch today. That's all. Peaches—bruised to death, I bet—swimming in that disgusting syrup."

Horace slumped back into his chair and gave a nod of re-signed understanding. Anita hadn't told him explicitly that their daughter was still being kept under watch. But the operation was so simple. Maintaining it felt effortless, so why say anything? It didn't take much for that other girl at the school to inform her mother what Dandy did and didn't eat, and it didn't take much for that other mother, Marie, a coworker at the bank, to inform Anita in turn. It was just a bit of chatter, as easy as that, but a much more sensible use of time because it had an actual purpose.

All the baggy clothing Dandy had begun wearing around the house after she started high school couldn't disguise the fact that she was getting even thinner. The first time she was caught in a lie about what she had eaten, she attempted to hide her spindly legs underneath her enormous sweater, knees pulled to her chest, rocking back and forth on the floor with an expression of fury and bewilderment. She grew more and more paranoid after that, unsure how Anita could tell when she was lying or telling the truth. She distanced herself from all of her teachers, began casting off her old friends, and refused the possibility of new ones. Her mood became cheerless and complaining, her general effort anemic at best. She spent an increasing amount of time on the internet and began to decline intimacy, if it could be called that, with anyone who was familiar.

Horace patted Anita's arm affectionately and said he would take care of the after-dinner cleanup, as if he didn't do exactly that every night. While he washed dishes, the room filled with fine blue shadows and she remained seated in the guest chair. Back when they were new parents and the going got tough, he'd try to reassure Anita by telling her, half jokingly, "Don't worry, this is just a trial run. The first one is always an experimental child." As though botching the care of one life was fine if you assumed other lives would follow. As if, despite being old when this first child was born, they were certain about having more. As if Anita herself, who had no siblings, didn't know that the result of most experiments is failure.

A lot of people assumed Dandy was a nickname for Dandelion or some other ridiculousness, which Anita took as an insult, and which was maybe what made the other mother, the mother of the actual spy, say mistakenly one day that the girl was "as thin as a *weed*." But Dandy ("Fine and dandy," Horace used to say in his imitation white man voice) was short for Dandridge, as in Dorothy. ". . . a Black woman of accomplishment in a very difficult time," Anita said out loud now to no one. Still pleased with the phrase, she told herself she would use it again the next time she lectured her daughter. She could go in there right now wielding it. But it was impossible to get up from her seat. She couldn't ex-

tract Dandy's awful, pornographic remark from her mind. The
girl seemed hell-bent on acting as if she'd had absolutely no home
training at all. She had spoken atrocities to Anita before, but this
was by far the worst. A blasphemy.

As she brushed her teeth and wrapped her hair for bed, Anita
had a premonition. She knew she wouldn't be granted the sweet
rupture of sleep, the mercy of closing her eyes against the blight
of one day and opening them to the clean promise of another. Her
sense turned out to be correct. Lying in bed, she was unable to
free herself from the agitation of her thoughts. Time passed with
a strange combination of speed and sluggishness, discarding her
willy-nilly into the pit of night. She turned away from Horace,
who was sound asleep, and finally allowed her whole body to
shake from sadness. But then her breath caught. Horace's arm
had fallen over her like a plank of wood. Anita could smell the
spiciness of the curry through his pores, the slight tang of musti-
ness from his armpits. She wiped her face as he began to whisper
some comforting words into her ear. It turned out he was awake
after all. She listened, but more to the soothing sound he was
making than to the words themselves. She didn't really want to
hear any words. His touch and his tone had a sedative effect.
She noticed her breath slackening. As she began to drowse, he
pulled himself closer to her. He continued to whisper, but the
sound gradually altered, issuing more from his throat. Her eyes
widened as she listened more carefully to him. She felt it as he
pressed himself against her, wriggling his hips slightly but firmly,
erect. One of his bulky legs edged over and around hers, locking
her entirely in a carnal embrace. It didn't take much to deter him,
however, just a disappointed utterance of his name, said almost
meekly despite the rage filling her chest. He knew exactly what

she meant—*no*—and he immediately gathered the heavy splay of his limbs from her body and curled himself away.

As a married couple, the two of them had sex only now and then, having settled into a schedule of lovemaking known only to Anita. She couldn't remember the last time they'd done it spontaneously. Refusing to grant Horace any further acknowledgment of what he had attempted, she gave him nothing more than the silence of her back. And she knew he would remain facing away from her too, frozen in his posture of embarrassment.

But he couldn't be more embarrassed than she was, degraded even. He must have lost his mind, trying something like that, as if he had forgotten who and what they were—who and what *she* was. And tonight of all nights. After what their daughter had said earlier. Despite the filth that had come out of the girl's mouth. Anita dwelled on his reckless lack of consideration until she noticed the sky starting to shed its darkness. Even the barest trace of twilight was somehow enough for her thoughts to become more expansive, to take new turns and pursue different paths. Horace eventually got up to begin his deliberate ritual of getting ready for work, and by that point she was convinced that the nature of his attempt had been even worse than she'd imagined. He hadn't thrown himself on her that way despite their daughter's nasty words, he had done so because of them. They had apparently stirred something in him, a sensation as agitating as Anita's anger.

She felt so discombobulated that for the first time in almost three years she called in to say she needed to stay home from work. She remained in bed instead of making breakfast for the family. Horace peeked in warily at her a few times and then, after an interval of silence, soaked thick with masculine helplessness, she heard him opening and shutting cabinets and the refrigerator to throw something together—something pathetic, no doubt. Finally, after another lull of familial expectation, he and Dandy zipped up their coats and left for the day.

At first Anita enjoyed some measure of ease, but it didn't take long for her to realize how infrequently she spent time alone at home. In rooms, yes—the kitchen, the bathroom of course—but those were transitory solitudes. She thought of them as preparations. For tasks that were nearly always at hand. Now, however, as she moved about with neither her husband nor their daughter in proximity, the space contracted. Oddly, it felt less like a house instead of more. The walls seemed to tighten, and in her imagination they collapsed into something like a frame around a spot of murk on the kitchen ceiling, which she fixated on even though she couldn't do anything about it. Glancing at a clock, she was surprised to see that it was only midmorning. She considered reporting late to the bank but didn't want to draw that kind of attention to herself. Instead, she decided to take a walk.

Anita found, however, that the concept was foreign to her. Her preference was for destinations, not for wanderings, the fact of arrival rather than the fraud of roaming under a spell of impressions. With her gloved hands stuffed into her coat pockets and her scarf wound snugly around her neck, she unthinkingly made a beeline for the subway station and then to the local fruit and vegetable market and then to the dry cleaner's. Each time, she stopped short before entering and asked herself what in the world she was doing. With sustained focus she managed to walk more slowly and frivolously, but despite her leisurely pace she soon became exhausted by the mental effort involved. She felt as though she was very far away from the house. After a while she found herself crossing a broad street and then she sat on a bench. Her watch told her it was nearly afternoon. The air was raw and gray.

"They sure are something, huh?" a raspy voice said.

When Anita glanced over, there was someone she hadn't noticed before, also sitting. It took a few moments for her to settle on any facts about the stranger, who seemed preoccupied, but Anita decided that the voice and body belonged to a woman, perhaps close to her age. Her large shapeless torso was oddly twisted. Now that the drapes of her concentration had been parted, Anita also saw that there were other people, all around, standing precariously still or in full stride. The bench was on the lip of Prospect Park, she realized, just outside of a playground. "Not a day goes by that they don't crack me up. Am I right or am I right?" It was the woman with the raspy throat again, but the quality of laughter that followed, clean and shrill, was entirely unexpected. "Hey, are you saditty or just hard of hearing?" she added.

Anita didn't respond.

"You're from around the way too, so you know how it goes."

"Excuse me?" Anita said.

"Don't act all inclined unless you want to be straightened out."

"*Excuse me?*"

"You're excused."

"Are you talking to me?"

"Maybe there *is* wax in those ears. Well, don't worry. I can be just as loudmouthed as anybody." Then the woman, distracted again, cried out, "Just look at them!"

Her body was contorted for a reason, so she could peer into the playground behind the bench. Several small children, too young for school, romped around on the equipment as parents and caregivers looked on, but two kids in particular, the rowdiest ones, held the woman's attention. They were about the same size, both crouched close to the slashing swings, and they wore hooded

purple coats that obscured their faces and stiffened their movements. They rolled a marbled ball between them, shrieking with
such flagrant, ungoverned laughter it was as if they had found the
greatest source of merriment in the world.

"I swear they must be geniuses," the woman said. "I swear to
God!" She released the twist of her body and faced Anita directly.
Her packed-tight skin, faintly pocked, suggested plentiful eating
and questionable hygiene, exactly the habits of the kind of person
who would be raising little hooligans. She wore a purple coat too,
though it was a bit more faded and threadbare. She smiled tooth-
ily when the children shrieked again. "You got any of your own?"

Anita hesitated and then shook her head.

The woman chuckled and leaned in. "You sure?"

"I don't have any children." Usually she had no trouble
guarding her life from the prying of strangers.

"Me neither," the woman said with a shrug.

"What?" Anita looked pointedly into the playground again.

"Nope, they're not mine."

Before Anita could respond, the two children's cries turned
ferocious. They were standing now, and instead of rolling the
ball, they threw it clumsily back and forth, pelting each other
with it. Everyone had stopped to observe the blundering assaults.
The woman in the purple coat yelled at the children to stop, and
it was a surprise when they immediately did so. When she told
them to come on, they abandoned the ball and obediently ran
to meet her at the entrance. She fussed at them, but did so with
obvious levity, as if rehearsing an inside joke. The grinning faces
of the children were more visible now, their cheeks paled ocher
by the cold. When the woman extended her hands, each of the
children eagerly took hold of one. They too seemed to be in on the
joke. For a second that felt much longer, the woman lifted both

children off the ground simultaneously, opening an inch or two
of indestructible air beneath the soles of their thin, tattered shoes.
Then they walked off like that, all three of them blameless, hand
in hand, hand in hand, dangerously close to the street.

The noise of the playground resumed. Cars rumbled past.
Passersby talked to companions at their hips or to people across
distances. Anita's windpipe felt blocked and she was unable to
clear it without making a repulsive sound. As she looked cautiously
around, her eye caught on a colorful object, golden with vivid
blushes of red. It was the ball the children—were they boys or
girls, she suddenly wanted to know—had been playing with. The
toy. The weapon. It had rolled to the edge of the playground, close
to where Anita was sitting. Instinctively, she reached behind the
bench and through the wide gaps of the metal fence and picked it
up. It sat dirt-streaked in the palm of her glove. Though it retained
a rocklike firmness, it was flattened here and there into something
that wasn't a true sphere, and there were several spots of exposed
yellow-pink flesh. It wasn't a ball, as it turned out, but an immature nectarine. Filthy and wasteful. Anita dropped it into the first
wastebasket she could find and brushed off her gloves. When she
got her bearings she walked back home as quickly as she could.

Anita worked just as efficiently as usual over the next few weeks at
the bank but succumbed by and by to a state of torpor when she
was at home. Dandy's outburst and Horace's transgression merged
with the unusual encounter Anita had had at the playground. She
felt weighed down. She kept thinking of what to say to her family,
or about the incident outside—that woman and those children,
the odd disturbance of that piece of stone fruit—but nothing ar-
ticulable would resolve in her mind. Instead, she mooned around
the apartment, with little to convey to Horace or Dandy other

than her indifference. Her going through the motions resulted in a slacker atmosphere that seemed to coincide with the inaugural whiffs of spring. The meals, which Horace prepared, became bland, and the furniture, which no one cleaned, collected dust. Anita had even stopped giving Dandy her special drink.

One evening, during a dinner of overboiled noodles swimming in burgundy-colored sauce from a jar, she observed her husband and child, the relaxed set of their shoulders and the lack of tension around their mouths. They clearly were happier, though they had enough consideration for her not to be brazen about it. Dandy had made a habit of sitting at Anita's place at the table, however, as though the rearrangement was what had brought about the changes in the house and therefore needed to be upheld. It was unclear what her eating had been like lately at school—Anita had given up the habit of checking—but her appetite had been slightly better at home. She and Horace rose from the table. It was time for them to watch their favorite reality show, some nonsense they had recently conspired to enjoy together. But after Dandy dropped off her dishes in the kitchen, and left them there unwashed, she walked back haltingly. Her face was stricken and her hand was pressed firmly to her sternum. When Anita demanded to know what was wrong, Horace came out of the kitchen to see. Their daughter said that her chest felt funny. It felt tight, she told them. It hurt.

It didn't really hurt, Dandy would admit later, to the doctor at NYP Brooklyn Methodist. The sensation was alarming, but it never became more than a dull discomfort, an oppressive awareness of the possibility of pain rather than pain itself; and the most overtly dramatic thing about Dandy's hospital stay was the unyielding bureaucracy they faced when they arrived. But Anita expected bad news anyway. For weeks now, ever since the girl's malediction, everything had been worse than it appeared to be.

Dandy was back at home nine days later. Quiet, withdrawn, she stayed in her room and, as if following her lead, Anita and Horace spent the afternoon in theirs. It was hard to remember the last time they had been in bed together when they weren't awaiting the onset of nightly unconsciousness. Anita was on her phone, searching term after term until she felt she had increased her understanding a bit more. It turned out there was a whole new lexicon—it felt like an entire new language—that she would have to learn in order to fathom her daughter's existence. Lipids, autosomes, metabolic processes. An extremely heightened risk, eventually, of severe atherosclerosis. Campesterol, sitosterol, stigmasterol—sterols of many kinds. The key term, the defining one among all these polysyllables, essentially described a mutation in the genes. The disorder was, as she understood it, a bodily greed, which caused the blood and organs to cling to much more than they could safely bear. Dandy's possession of this chaos, or its possession of her, made her, in a way, what Anita had always wanted her to be. To date, medical literature had recorded only one hundred people in the entire world who were bound to the condition. By her very nature she was in peril, but also special, rare. The doctor had seemed fascinated, almost thrilled.

He had shown Anita and Horace the visible signs of what was otherwise unseeable. He indicated the girl's swollen Achilles tendons, and the small yellowish growths on her elbows and behind her knees. There was even one between the pinkie and ring finger of her left hand. Anita mouthed the word: *xanthomas*. They had all been there for months, Dandy admitted, but why hadn't she said

something sooner? More importantly, how was it possible that
Anita's hawklike eyes hadn't noticed them? The doctor responded
to this in an ambivalent tone, both censure and congratulation.
Then he said it was probably thanks to the twice-daily feedings of
that drink she had forced on her daughter that the condition—he
was careful not to say "disease"—flared up enough to call attention to itself. For someone with Dandy's genetic makeup, he said,
each of those cocktails, full of fat and sterols, was like a heart
attack in a glass. Anita immediately understood what he meant. It
was conceivable to say she had saved Dandy's life, and it was
conceivable as well to say she had nearly killed her. Each was in-
eradicably true. But now Anita wasn't sure what that meant about
the kind of mother she had been these past few weeks, whether
that span of neglecting her child had made things better or worse.

When she looked up from her phone, Horace was watching her. A few more seconds passed before he dragged his gaze
away from her face. In those moments, Anita saw something she'd
never seen in him before, an appraisal of her that culminated in
doubt, if not something worse. He could leave me, she thought.
He wouldn't, she was sure, but she could no longer say it was because it had never occurred to him. He'd had the thought—that's
what those crawling seconds had seemed to communicate—and
he would possibly have it again. After a moment of panic, however,
Anita told herself that a little skepticism in a marriage was fine,
healthy even. Or maybe what she was feeling was the release of a
pressure she hadn't known was bearing down on her. She almost
laughed, because whatever had just happened was almost funny.

By a trick of light, afternoon had imperceptibly given way to
evening. Anita got out of bed and said she felt like fixing dinner.
She hadn't done so since the day she made the curry, but Horace
just flipped a page of his magazine in response. When she left the

bedroom, she heard him shut the door behind her. She went to the girl's room, tapped on the door, and waited before entering. She didn't go far past the threshold. Despite the abiding brightness outside, the room was settled in a heathery darkness. The overhead light was switched off and the curtains were shut. Near the tops of two adjoining walls, fluorescent stickers were scattered about, spiked suns and crescent moons left behind many years ago by previous occupants. In bed, lying supine with her knees bent on top of the covers, Dandy didn't acknowledge her mother's presence. Anita wished the room were more illuminated. She wanted to examine her daughter, to find evidence of some kind, of any kind, as long as it was conclusive. She wanted to prove that she could. Through the focus of her attention, she managed to make out the rise and fall of Dandy's chest. Okay, so now what? Now what? What would a good, thoughtful, attentive, superheroic mother do now? What was she supposed to do? It was unbearable, Anita felt, to be a bystander to your own daughter's life.

"How are you feeling?" she asked.

Her daughter didn't respond.

"There's so much I want to say to you, but I don't really know what to say."

No response.

Anita remembered the lie she had told to the woman by the playground. *I don't have any children.* "Listen," she said. "You're the most important thing in my life, and now, now you must be scared."

Dandy's chest rose and fell, rose and fell, with no discernible change in her breathing.

"*I'm* scared," Anita said. By a degree or two, she could sense the light of day finally waning behind the curtains. "Well, okay. I guess I'll leave you be for now," she said. "Are you hungry?" She perceived then, or thought she did, an infinitesimal shift, a faint flicker of motion from the bed.

"Yeah, whatever," Dandy said in a stale voice, as though she hadn't used it in a very long time.

I love you, Anita cried, but only in her mind. "I guess I'll go get some dinner on the stove then," she said. After a brief hesitation, she left and quietly shut the door behind her.

"This is a house," she caught herself saying as she passed through the living room.

In the kitchen, she opened the refrigerator and peered inside, remembering when Dandy was nine and insisted on calling it the "icebox." The doctor and the dietitian had been clear. There was little confusion about the foods her daughter had to avoid now, and for the rest of her life. However long that would be. However long they could stave off any blockages of her blood. The list featured nuts and seeds, margarine, vegetable oil, shellfish, chocolate, yolks. That morning, for the first time in weeks, Anita had shopped for groceries, and for the first time in years she had done so without buying avocados. And instead of whole eggs, she purchased liquid whites. What might Dandy say about it? She'd say it was snot in a box. *Don't be so vulgar.*

Dandy had to take medications too. The diet alone would make some difference, but almost any food at all posed considerable problems. Anita chuckled dryly at the conundrum, then she laughed again more freely. It was almost like her daughter had known it instinctively, that food, so many foods, could enter her body and turn toxic. Weren't there animals that could do that, somehow detect with fine accuracy the venomous things of the world? Anita would look them up later on her phone.

She felt exhausted all of a sudden, so she decided to make something quick, just a simple stir-fry with rice. She cleaned and chopped broccoli, carrots, green beans, bell pepper, red onions, scallions. Despite the medley of color, however, the piles of vegetables looked drab on the cutting board. Anita gazed up at the mark on the ceiling as a wave of despair knocked against her. The doctor had said she should cook with water instead of olive oil, another sly poison. "Water," she said aloud, incredulously. *No.* "This is a house." Instead of doing that, she found some celery, some garlic and ginger, and a yellow onion, and she decided to use them with some of the carrot. It would take significantly more time, but she was intent now on making a fresh stock. She nursed it for well past an hour, until its fragrance was rich and bold. "This is a house," she said, and the house remained quiet. She would use this to cook, adding just a little at a time to the pan. The rest she could use tomorrow for a soup. As the vegetables brightened on the stove, she spiked the dish with wine and more ginger and other spices, happily improvising. She sampled the food as she went, and was pleased with how the flavor began to evolve. This was a lot of labor for something so simple, but it was good. Damn good.

The vegetables were done right before the rice cooker sang "Twinkle, Twinkle, Little Star." Anita turned off the burner and fluffed the rice. She set out three napkins and three sets of utensils on the table. She set out the vegetables on a serving plate, the rice in a serving bowl. She prepared one of Dandy's medicines too, a chalky powder mixed into a glass of orange juice, the new concoction she would have to drink twice a day. Outside, the sky had finally relented to the fact of evening.

She announced that dinner was ready, and waited before she sat down. She wasn't sure how Dandy would arrange herself at the table. When no one came, she made the announcement again, even louder this time. She was hungry, so she knew they must be too. After a few moments, there was the sound of a door opening and then closing. Then it happened again, a door opened and it closed. But Anita didn't see her daughter or her husband. *Where are they? They sure are something.* She stood there by the little table and told herself to keep waiting. *Be patient. They'll come. This is a house, this is a house, this is a house.*

THE HAPPIEST HOUSE
ON UNION STREET

The next unusual thing was how quickly the pumpkins out on the stoop began to rot. They seemed to be telling Beverly that her suspicions about the other oddities, such as the arguments between her father and her uncle, were correct. She had heard the two men argue before, of course, usually about whoever was renting the third floor of the town house, but recently the fights had become more frequent and more intense, as strangely heated as that summery October. Late Sunday morning another argument had woken her up and drawn her out of bed, and as the cadence of the men's voices led her down the hall, past the framed feel-good photographs taken by her grandmother, her nostrils filled with the aroma of bay leaves and cloves that always came from the kitchen. In order to hear the men more clearly but without being detected, she sat cross-legged on the floor near the refrigerator, in the one corner that never got any sunlight and felt therefore like a hiding place. The sliding doors to the living room, where the men were, hadn't been closed completely. So

from the darkness of her refuge, while she breathed in the smell
of her grandmother's cherished simmer pot and worried the soft-
pink Band-Aid on her arm, Beverly could also catch glimpses of
Uncle Rayford and her father, Raymond, pacing back and forth
as they argued.

"How *you* gonna tell *me* what's irresponsible? You of all people."
It was her father talking, the strain of impatience in his rising voice
so distinct. "And whose child you think she is anyway?"

"As much mine as she is yours," her uncle said.

"It ain't the same, Ray, not at all. You act like one of her little
friends. All you do is play. What, are you eight years old too?"

Uncle Rayford stopped pacing for a moment between the open
doors, much of the gap filled by his lanky body and picked-out salt-
and-pepper hair. "All I know is, baby girl was perfectly fine when
she was with me. But a few hours with you and it's flashing lights."

Yesterday had been unusual too. Beverly had cried, a little,
when she first heard she'd been taken away in an ambulance, but
only because she'd missed the entire ride—had been out cold the
entire time—which was a boring thing to do. A year or two ago,
she would have said it was yawny, a term she'd been somewhat
upset to discover she hadn't invented herself, but she was past the
phase of making words up. Now the idea that so much could happen beyond her awareness frightened her, as did the suggestion
that she was either her father's girl or her uncle's. To her, it was
obvious: she belonged equally to both of them. She loved running
up and down the town house's staircase with her fingertips tracing
the mahogany banister, the way the two of them must have when
they were her age; she loved going between her uncle's apartment
and this one, where she and her father lived. (Never up the stairs
to the third floor though; whoever lived there would usually stay
only a month or two at most, and so would remain a stranger to

her.) She wished she could bring the laptop into the living room so she and her father could sink into the sofa cushions and spend time watching more videos of the Korean lady eating her food. Then she could dash downstairs to hang out and dance with her uncle. But the two men kept on arguing. And the doctor had said Beverly should take it easy for a while. She touched the sore spot on her arm and glanced up at the high ceiling because Mr. Reed, the current third-floor tenant, could be heard laughing. Then something occurred that felt more interesting than the chest-hurt of crying: a thread of longing unspooled from the pit of her stomach toward her father and uncle. She was filled with the desire to follow the thread and make peace between them. She could help them remember who they were, Ray and Ray, and remind them that just a few days ago the three of them had carved pumpkins together. Though that hadn't gone normally either, and neither of the men seemed to care that they had started to go rotten.

"It's like the doc said, man. Girl was dehydrated. Simple as that. Shit happens. Kids get sick."

"Who you trying to convince," Uncle Rayford said, "me or yourself? As I recall, Mama never had a problem with either of *us* passing out for no reason."

Beverly inhaled a bellyful of the simmer-pot smell and thought about her late grandmother, her namesake, a woman she never got to meet. It must have been odd for her to have twin boys who in so many ways were so different. You could see it in their baby pictures. Rayford pleased and plump, with the kind of big creased thighs adults liked to nibble on and fuss over. Raymond eternally scowling, his mouth already set to curse, his body thin and stiff like a piece of jerky. They did grow to look more alike though. There were albums full of photos, taken in this very house, in which they wore exactly the same clothing. The best ones, the feel-good ones, were hung in the hall. Superman shirt and navy shorts, Superman shirt and navy shorts. Striped denim overalls with matching railroad cap, striped denim overalls with matching railroad cap. Easter Sunday suit, Easter Sunday suit. Plaid footed pajamas, plaid footed pajamas. And so on, and so on. But there weren't any stories about them pulling any of the pranks you would expect from twins. Apparently there had been none of the old switcheroo. Which was too bad, Beverly thought. She liked the idea of them scheming together to fool people silly enough to ever mistake one for the other. And she felt sure that her grandmother, said to have been a woman of mischief, would have enjoyed it too.

"Something ain't right," her uncle was saying now, "something ain't right."

"Nope. Don't even try it, Ray."

"Well how come when I asked her about what happened, she turned away from me, talking about she don't remember? You and me both know good and well that child is saucer-eyed. Just like her mother. She don't miss nothing. Any other time, she'd run her mouth and tell me everything, the whole history of the world, from in the beginning until kingdom come."

"Maybe she ain't want you to feel bad," her father said.

"Bad about what?"

"Maybe she ain't want you to feel bad 'cause she knows it was *your* fault. You the one. Got her running amok all the time, dancing around and cooning."

"Come on, Ray, why you gotta talk like that? Lower your voice."

"Got her crawling down on the floor like a little roach, spinning herself silly. You wanna know what happened? Okay. It was all, *Look at me, look at me. Look what Uncle Rayford taught us yesterday.*

Couldn't stop herself. Girl passed out showing off, trying so damn hard to be you."

Well. That wasn't how Beverly recalled it. One thing her father didn't mention about yesterday was how annoyed he'd been with her. Instead of letting her spend time with Uncle Rayford, as was usual on Saturdays, he had decided out of the blue that she would accompany him on his plumbing jobs. He took her from home to home, and at one place, a house in Lefferts, his voice grew very soft and nearly sad as he directed her gaze to all the features of the interior that excited him—fixtures made of blown glass, walls accented with copper, a bathroom with vintage trough sinks and brass faucets. They were the kinds of things he would talk about adding to their house one day, though he hadn't talked that way in a while. As he dragged her from the bathroom to the kitchen, he also tried to interest her in the finer points of his work, explaining that controlling the flow of water to suit our needs was "a kind of magic," telling her that most toilets function because of "a gentleman's handshake with gravity itself," and, attempting to make her laugh at a bit of silliness, pointing out that there was a certain pipe that was called "of all things, a nipple!"

Whenever he said something, Beverly looked up smilingly, attentively, from the game she was playing on his phone, but the truth was, she found it all extremely dull. She would have preferred to be with her uncle, practicing her house dances outside on Eastern Parkway or at the studio in the city where on some weekends he taught classes for a little money. And then maybe taking the subway to Flatbush to get ice cream—peanut butter for her and Guinness for him—from the old shop run by the sing-talking Rastamen who, Rayford frequently told her, retained the sound of West Africa in their mouths. Still, Beverly kept smiling at her father, but it must have been that her smiles appeared forced, or that the laughter he sought came a beat too late. In any case, a switch flipped and he got visibly upset. He got so angry he snatched his phone away from her, and when it was time for lunch he refused to take a break so they could eat. He completed his work at the Lefferts house with a rugged silence that made her own silence feel like a jail.

As they walked back to the town house later, as the sky took on the first tincture of evening, he didn't react when she pointed out all the other pumpkins also rotting on the stoops lining Union Street. He didn't notice the smudges on his beloved stained-glass entryway as they went inside, and even though it was dinnertime he didn't seem to have an appetite. When Beverly suggested that they get out the laptop and watch one of the mukbang videos they loved, he refused. Occasionally, when Mr. Reed got loud, her father glowered up at the ceiling; otherwise he just brooded on the sofa.

In an effort to lift his spirits, Beverly put on a little show for him in the living room, a show that was also a way to practice the new steps Uncle Rayford had taught her after he picked her up from school on Friday. But she quickly saw that her performance wasn't having the effect she had intended. Every shimmy of her shoulders, every dip and glide, every shuffle of her feet on the parquetry, seemed to stoke her father's anger. He wouldn't even look at her. He just breathed loudly through his flared nostrils, and the knobs of his jaw pulsed on both sides. Why did he tell Uncle Rayford that she couldn't stop herself? Once she saw his utter lack of interest, that was the easiest thing in the world to do. The problem was, he wouldn't allow it. He refused to grant her a real audience, but he wouldn't free her from her performance either. When she invited him to join in, to dance along with her the way her uncle did, he smiled sadly at the ceiling. "Nah, you go on," he said dryly, still not looking at her, but with an odd expression, a small, stingy grin. "Keep going. What else he teach you? Yeah, okay. Keep on. Do another move." Even when Beverly complained that she was getting tired, he urged her on from the sofa, his eyes going every which way but at her, clapping in a harshly mechanical way that didn't sound like music at all. So she shuffled, she shimmied, she spun, she practiced her floor work on the hardwood before rising, with easy smoky elegance, back to her feet, knees bent, one-two-three, close-rotate-reach. Beverly grew increasingly exhausted, her mouth drying, sweat stinging her eyes, and she began to feel woozy and sick to her stomach too, but she didn't complain, she just concentrated on her father's robotic clapping as it sped up, more felt than heard now, and on his dispassionate voice insisting more more more. She willed her body into another spin and then she stopped on a dime, but the room whirled around her again and kept whirling until suddenly it lifted away from her, as though a hand had gripped the town house and ripped its frame into the sky. The next thing she knew, she was in the brightness of a hospital room and there was a white lady wearing white, a nurse, sticking an IV into her arm.

And what Uncle Rayford had said wasn't really true either, Beverly thought now. Everything? Why would she ever tell him *everything*? It wasn't a good idea to do that with anyone. Earlier that week, on Wednesday, when he picked her up from school the afternoon after the pumpkin carving, she hadn't told him everything that was on her mind. He'd shown up wearing track pants and his favorite T-shirt, the old yellow one that read ZAIRE 74 in faded blocks of green and orange lettering. His clothes announced that he was in a good mood, and as they walked together he confirmed that he was, going on and on about the miraculous fact of another beautiful day. Over eighty degrees, for the fifth time this month even though it was late October. It meant he could teach

outside again, which he loved. On such a warm, summer-haunted
afternoon, his students, mostly teenagers and people grown but
not yet old, were more likely to show up, and he was more likely
to attract the curiosity of passing strangers. Uncle Rayford was
a man of the community and a healer—those were titles he had
given himself—which meant that out on Eastern Parkway, he
showed people in the neighborhood how to take care of their bodies. Beverly watched him rise from the bench where he liked to sit,
and right there, on the island between Nostrand and New York
Avenues, he became a kind of preacher too—that's how she sometimes thought of him, like one of the robed men at the sweltering
church her mother took her to in Maryland. As the sun shone on
him, Rayford taught a lesson on how to channel energy, which
became a lesson on how to stretch and strengthen the muscles,
which became a lesson on how to hydrate and eat and breathe.
How to scope out danger and defend your body too, but when
those lessons hardened people's faces and made them too serious, he changed tack and lightened the mood by teaching them
house, which was what Beverly had been waiting for all along.
It embarrassed her that she used to think the dance was called
that because he had invented it, as well as the music, in the house
they lived in. It wasn't true of course, and house, he told them all
that day, as he had told her many times, was for anyone in touch
with their soul. "All a soul is," he said, "is the music in your body
turned up loud enough for everyone to hear." Some of those who
had shown up to learn from him were scruffy, the type who looked
like they might jump you, the type she used to assume you might
need to defend yourself against—*bums* is what Raymond would
have called them, *old dusty bums*, *knuckleheads*, or *thugs*—but since
Uncle Rayford didn't mind, since, in fact, he warmly welcomed
them and they turned out to be kind, she didn't mind either, and

so she enjoyed another day of learning what it meant to be a girl of the community. She danced happily beside them, and had no trouble blending her music with their own. She loved these lessons, more than the ones he taught with more formality at the studio in the city, and she saw how much this string of oddly warm days meant to him as he led the movements, offered gentle corrections, and laughed, telling them all to relax. "Relax and get free!" he said to them, though he was looking specifically at her. So there wasn't any reason to mention her observations about the trees that shaded the bench he liked, how unsettling it was that their leaves were still so green this time of year, so close to Halloween, without even a hint of blushing orange, yellow, or red. No, she decided, smiling at the thought of her dirtied palms and her sweat, this could be added to her box of secrets, to the collection of white lies, sneaky behaviors, and notations on beauty she pledged to keep to herself.

Her father's voice was still going in the living room, and though it wasn't as loud as it had been before, it felt more danger-ous somehow, like one of the small knives Beverly could see on the kitchen counter, the ones from the set he sharpened frequently and had warned her never to touch. When she scooted forward to hear him, the muscles in her legs and shoulders told her they were sore too.

"And don't think for a second I'm not on to you," he was saying. "I know what you're doing, coming at me like this. Projec-tion, that's all that is. You been doing it since day one."

"I don't know what the hell you talking about," her uncle said, and again a slice of his glorious graying hair came into view.

"Oh, you know all right. You *been* knowing. It's been this way from jump. Well come on, let's have it out now, all the way. Let's do this, right now. It's time. It's past time. Just admit it. I want to hear you finally say the words. You got duped."

Beverly made sure she was still undetected and then stood to run her finger through the maze made by the pattern of vines on the laminate countertop. Since her father and her uncle weren't discussing her anymore, and since she couldn't really grasp what they were talking about at the moment, the fight was less interesting. But the combination of meanness and glee in her father's voice made her think again about her father's unwillingness to let her stop dancing. His tone was nearly the same as it had been yesterday, she noticed, so he was probably also forcing Uncle Rayford to do something he didn't want to do. And what did it mean to get duped? Beverly couldn't look it up now without the dictionary, or without her father's laptop or phone. The only thing that kept coming into her mind was *droop*, a pleasing word despite its childish sound, a good one for the faces they had carved into the pumpkins. Upstairs, maybe in response to the ongoing argument, Mr. Reed turned on his jazz music. Beverly didn't like Mr. Reed. He had almost ruined the pumpkin carving by causing yet another fight. It was so bad that she had hardly slept since, at least until she'd ended up in the hospital.

Beverly was always excited about carving the pumpkins. It was a tradition, one of the last activities of the year that she did with both her father and her uncle. Her father didn't go trick-or-treating, and her uncle refused to celebrate Thanksgiving with them. He said he hated it. He called it *a day of mourning*, a phrase that Beverly would go on to think about often during her life.

The evening before the lesson on Eastern Parkway, on Tuesday, Beverly, her father, and her uncle had all been together in the light of the living room's lamps, a quality of illumination that reminded her of pearls. They had covered part of the floor with layers of newspaper and flattened grocery bags, and she had already used the black marker to draw her own face, with large rounded eyes, onto one of the pumpkins. The next step was to draw Ray and Ray, who had to be exactly alike, almost, with half-moons for eyes and wide grins, the only difference being that one would have whiskers like a cat to represent the hair on her uncle's face. The thought of the two of them as kids doing this with her grandmother pleased her. But when she looked up to study them, their expressions weren't alike in any way. They were both examining the materials they had gathered—the knives and paper towels, the ladle, two bowls for the pumpkin seeds and guts—but Uncle Rayford's mouth was sad, his gaze dull and distracted, and Raymond's face was hardening into a fossil, another word she liked and had, when she first heard it, immediately decided to keep. Mr. Reed's jazz was going that evening too, and her father didn't seem to like it.

"Reed pay October rent yet?" he asked.

"I don't know why you still worrying about rent," her uncle said.

"I know he ain't pay it."

"Why you ask me then?"

"That's your peoples."

"*My* peoples. All right."

"He ain't pay all of September neither."

"All right."

"How is it that this shit is still happening, Ray?"

"Daddy, language," Beverly said.

"That's right, baby girl. Remind your daddy that a young lady is present."

"For God's sake," her father said. "We're in it up to our eyeballs, man. We need every cent we can get. It can't keep being like this."

"Beverly, ask your daddy exactly how it is he wants it to be."

"Uh-uh, no. We're not playing that game," her father said. "Don't talk to *her*. You talk to me."

"Ask your daddy to tell you exactly who it is he wants to have up there on the third floor."

"Somebody who can pay the damn rent!" Her father stood and walked over to the biggest window. He leaned his hands on the sill with his back to them, his shoulders pressed close to his ears. On either side of him, the curtains were still. From outside, he might have looked like one of his mother's photographs.

"Language, Daddy," Beverly mumbled. But he didn't seem to hear her; no one did. Mr. Reed's music had gotten louder. Beverly was holding the marker so tightly it hurt. She let it drop from her hand.

"Oh, there's plenty of people like *that* coming here," Uncle Rayford said. "Ivy League kids, bankers on the come-up, so-called entrepreneurs with their hands in their parents' fat pockets. Manhattan people. Vacation-home people. Plenty of them. Those the kind you want."

"As long as they can pay the rent."

"Baby girl, ask your daddy why it is he's scared to have someone who looks like you up on the third floor."

Beverly frowned. Mr. Reed didn't look like her. She tried to see all the people she could remember living up there, and though there were a few she had missed while she spent part of the summers away with her mother, she didn't think any of the tenants resembled her at all.

"If you had your way," Uncle Rayford continued, "you'd have a couple of Beckys living up there."

"That's bogus, man," her father called over his shoulder. "That's BS and you know it. It's not about Black and white."

"If it was up to you, you'd probably have a couple more of them down where I'm at too. Instead of me."

"It *would* be nice if your money was regular."

"But guess what, Ray, it's never been up to you. Ma left the house to *me*. And we both know she did it for a reason."

As Mr. Reed's music shrieked above them, her father spun around with a deadly gleam in his eyes. His face was so ugly, which was distressing, because Beverly had always thought of him and her uncle both as quite pretty, which in her opinion was a much better word than *handsome*. She could feel in her own flesh that her father was shaking.

"Tell the truth to shame the devil," Uncle Rayford said, laughing. "I wish you could see yourself. Look at you, mad as hell." Then he smiled down at Beverly. He picked up the marker she had dropped earlier and handed it to her. "Why don't you show your daddy what he looks like right now. Go ahead and draw that old mean mug. Put it right there on the pumpkin."

She grasped some of what was happening, but not, at the root of it all, why, which she knew meant that she couldn't claim to understand it at all. Her uncle kept saying her name and giving her commands, but not in a way that seemed to have anything to do with her. She couldn't move.

"What's wrong?" he asked. "Here, let me help you." Then he scooted beside her and took hold of her left hand, the one with the marker, wrapping his fingers tightly around it. He grabbed a pumpkin by its stem and moved it closer so it was within her reach. "Look how humongous his eyes are, even bigger than yours, baby girl," he said. Taking his time, he made her draw on the pumpkin's ribbed shell, first one large, rough circle, and then another across from it. "And look at those nostrils flaring."

Beverly tried to resist but her hand was much weaker than his. She watched as the lines he forced her to make on the pumpkin slowly became possibly the ugliest nose she had ever seen, far from the beautiful African nose Rayford had told her they all possessed. This one looked more like the snout of a swine. When he made her hand draw the beginnings of a scornful mouth, her father cried out for Uncle Rayford to stop. Then, as the music blared upstairs and the two men in the room stood like people about to fistfight and made a commotion yelling over each other, Beverly, feeling alone now, stared at the incomplete face on the pumpkin, its mouth no more than a sidelong streak of dirt. Her father didn't look anything like that. She rubbed at the black marks but they had already gone dry on the shell. It was only when her chest began to hurt and the men lowered their voices and rushed over to her that she realized, with embarrassment, that she was crying. They apologized and said the soothing, calming things that always made her feel better despite her annoyance at being treated like a baby. Together, with Mr. Reed's jazz moaning from the ceiling, they helped her draw a smile on the pumpkin. It was pleasant enough in its own right but asymmetrical, and grotesque beside the nose and eyes. "This is gonna have to do," Uncle Rayford said, and Beverly figured he was right. After some thought, she decided to replicate the face on the remaining pumpkin, making sure to add the cat whiskers for her uncle. After the men cut out the lids, she reached into the pumpkins to grab the strings of seeds and then ladled out the guts. Her father and uncle, speaking to her but not to each other, wiped the pumpkins' outsides clean of any mess, and then they assisted while she carved the faces she had drawn, mechanically following the lines. Her father and uncle each brought their own pumpkin outside and set it on the stoop. Then there was the last part of the tradition, her grandmother's favorite, which Beverly, with the men's supervision, mostly did herself. She brought the bowl of seeds into the kitchen, cleaned and dried them, and seasoned them with lemon pepper, garlic, and salt. Her father helped her place them into the oven's heat. Even now, as she traced her finger through the vines on the countertop, she could taste the roasted seeds on her tongue.

"Look, man," her uncle was saying in the living room, "I already told you. It's gonna be fine."

"Fine? Fine how?" her father said. "Explain it to me, Ray. Make it make sense."

"I'm talking to some people."

"What people? Those bums you spend all your time with? What they gonna do, help you rob a bank? They got law degrees? They passed the bar? They work pro bono? I think not. I think the hell not. You know what, let's just say you've done enough talking. All you do is flap your gums. *I'm a man of the people, I'm gonna heal the community*, blah blah blah. Mr. Crown Heights himself. Mr. I'm Blacker Than a Thousand Midnights. All that talk and you got duped, just like I said. And by some damn white men, of all people. Ain't that some shit."

"It was theft."

"And the accomplice is as bad as the thief. Fact of the matter is, *you* did this. You just signed it all away."

White men. White men? Beverly stretched her mind further back and remembered a day, near the beginning of spring, when three *strange* men—often another way of saying white men, but not always—had spoken to Uncle Rayford outside the town house. Of the three, only one was white. The other two were the kind she had seen at block parties and cookouts, or out on the Parkway learning house and other lessons from her uncle as traffic sped by. The main difference was these men wore business suits. The white man wore a suit too, a dark blue one that was less nice than the other ones, but he didn't do much of the talking.

That afternoon wasn't quiet, but it was serene and warm, the sky faded blue like an Easter egg. Wads of gray and white cloud stretched themselves until they vanished. School was over for the day, and Uncle Rayford was sitting behind Beverly, braiding her hair. Playing children screamed as they passed, and strolling adults greeted Beverly and her uncle, which was the way of the stoop. He wasn't quite as gentle as her father, so sometimes, as he pulled the comb through, or grabbed sections of hair to begin a new plait, her scalp felt tender. When the strange men stopped by, Beverly heard her uncle say, "Back again, huh?" The white man among them, who had abnormally large hands, smiled. He said that if they were persistent, it was only because their organization believed in helping people.

One of the other men, to his left, said, "It's a beautiful home, Mr. Cureton—or can I call you Rayford?"

Her uncle laughed dryly. "Rayford's fine if you're familiar."

The man to the right said, "Beautiful is right, but what are you gonna do, Rayford?"

"Let's face facts. The property is distressed, and that's a big problem."

"The house is depressed?" Beverly asked. Her uncle used that word to describe her father sometimes, when he was gloomy, though the house never felt that way to her. But Beverly realized her mistake even before she noticed the men at the bottom of the stoop looking at each other and smirking.

"My grandfather bought this house," she proclaimed, to re-assert her authority. "It's two hundred years old."

"Not quite that," her uncle said. "But you'll see it to two hundred. Get it right now. When did he buy it?" he asked. This was one of his tests.

"Nineteen fifty-seven?" she said.

"You asking or you telling?"

"Telling."

"Mm-hm, good. And why's that important?"

"You can't know where you're going unless you know where you've been."

"There you go." Then he continued the test. "How much money did it cost?"

"Eight thousand dollars."

"Nope. Seven thousand six hundred dollars."

"That's what I said."

Uncle Rayford laughed. "That's some funny math you doing, but okay. Well what's so special about all that?"

"Grandpa's parents used to be slaves—*en*slaved," she said, before her uncle could correct her about this again. That part of the story had always chilled her. It was frightening to think about. You took only three or four steps back, hardly going anywhere at all, and you ran so quickly into a thing like that.

"That's right," her uncle said, and at this point he stood and walked down toward the men. "You see, isn't it a remarkable story?" he said to them. "From the *slave* ship to *home owner-ship*"—he snapped his fingers—"in the blink of an eye. How unlikely is that? Those are some mean odds, wouldn't you say? Well, that's what my family does, gentlemen. That's how we do. That's our story. We get nose-to-nose with the worst of problems and figure things out on our own."

"That story's a great one, no doubt, but it's more common than you think," said the man on the left. "We've heard versions of it before, from people all over Crown Heights . . ."

"Bed-Stuy, Prospect Heights, East New York, Brownsville," the man on the right said. "Up in Harlem too."

"It really fills you with admiration," the first man said. "For our ancestors. And how hard they worked so that we could be here, living the kind of lives we do."

Her uncle chuckled. "Oh I see what's going on. This is why he brought *you two* along this time, huh?"

"It's not like that, Rayford. Our parents and grandparents lifted each other up, all right, and it's up to us to keep that tradition alive. And that fortitude. We owe them that."

"The traditions *are* alive," Beverly said. She didn't care when they all stared up at her. She loved all the family's traditions: church on Easter Sunday, the West Indian Day Parade after she returned from her mother's house in Maryland, carving pumpkins and roasting seeds in October, Thanksgiving dinner with her father, the Ailey dancers with her uncle on Christmas Eve, not to mention the nearly constant pleasure of her grandmother's simmer pot.

"Is this your daughter, Mr. Cureton?"

Uncle Rayford turned his head to look at the white man. "That's right."

Beverly smiled. She already felt like she was the child of both Rays, and it was hard to imagine anything could change that, but she deeply wanted her uncle to say yes, now, to this man.

"What's your name, sweetheart?"

"Nunya," her uncle told the white man, whose expression became confused.

The man on the left raised his palms as if to show they were clean. "We completely respect that, Rayford. Completely. Now, judging from how much pride you have about this place, I'm assuming you grew up here, is that right? Well, what about her, your daughter?" He turned to her now. "You're already a big smart girl, I can see, but you've got a lot of growing up left to do, don't you, and that growing-up should happen here, shouldn't it?"

Beverly rolled her eyes. The things the man was saying now were really obvious and really dumb.

"And *your* children too," he continued. "Your children and your grandchildren. They should grow up here too. On and on down the line."

This is boring, Beverly thought. She wanted to hurry and get her braids over and done with.

"Look," said the man on the right, "Brooklyn's changing, we all know that."

"Forget changing. Might as well admit it's already gone," said the other man.

"Twenty, thirty years ago, nobody gave a damn about this place."

"Nobody, huh?" Uncle Rayford said.

"You know what I mean. If you were in the city, cabbies wouldn't even want to take you across the bridge. Some would refuse outright. You know how it was. But now . . ."

The man on the left shook his head. "My family has a place in the Stuy, an amazing brownstone. Almost as fine as what you have here. If it wasn't for Homeowners' Relief, we would have lost . . . we would have lost . . ."

"Lost what?" Beverly asked.

The man smiled up at her painfully. He appeared to be thinking hard about what to say, which was annoying. When adults did this to her, it felt like they were giving themselves permission to lie.

"Let's go talk on the corner," Uncle Rayford said, cutting in before the man could continue. "Bev, stay put for a minute."

"But my hair," she whined.

"I'll be back in a second," he said. "Don't move a muscle. Why don't you practice your freezes?"

She pulled the comb out of her hair and watched her uncle walk to the corner with the three men. They talked for a bit and then the white man took out some papers, which they examined on the hood of a car. Then they talked again and forever, long enough, Beverly thought, for her to grow up and have all those kids and grandkids mentioned earlier. When they approached the house again, she heard her uncle say, "I'll think about it."

"Why don't you take my business card?" the white man said.

"I said I'll think on it."

"There's no harm in taking a card, Mr. Cureton."

Her uncle gazed down the street and tasted the top row of his teeth. He ended up taking the little white card reluctantly, using his thumb and forefinger.

"Go to the website and check us out," one of the other men said. "Most of the information you'll need is there. Plenty of testimonies too. But if you still have questions, call me personally. My number's there on the back. We won't bother you anymore, Rayford, but I really hope you consider us. We do good work. We're building a great track record of helping people, our people, neighborhood people. You and your daughter have a blessed day."

Her uncle slipped the card into the back pocket of his jeans. He shook hands with him and the other one, then waved halfheartedly to the white man. The three of them left.

"Don't look like you were doing your freezes," Uncle Rayford said to Beverly. He resumed his place behind her on the stoop.

"Do you like those people?" Beverly asked. She felt him stick the end of the comb back into her hair and take three sections of it in hand.

"We'll see."

"We will?"

"They might be all right." He started on a new plait.

"I know what *depressed* means," she asserted.

"Of course you do."

"I know that's not what our house is."

"No, baby girl, it isn't. How many times have I told you? Remember what your grandmother used to say."

Beverly couldn't help but grin.

Back in the now, in the shadows of her hiding place, she realized she had forgotten to look up the word the strange men had used. She thought for a while about her error, about how you could sometimes wrong your way into a right, how you could stumble your way into a dance. She put her hand on the kitchen's slightly yellowed wallpaper and asked, whispering, "*Are* you depressed?" The house didn't respond. When her father was happy he couldn't stop talking, but when he was depressed he hardly made a sound. Then again, sometimes being quiet was a good thing, like when she meditated with Uncle Rayford, or when she and her father watched the mukbang videos, which was like meditation too. Beverly had to admit that it was confusing.

She was feeling exhausted again, and her limbs ached. Her father and uncle were still arguing back and forth, but what they were saying—about legal fees and medical bills, and about numbers, thousands, millions—just floated away from her weary mind. She lay down, right on the kitchen floor, and closed her eyes.

When she opened them, she was back in her bed. Through her curtains she could see it was night outside. She lay still for a while, until sounds she recognized reached her ears. She got up and went into the living room. Her father was sitting there, the room dark other than the light coming from his laptop. He was holding a can of beer, she saw, and there were three more cans crushed on the table beside him. The sounds she had heard were coming from the laptop, sounds of the Korean lady speaking and chewing her food. Beverly looked at the screen for a while, at the various dishes of food spread out in front of the lady, at her pink lipstick and the red stains of sauce. Beverly recognized the sweater the lady was wearing. Maybe this was one of the videos they had already watched.

"Daddy?" Beverly asked. She felt a depth of tenderness that was rare even for her, as though seeing him after a very long time and recognizing who he was. He was her father.

He took a sip from his beer and kept staring at the screen. He always stared at the videos this way, as if the eating was a form of magic and he was under a spell.

"You're watching without me, Daddy."

Her father smacked his lips and his eyebrows lifted on his forehead. "So you're up, huh?" he said. "You must be hungry."

But Beverly wasn't hungry at all, and it felt too late to eat.

"I'm gonna cook us up some dinner. Not just any dinner, we're gonna have ourselves a feast!" He stood, drank deeply until he finished his beer, and crushed the can.

"What about Uncle Rayford?"

"It's just gonna be you and me," he said. "It'll be like Thanksgiving came early."

She followed him into the kitchen, which smelled only faintly now of her grandmother's simmer pot. She stood there wondering who had found her in her hiding place, who it was that had carried her to bed. She asked her father but he ignored her. He took pans and other pots out from the cabinets under the sink, and then he began rubbing his hand along the countertop, as if to wipe away the maze of vines. He still seemed to be under the eating spell.

After watching him for a while, Beverly started to back away. Her father didn't seem to notice. She went downstairs and quickly found Uncle Rayford. He was sitting in a chair in his living room with his eyes closed and his fingers pressed to his temples. He seemed to be thinking hard. Despite her sore muscles, Beverly threw her body onto him and gave him her most powerful hug.

"Hey, baby girl."

"Uncle Rayford."

"What you doing up?"

"Uncle Rayford," Beverly said, "you're my daddy. You're my daddy too."

He stood so abruptly that she fell away from him. Then he held her at arm's length by her shoulders. His face looked stern, even more like her father's than it usually did. He said, "Go on up and back to bed, okay? I can't play around with you right now."

Beverly stared at him before going upstairs. In the kitchen, her father was hidden behind the open refrigerator. He still didn't seem to notice her. She snuck over to the counter, where several ingredients for cooking had already been set out, and she took one of the knives from its set. She left the kitchen. Slowly, quietly, she opened the front door of the house, stepped outside, and closed the door carefully behind her.

Even though she was wearing only her pajamas and it was nighttime in October, she wasn't cold. This October was different, she reminded herself. At her feet were the three shadowy shapes of the pumpkins, clustered together. She sat at the top of the stoop and examined the two that were her father and her uncle. Their mouths were completely warped, and the holes she had carved revealed through webs of cottony mold the deep purplish black within. No longer fat and round, now discolored and collapsing into themselves, they looked even worse than they had be-

fore. Hers, she noticed, was decent by comparison. "You need to
be fixed," Beverly whispered, and as she held that pumpkin by the
stem, she dragged the knife's edge along the rim of one eye. But
the decaying shell came apart and the edge of the knife pierced
her other hand. She watched the sluggish crawl of her dark blood
but didn't make a sound. This was dull too, she decided—her
notion about the pumpkins and the cutting, even the surprise of
blood—all disappointing despite her theatrical intentions. None
of it meant a thing.

Beverly startled when she heard the door open behind her.
But it wasn't her father, and it wasn't her uncle either. Mr. Reed
stood looking down at her through the flashing circles of his
glasses. She felt his gaze shift to her hand, to the knife, and then
back up into her eyes. She bristled at the warmth of his concern.
His mouth strained open within the silvery nest of his facial hair
and he asked if she was okay. She quickly replied that she was
fine. He nodded for an unusually long time, but instead of continuing on his way he placed his hands on his knees and lowered
himself with a drawn-out groan until the two of them were sitting uneasily together. They remained there on the stoop and
stared at the night. It was so peaceful and still. Beverly could
smell her father's cooking through the window. With her bare feet
she weakly tapped a sequence of her uncle's steps.

She thought about what the first Beverly would have said to
her misbehaving sons years ago in order to set them right. The
answer was obvious, family lore intimately known. "This here
is the happiest house on Union Street," she said aloud, reciting
her grandmother's affirmation. "The most happiest." Mr. Reed
didn't utter a word in response, and, remembering this, she would
always feel gratitude and resentment.

THAT PARTICULAR SUNDAY

There are times when a family has an aura of completion. Remembering such a time feels like gazing at a masterpiece in an art gallery. You might find yourself taking one or two steps backward to absorb the harmonious perfection of the entire image. Or you may be lured by it, drawn to it, inching closer to study every fine detail of composition, the faultless poise with which each element confirms the necessary presence of the others. Take the figure of the son, who hurtles into the foreground of the picture, claiming his position in a web of femaleness, affixing himself to the very center of its adhesive heart, because he belongs there, or so he believes with the wild unblemished certainty of a boy's imagination. Like everything else in the image, he never changes. *Yes, that is my mother,* his presence announces. *And those are my aunts,* he seems to say. *And this*—of the girl closest to him, her expression as breathless as his own—*this is my cousin. My companion. My closest friend. Her soul is the identical twin of mine.* The absence of the father doesn't matter one bit. The absence of the siblings doesn't matter much either, even though the son will love them hopelessly. Helplessly. They belong to a different elsewhere, a time yet to come, with another brute of a father to come, and the circumstances of their lives will frenzy the family, purpling it, cloying it until it is spoiled. Then it will be no different from any ordinary clan. Unpleasant to regard. An eyesore.

The apartment building is now in a state of ruin. Last month, on a Sunday too recent to be called the past, my cousin Mary stood with me on Adelphi Street, in front of the place where my mother and I lived when I was a boy. It was a brisk autumn Sunday, unusually seasonal, the afternoon bleared by a thick, dun blanket of cloud, by the livid shadows of new high-rises. Mary's infant daughter, comically bundled, stirred in the stroller, chaotic even in her sleep.

"Come *on*," I repeated.

"Do we have to?" she asked. "It's so silly."

"I'll beg, you know I will. Don't make me do it."

"Fine," Mary said. "Let's just get it over with. Lord knows I don't want you to sound any more pathetic than you already do."

On the count of three we sang together, the way we used to on Sundays, literally music to my ears: "*Four-B, that's me!*"

Mary frowned and shook her head. "I don't know why you're grinning," she said. "I really don't. We sound awful."

I laughed at her.

"We do. Like a couple of strays in heat."

"Two cats, caterwauling," I said, indulging myself.

"And the song—if *that's* what you want to call it—it's so embarrassing. It's just . . . a nothing. Less than nothing. Is that all we could come up with?"

"We were children."

"Oh, were we?" she teased. "Like that justifies it. We must have been two of the dumbest kids who have ever lived. I pray Nina doesn't take after me, if that's the case. And if that's the case, that means you might be a bad influence. So maybe it turns out to be a good thing that my baby's grown cousin, who claims to love me, and who has all the time in the world, makes absolutely zero effort to spend time with her, much less help out."

"Grown going on geriatric."

"That's your excuse? What, you have some infirmity I don't know about? What is it, arthritis? Dementia?"

"I don't know," I said lazily, lawlessly. Underneath the canopy of the stroller, the baby continued to dream. Her sinister little fists contracted, two knots spasming at the ends of her coat sleeves. I looked at the cracked stoop of my old home. The peeling paint on the facade giving it the appearance of scales. "Kids just aren't very fun at this age," I found myself muttering. "I didn't even know you were bringing Nina along."

"I'll be *bringing Nina along* pretty often for the foreseeable future. Doesn't matter how I or anyone else feels about it. It's kind of a part of the bargain."

"Don't get me wrong. I'm not unhappy to see her. It's really nice to see her. A really nice surprise."

"Oh don't get all earnest on me. You need to loosen up, Aaron. Relax." Mary observed me closely for a moment and then added, "There it is. Your *other* expression. Yeah, that's it for sure. There's the grin, and there's the grimace. They look so much alike . . ."

Feel alike too, I thought, the sensation of each slicked onto my face. "But you could always tell them apart."

"Not even remotely true. It's as clear as day to me now, but when we were young I had no idea."

"That can't be right," I said. "You knew me better than anybody, better than my own mother did."

"How is she, by the way?"

"I don't know," I said, loudly for some reason, nearly stentorian, the blast of my own words like a protest in my ears. Then more quietly: "I sent her some cash last week."

"Yes, moneybags, I'm aware. Your mother told mine. Told me too, as a matter of fact. I talked to her on Thursday. You should give her a call too. She's starting to think she didn't raise you right." Mary crouched down to decipher Nina's fussing. She spoke softly to the baby, sounding almost, painfully almost, like her old darling self. "And how are your brothers?" she asked, looking up at me.

My spine felt rigid, rusted into the shape of a question mark. On its own, my right hand rose, smoothed the lines of my forehead, concealed the show of my teeth. "I don't know," I told her. The images that include my brothers and their troubles aren't ones I've ever cared to examine.

The sabbatical nature of Sundays had everything to do with the time I would spend with Mary, time which never had to be announced. My mother would simply watch, pleasantly at a loss, as I dressed in a clash of color, down to the mismatched socks, and, soon after, I would throw my small body into her arms and we would leave without saying a word. Or, more rarely, our intercom would buzz. On those Sundays, Mary and I played or read or watched television together in 4-B, or maybe we romped in the local park, but more typically my mother and I would leave the neighborhood behind. What I'm referring to now is the actual past, the genuine past, the Sundays that had the patina of the golden age, time's verifiable signature. My mother displayed almost no confusion then. Matters were simpler. She didn't call me by the name of one of my younger brothers, that casual error she makes now. She couldn't. It was years before Keith or Rashard would even be born.

We lived in the neighborhood before it was a real estate agent's dream. The historical record describes that era of Fort Greene with words like *abandoned*, *poverty-stricken*, *crime-ridden*, and with references to *crack*, words that are impossible to believe or even tolerate given the form and mood of my memories. As my mother and I strolled through and away from the area on a typical Sunday, toward the subway station that would take us to the part of Brooklyn now called Little Haiti, the corners, windows, and stoops were florid with faces and brilliant patterns of clothing. Far from abandoned, everything was proudly and ostentatiously claimed. Sometimes Leora, the liveliest of my aunts—dead now—would be with us, jutting her mandible out at catcallers, teasing my mother for telling me to "talk proper," calling her "girl" in twelve different tones, tapping me on the shoulder to point out a squirrel spiraling up a tree. Walking between Aunt Leora and my mother I had to step double-time to keep up, but I made sure to go slowly enough not to interfere with the delicious sensation of being drawn along by them, the dampness of my palms like a glue that stuck my hands to theirs. As long as I live, I will never forget the tug and pulse of that neighborhood feeling, that family feeling. *Here it is, and here I am.*

My mother and I would emerge from the Newkirk Avenue station, turn three corners, left-right-left, and arrive at Mary's apartment, where she lived with her mother. Mary's father lived there too, as a matter of fact, but in my memory he was always away at one of his jobs, even on Sundays, so I hardly ever saw him. Though he didn't appear in the picture, he was an essential source of its warmth, its cadmium-yellow light. Even then I understood that the quality of the light in their home, which could be dimmed or brightened at will, had an essential connection to the fact that he was never there. So did the abundance of rooms it contained. So did the pure fleecy whiteness of its furniture and carpeting. Aunt Arlette was the virtuoso of their home, which she didn't hesitate to remind my mother of during our visits, but I knew, even if I didn't have the word for it yet, that my laboring uncle was the patron. While Mary and I were in her playroom, we could hear her mother's voice speaking about her latest acquisition, a new wall hanging or set of curtains, a vintage lamp, a coffee table topped with an oval of glass, a Christmas spruce that they would keep for years and that was also white, a color so enchanting that I laughed in confusion during a subway ride back when my mother told me to stop running my mouth about it. "I can see why you would be so impressed," she said, "but that doesn't change the fact that it's artificial." It was my mother's tone that confused me. Her judgment rested on a word that made me understand it in the Latin sense, a way of praising the tree as a work of art.

It's difficult to say how many years they lived in that apartment, but not because of a failure of memory. I could state something like *Mary and her mother (and her father) lived just off of Avenue D in Brooklyn for eight years, from the time I was four until the time I was twelve.* But this kind of boiled-down nonsense might as well be in a newspaper clipping, or an obituary. It's the kind of thing I find difficult to bear. It doesn't mean a thing. It doesn't capture what it felt like to be there. The depth of feeling that was reliable and unvarying. There, Mary and I would kneel to drive our talons into the plush of their carpet and watch them disappear. There, we would puppeteer her dolls through dramas so improvised we would stun ourselves into contemplative silences. There, we eavesdropped on our mothers, who sat in two of the dining chairs, opposite the white sofas and glass table. As they sipped coffee they would parley, Aunt Arlette's word—"It's not gossip," she said to us, "if you're actually interested in people"—and some-times, or so Mary told me once, the coffee would be spiked with rum, though only now and then, according to Mary, and only a nip, because their father—our grandfather—was an alcoholic back when he lived in his ancient time. Mary and I would peek in on our mothers shortly before dinner, which was earlier at their apartment, and we were purposely bad at our spying. We wanted to be caught. Without fail they would call us over, and I would sit on my mother's lap and Mary would sit across from me on Arlette's. They would groom us—licking a fingertip to wipe away a smudge or a patch of ash, picking nits of lint from our heads, tucking in any stray feathers of hair, checking that the seams of our clothes were intact—and then their parley would evolve into something else, a maternal show-and-tell in which Mary and I were the exemplars of girlhood and boyhood. They would take turns, emphasizing Mary's charm, or my intelligence, her way of making people laugh, my way of avoiding trouble, the brightness of her smile, the length of my eyelashes, her lovely teeth, my lovely hands, her love of reading books, my love of telling tales, her curi-osity, my gentleness, and so on. "It's too bad the two most sublime Negro children ever to appear in God's universe are related," Aunt Leora said once when she was also there, probably on one of those spiked-coffee Sundays. "Otherwise you could just go ahead and marry them to each other!" As far-out as the comment was, it was still entirely consistent with the feeling of being there, though whenever I've brought Leora's joke up with Mary, she says she doesn't remember it. "*If* it happened," she told me recently, "I'd bet every penny I have that you and Leora were the only ones laughing." But it did happen—I know for certain that it did—and I know without a doubt that there was no division among us.

That Sunday unfolded the way every one of them did. The

show-and-tell eventually had to end because Aunt Arlette had to
get up and make sure the food in the kitchen didn't burn. When
she stood and Mary slid from her lap, I scooted from my mother's
at the same time. The two of us returned to her playroom con-
secrated, and we played another quick game before dinner was
served, vibrating like little gods. That day we shook from the raw
sugar of curiosity. She was sublime and so was I—whatever the
word meant, that part of Aunt Leora's joke sounded too good
not to be true—but sublime examples of what? What *was* a girl
anyway? And what, for that matter, was a boy? We knew where
the answers, under lock and key, were supposed to be kept, so we
also knew what had to be done. Mary hiked up her dress and I
unzipped my pants. We each slid our thumbs into our own waist-
bands and rolled down the front of our Underoos, but only so far.
Our pre-dinner game that week was simple, quick, conclusive:
she poked twice at the smooth skin over my bladder and I poked
twice at hers. That's all it took for her to state what was obvious.
"*Boy* and *girl* are garbage words," she said, and I agreed. We took
down her hardbound dictionary and neatly sliced both terms and
their definitions out with a pair of safety scissors. And as Aunt
Arlette began calling us back to the dining table to eat, we turned
pages by the handful in search of the word *sublime.* As far as we
were concerned, what we had done with the scissors had pruned
the English language itself, and improved it. Still, I'd been hesitant
to bring up this particular detail of that Sunday with Mary, who
is quickly becoming the queen of contradiction, but when I finally
did I was surprised when she nodded in response, clearly amused.
"I remember that foolishness," she went on to say. "The things
children do . . . We thought—the two of us *actually* thought—that
we were the same."

But we were the same. We fell out and shrieked at the same

jokes, and the convulsions of our whole-body laughter made us sink deeper and deeper into the white carpet. We were bored or repulsed by the same things: most cartoons, car chases in movies, almost all commercials and ads. Neither of us was interested in having a pet, and we found the fact of domesticated animals itself sort of sad. Though we were purposely inept at spying on our mothers during their parleys, we both had a keen interest in our other aunt, Thérèse, and made sure to pay special attention to any talk of her. Thérèse was the oldest of the sisters, and her appearances were even more irregular than Leora's. She was on the very edge of the picture, and receded pretty far into the background, virtually out of the frame. You might not have noticed her at all if it weren't for her triangular bush of shoulder-length Donna Summer hair, complete with a sturdy fringe of bangs that nearly covered her entire forehead. During the parleys, her hair was sometimes referred to as a wig, and our mothers seemed to suggest that she had many wigs, possibly dozens of them. Mary and I never saw any of these, which made us think our mothers were fabricating lies about her hair in the interest of sibling fun, and maybe out of sibling jealousy, but that didn't stop us from wanting wigs of our own. For at least a few years, we both put them on our Christmas lists. Neither of us ever got one.

I don't remember Aunt Thérèse ever being at Mary's apartment. She must have known that her younger sisters needed time and space to make their harmless jokes at her expense. Or she might have suspected that during the Sunday parleys our mothers referred to her as Theresa, the name our alcoholic grandfather insisted on giving her when she was born. "Thérèse" was her own modification, a gift she had given herself when she turned eighteen. Our mothers honored her preference when she was present. Only Leora called her Theresa to her face. This would

happen on Adelphi Street, in apartment 4-B, which lacked the
dazzle of Mary's place but had a more subtle magic of its own.
The fact that it could hold all of the sisters at once, even Leora
and Thérèse, was proof of this magic. This usually happened
two times a year, once in June or July for a "cook-in" and then
again in November for Thanksgiving, which we celebrated, of
course, on Sunday. Thanksgiving belonged to my mother. She
would roast a turkey and bake macaroni and cheese, which everyone would eat with polite appreciation, but what everyone really
looked forward to was her fried chicken, which Aunt Thérèse
would tell Mary and me was the best. "The absolute very best,"
she said to us the year she stopped eating turkey, when twice as
many chicken bones ended up on her napkin. It must have been
the following year that she declined both the mac and cheese and
the chicken, when she looked around sort of helplessly at everyone
else fixing their plates and quietly asked, "Is there any sal-mon?"
She pronounced the *l*. My mother seemed to panic and was ini-
tially unable to speak, because, I thought, of that *l*'s unwelcome
presence. But I realized it was because of the apparent absence
of any food her sister could eat. "I—I'm absolutely sure I have
something here that you'd like," she said, and opened the door to
the freezer. Aunt Thérèse stood beside her and they both stared
as the vapor cleared and revealed all the crammed-in containers
of goods. "Ah," my aunt said after a moment, still staring blankly
into the compartment, "just a little sal-mon would be perfect." At
this point, Leora jumped in. "Theresa, you'd never go around demanding *sal-mon* if we were back home in *Suf-folk*," she said, fon-
dling both *l*'s with her tongue, "so what makes you think it's okay
to do it here?" Thérèse's eyebrows shot up and retreated behind
her bangs. I've told Mary that this expression, which we saw so
often, seemed to communicate any number of things. Fear, long-

ing, happiness, curiosity, surprise. But she said I was overthinking it, and that it happened simply as a result of anyone alluding to the small town in Virginia where each of them was born.

I don't know about that—causation, correlation—but it is accurate to say that the mention of Suffolk was directly followed by the vanishing eyebrows. And that wasn't the only disappearance. For a few moments, something seemed to vacate the room. Judging from my mother's eyes, its escape route went along the ceiling, through the hanging maze of Boston fern and devil's ivy, and out the living room windows. All the women gazed there silently. I've had to tell Mary what happened next, because she didn't remember.

"You said, 'What are you all looking at? Is somebody out there?'"

"Is that what I said?"

"Well, you've always been a breaker of silences. You never could tolerate them for very long."

Aunt Thérèse said nobody was there. My mother said, "Everybody's here." "Of course everybody's here," Aunt Arlette added. "So what are we waiting for? I'm hungry. Who's saying grace?"

Leora gave each of her sisters a curious look and then made a space to sit between me and Mary. As Aunt Thérèse said grace, praising God for the bounties of food and family, the two of us watched her and her plate piled high with iceberg lettuce and candied yams. During the meal, we observed how she held her fork between bites, balancing it lightly among her fingers, how her elbows and forearms never touched the table, and then we tried to imitate her. The way she ate, with unhurried relish, strikes me now as the image of her authority, illustrating all the pride and elegance she had fashioned for herself throughout her life. She

made that peculiar salad seem like the most mouthwatering dish
in the world.

Not long after that Thanksgiving gathering, during an early
weekend in December, the first snow of winter arrived. By Sunday morning, what had started as a shy dusting became a steady
concentrated fall. The flakes looked so large and finely detailed as
they slipped past my window that I was sure I could name every
single one of them if I tried. I was excited as always to see Mary,
to show off the new socks and snow boots I had gotten for my
birthday. I wasn't dressed yet though, because my mother hadn't
come in to watch me. When I called out to her, she stormed into
the room and asked why I wasn't ready yet. "I was waiting for
you," I said. "You're getting a little too old for that, Aaron," she
told me. "Now hurry up and get your clothes on." The edge in
her voice rattled me, and sometimes I think of it as the seedling
instance of a sound that would start to recur years later, though
by then it would become sharper and more tremulous, and she
would have called me Keith or Rashard, if not both, before cor-
recting herself. It's easy for me to dismiss that thought, however,
because back then things were so pristine. My moments of doubt
are pebbles compared to the mountain of what I know to be true.
Here's a truth I'm almost certain of: She smiled her usual Sunday-
morning smile at me before she walked away. She must have heard
how harsh she had been, and so she offered an apology. Wanting
to please her, I rushed to put on my green pants and my orange-
and-gold-striped turtleneck. I pulled on my socks, one each from
the new pairs. Just as I began to wedge my heel into the socket of
a boot, our intercom buzzed. So Mary was coming to our apartment this week! I was more than fine with that. In fact, I preferred
it. It meant we could go to the park and play in the snow.

I ran in my socks to greet her, but was surprised to find not only Mary and her mother, but Aunt Thérèse and Aunt Leora too. The four of them were crowded together just outside the doorway, the slush that rimmed their boots melting onto our welcome mat.

"I just need to grab my coat," my mother said.

"Why is everybody here?" I asked.

My mother looked back at me. "You're still not ready? I told you to hurry up."

"But why are they all here?"

Mary erupted with laughter, but not in a teasing way. She was delighted that she would get to share the surprise. "Didn't anybody tell you? We're going on a trip today. To see our other aunt. Don't you get it? Don't you hear what I'm saying? We have another aunt!"

I couldn't begin to understand what she meant, but I went outside with everyone else, somnambulating behind the rest of them. We piled into a rented minivan and Aunt Leora, the only one of the sisters who was both willing and able to drive, sat at the wheel. We sped past Fort Greene Park within the first thirty seconds of the drive, and as we went by I think I was the only one who turned to look at it. Sitting next to me, Mary faced directly ahead, squinting a little, beaming softly and warmly. She seemed happy about this radical change, this break in our routine. Calmly expectant. Her demeanor began to rub off on me, and when she blindly reached her hand across and took hold of mine, I told myself not to think in terms of something broken or twisted. Instead, I thought of my mother's bush lily, which had been in her care almost as long as I had. Late the previous year, she had repotted it and had stopped watering it so often. In the new place she had given it, with less direct sunlight, it cooled and settled, and in March it flowered for the very first time. I imagined us all as a cluster of those orange winter blooms, and now, joining us, there would be another bright flower.

Mary scoffed when I reminded her of that drive. "You mean to tell me you were sitting there thinking all those fancy thoughts? Well, let me assure you that we were none the wiser." She claimed I was actually terrible in the car—"fidgety, whiny, carrying on like a child possessed"—but the truth is I was excited and probably just a bit more demonstrative than usual. "You can't spell *demonstrative* without *demon*," she joked when we were together last month, and after she said it I had the revelation that while adulthood had changed her perspective, motherhood had gone even further and shifted her allegiances. I could see it in the way she acted in response to Nina. In Mary's bleary, darkly encircled eyes there was anticipation of trouble and the frightened assumption of the worst. My cousin is now a mother, an exhausted mother who will likely raise her daughter on her own, so I know I'm not being totally fair. Exhaustion can drain your willingness to entertain the marvelous. But that unwillingness can provoke exhaustion too.

I remember asking, maybe more than once, "How long does it take to get there?" I really wanted to know. Aunt Leora's reply, however, was "Nine million years." She didn't talk much during the drive. None of the sisters did. They sat in front of us enclosed in their own mostly uninterrupted silence, and what they did say hardly even rose to the level of chitchat. A word was spoken now and then, but for all it meant or inspired in response it might as well have been a cough or a sneeze. They must have been as anxious as I was to get there, wherever we were going, wherever this new addition to the family was, and it couldn't have helped that the drive was slowed and hushed by the weather.

I had been afraid to ask where *there* was, afraid I would discover that Mary knew infinitely more than I did about the mys-

tery of our new aunt, and that I was the only one entirely out of
the loop. But when we finally arrived, she seemed just as per-
plexed as I was. We had parked between two brick buildings, a
small one and a much larger one that reminded me of some kind
of school. If I had encountered it later in life, I would have said
it was like an administrative building on the campus of a liberal
arts college. It had eight stories and was topped by a white clock
tower, which could be read easily because we had traveled to the
very edges of the snow. Gazing up through the thin powdering, I
saw that it was nearly three o'clock. The drive hadn't taken nine
million years; it had been about four hours.

"Where are we?" I asked.

Aunt Thérèse said, "I believe we're in Maryland."

"Not quite," Aunt Leora said. "This is still Pennsylvania,
though we are really close to the state line." But that wasn't what
I meant.

We went inside the larger building and down a hall until
we met an official-looking white lady behind a panel of glass. As
Aunt Leora spoke to the uniformed woman, Mary and I stared at
a series of plaques on the opposite wall. Mary's lips moved as her
eyes scanned one of them, and I read alongside her, only partially
comprehending the words. I imagine that the statement you can
find now is the same as it was back then:

In 1903 the Bluestone Recovery Center began as Camp Blue
Ridge, a sanatorium for patients with tuberculosis under the
leadership of Dr. Gerald K. Hamilton. Camp Blue Ridge was
renamed the Hope Sanatorium in 1906, Bluestone Sanatorium in 1919, and the Horace B. Wilson State Hospital in
1958. The Department of Health closed the Wilson State Hospital as a sanatorium in 1970, and under the Department of

Human Services it reopened as the Bluestone Recovery Center to serve persons with histories of psychiatric illness and persons with histories of incarceration. Residents of the Center have exhausted other placement alternatives, are considered psychiatrically stable, and do not exhibit any behaviors that would put themselves or other residents at risk of harm. The Center is committed to maintaining the highest standards of compassionate long-term care for our residents in order to assist in their recovery. The ultimate goal of the Center, as much as possible, is to help every resident return home to their family or their community.

I've asked Mary about this. She tells me that what has stayed with her much more than the wording on the plaque was how painfully lit that hall was. "It felt like the kind of light that burns through everyone's skin and exposes your bones," she said. "It made me scared for her." Though it's true that there was a radiant intensity to the place, what Mary misses in her memory of that light, I've thought, is the people walking slowly through it, so slowly that they may as well have been floating, and it seemed too as if all of them wore the most serene smiles on their faces. They raised their hands to welcome us, or nodded their heads to acknowledge us as they passed, and they said hello to us in thick whispers, as though their mouths were lined with felt. They whispered it so often the word rang softly through the hall like an echo of civility. So my impression isn't of the light itself, but of what it illuminated. An emphatic, empyrean bliss.

Aunt Leora stepped away from the panel of glass and led us into a room with many chairs. There were no other people there. We took off our coats and she gave us each a sticker that read

VISITOR to affix to our sweaters. "We can all go in," she told us, "but only two at a time." As soon as she said this, I took Mary's hand and began swinging it in the space between our seats. When she turned to look at me, I winked at her with both eyes. Soon the other door in the room opened. A different uniformed white person, this time a man, stepped in and said, "All ready for you." Aunt Leora and Aunt Thérèse stood up.

"I guess we'll go first."

"Lead the way, Theresa," Aunt Leora said before they went through the second door. "Age before beauty."

While they were gone, it was just as quiet as it had been in the minivan. The room we were sitting in was windowless, a bit faded, a bit grubby, and less brightly lit than the hall. The geometries of the wallpaper held my interest more than the landscape paintings did. Sweetened air seemed to be pumped into the room but I couldn't figure out its source. I swung Mary's hand faster, arced it higher, hoping it would be our turn next. The door opened after a while and Aunt Thérèse burst through it. More calmly, Aunt Leora followed. Aunt Thérèse sat and then immediately stood again.

"I think I need some fresh air," she said.

"Since when are you a woman of the outdoors?" Aunt Leora asked.

Aunt Thérèse drove her arms into her coat. "You don't *always* have to have something smart to say. It's not *always* the right time for your sass."

This banter amused me. I imagined they behaved exactly the same way as little girls, briefly squabbling in the middle of a delightful game.

When Aunt Thérèse left through the first door, Aunt Arlette

stood over me and Mary. She watched our hands swinging, swing-ing, swinging. "Will you stop playing around?" she said. Then she grabbed Mary's other hand and pulled her away from me. I watched as my cousin, walking stiffly on her heels, was taken through the second door. For some reason, she didn't look back at me.

"How was it?" my mother asked Aunt Leora.

"How do you think?"

"That good?"

"Oh, even better," Aunt Leora said. "You don't even have a clue."

"This was your idea."

"And I don't regret it at all. *This* is what a family does."

I realized they weren't going to say anything about Aunt Arlette's unnecessary cruelty, taking Mary away from me, so I stopped paying attention. I lost myself in the wallpaper. I filled my lungs with the room's sweet air and went back and forth about whether I liked it.

When Mary returned, her face held an expression of awe. Her mother, walking behind her, guided her into the room by the shoulders and sat her down in a chair that wasn't close to me. Mary didn't look at me or speak to me. But I got to my feet quickly. It was finally my turn.

"You got a child too? *You?*" This was how my mother and I were greeted when we went through the second door. The voice, which was loud, even shrill, belonged not to an orange blossom but to a plain woman seated in a peach-colored armchair. Other than the uniformed man, who observed from a far corner, she was the only person in this new space. It was larger than the one we had been waiting in, with many arrangements of various arm-chairs, sofas, and tables, like a showroom's display of furniture.

If there had been lots of people, they could have sat in clusters of three or four, pretending they had achieved some privacy.

The first flash of thought I had about the woman as my mother and I sat on the sofa across from her was *This is my enemy.* I was on high alert, ready to protect my mother and myself, to defend our authenticity as parent and child, but I reminded myself that this person was supposedly my aunt, and there was something about her appearance that caused my feeling to dissolve. She was wearing a floral-green housedress and kept running her hands up and down her bare arms. Her short hair was braided into flimsy cornrows. Like the people in the hall she maintained a smile, and she rocked forward and back slightly as she watched us with her active eyes. She reached toward the warped magazines on the table between us, but then drew her hand back and started rubbing her arms again.

"Are you cold?" my mother asked.

"It's the other building that has the haints. This one is fine," the woman said.

"What?"

"Ghosts make you cold, Tweety. Everybody knows that."

I immediately turned to my mother, but she didn't say anything about being addressed as Tweety. All she said was, "You're right. I had forgotten all about that."

"So you're a pharmacist."

"I work in a pharmacy."

The woman's smile widened. "Just tell people you're a pharmacist."

"Are they taking proper care of you here?" my mother asked.

"I'm doing okay."

"You'd tell us if you weren't getting proper care."

"What's proper? What's improper? I'm doing fine."

"I'm relieved," my mother said breathlessly. She took a long look at the man in the corner and then said, "Isn't that Mama's dress you have on?"

"Pretty sure it's mine now," the woman mumbled. Still rocking, she looked down. Wide lanes of her dandruffy scalp were exposed between her braids. She fingered the hem of her dress, and I could see now that it was in a shabby condition.

"What's your name?" I asked.

Her face flew open and stabs of keening laughter cut through the room. It sounded like she was remembering pain. "What kind of manners have you been teaching him? A true Southern gentleman would offer his hand and state his own name first before asking for mine."

"He's not a Southern gentleman," my mother said.

But suddenly I did want to be a gentleman, Southern and true, and there are times I think I've never lost this desire. As instructed, I offered my hand and told my aunt my name.

"That can't be right," she said. "You don't favor any Aaron *I've* ever known. You look more like a Buster to me. There you go. Tweety and Buster. Now that's something. That has a nice ring to it."

My mother stiffened and drew her shoulders back. "Aaron," she said, "this is Claudia. My younger sister. She's the baby of the family."

Claudia's laughter shot through the room again. In the image of our family that I hold most dear there are tiny spatters and slashes everywhere, but you have to get very close to the canvas to see them. To the untrained eye they might look like flaws, errors, but they are the marks of Claudia's laughter, and there is a design.

The two of them continued talking as my mother sat stiffly

beside me. Her posture seemed to alter the sound of her voice, muffling it, and everything she said seemed patient and thoughtful and civil, full of the courtesies she used when she spoke on the phone to people she didn't personally know. I made the necessary adjustments in my mind. Leora wasn't the youngest of four sisters. Claudia was the youngest of five. Claudia. My aunt Claudia. Mine. Once I had worked things out, I was ready to join the conversation, but my mother suddenly announced that we should get going. "Before it gets dark," she said. "Y'all just got here," Claudia replied. "I know," my mother insisted, "but we have a very long drive."

It was beginning to turn dusky outside, the sky the color of lavender, and the snow came down more heavily than before. As we walked through the parking lot, I made Mary watch me catch the flakes on my tongue. During the ride back, Aunt Arlette, Aunt Thérèse, and my mother kept saying over and over how nice the visit was and how glad they were that we did it. And they kept saying we should plan to come again sometime. Through this litany they forged an agreement, and I couldn't help but grin in response. Mary was staring at me. She held her hand out across the seat and I took it. No one said anything about when Claudia might return to the family. Silently, Aunt Leora drove on.

Aunt Thérèse was the first to be dropped off, and my mother and I were next. When we got to Adelphi Street, Mary and her mother stepped out with us to say goodbye. We exchanged hugs and then Mary and I looked up at the windows of the apartment. We concluded the visit the same way we did every Sunday in the neighborhood. "*Four-B, that's me!*" we sang, though the words were a bit dampened as the snow continued to fall. It's this version of our singing, in the shifting white shadow of that particular Sunday, and its augmentation of our family, that I desire to re-create

WITNESS

whenever Mary and I return to Adelphi Street. I told her this
when I saw her last month, and I asked her if she remembered. "I
do. I remember every detail, or practically every one. I'll tell you
this though," she said. "I'm almost certain that that's not how it
happened."

But what else would she say? She has a baby to think about,
and the idea of a future better than the past to put her faith in,
no matter how bleak it is now, when the country and the world
seem to be unraveling, and when the nerve-shock of an autumn
day is that it actually feels like autumn. My cousin can argue with
me all she wants—on some level I understand that she has to, she
has no choice—but she can never deny the affinity we had or the
perfection of the many Sundays we shared. And she can't deny
what happened that evening after my mother and I went up to
apartment 4-B. Mary can't deny it for the most obvious reason.
The twin of my soul simply wasn't there.

My mother went directly to her room. I locked the front door
and followed her. When I came in she was on her hands and
knees, dragging various items from under her bed in the dark. I
turned on the light and the floor was a mess of shoeboxes and dust
bunnies, the cookie tins where she kept her needles and thread.
She pulled out a photo album with *Happiness* in golden sentimental cursive embossed on its worn maroon cover, though all but the
first two letters of the word had been faded by time. She sat with it
on the bed and I sat there too, beside her. As she flipped through
the album, which I hadn't ever seen, she would take out certain
photos, many of them Polaroids, and set them aside. She wasn't
explicitly showing them to me, but she wasn't hiding them either.
Eventually I figured out what made them special. They were all
photos with Claudia in them, as a baby, a little girl, an adolescent,
a young woman. It was difficult to recognize her at first, but once

I found her face in one of them I was able to identify her in all the rest. Some included all the sisters, all *five* sisters, others included combinations of just a few of them, and some featured Claudia alone. At some point there were no more of these pictures for my mother to remove, and she flipped without interruption through the rest of the album, humming pleasurably until we got to the pages that held no images. I could hear the snow, threads of it striking and melting against the window, causing the panes to sweat. What I could see of our neighborhood was beautifully abstracted by the misted glass. My mother reached an arm around and told me she loved me. She drew me in so close I could feel the rapid beating of her heart. Tweety and Buster, I thought. I was grinning so hard my face hurt. She closed the album and swept every loose photo into a pile.

BARTOW STATION

Jimmy shakes his massive head and frowns. "Are you kidding me, bro? You don't listen so good, do you?" When I don't respond, he adds, "Don't talk so good either."

We sit side by side on a bench in the locker room. Tying our laces. Most of the other guys are already in their uniforms.

"*This* dude," Jimmy says, projecting like an actor on a stage, "gets hired off the street like a damn unicorn and then comes in wearing some roach-stompers."

A couple of the other guys laugh, but most of them ignore Jimmy. They seem annoyed by him, and suspicious of me.

"And those socks," he says, shaking his head again. "White's no bueno. They gotta be black or they gotta be brown. UPS is military, bro. Atten-*hut*!" He stiffens and salutes.

I don't say anything.

"For real, get you some new shoes, quick, or your feet are fucked. I mean, they gonna end up fucked anyway, but still—"

"This is just a gig, man," I tell him. "I'm not here to collect a pension or anything."

"Bro, what the hell, lower your voice when you say some shit like that. People *kill* for these jobs."

The buzz of other conversations fills the room. As some guys start leaving, it slowly drains away.

Jimmy gives me a meaningful look. "You run fast, bro?" His head tilts left and then right, as if his neck can't hold it. "Fucking dog chased me in Bushwick. German shepherd. Looked like a sweetheart at first but then"—snap—"went rabid just like that."

More guys file out of the locker room. The morning meeting is downstairs.

"You run fast, bro?" Jimmy repeats.

I nod. I do run fast.

He smirks in approval and stands. Makes his hands into blades and pumps his arms, slicing the air around him. "You see anything looking pissed-off, you dip," he says. "Anything don't look right, run away. Be safe. Anything too sweet? Don't trust that either. Back to the truck lickety-split and slam the door shut, you hear me?"

My shoes—cheap oxfords, faux leather—are dull and worn. They squeeze the hell out of my feet, pinch my toes into curls. I've had them since I was a teenager. The last time I wore them was the last time I set foot in a church. In memory of my cousin. Troy.

Jimmy's snapping his fingers at me. "You be nice to the loaders, okay? Make life easy and kiss their ass if need be. And in the truck, it's gotta be like clockwork. No dillydallying or we'll never make all our drops. We're not out there to make friends."

He stands and hovers over me. "All right. Let's head down. Bosses gonna yell at you for those socks, but it might be tomorrow. They love to get you for the shit you did wrong yesterday."

I swallow the wad of spit in my mouth. We go downstairs and

get screamed at. Whatever the reasons are, I haven't a clue. It's
my first day on the job.

For a while, I work with Jimmy. Some of the other guys want him
to slave me real bad, knock the unicorn down a few pegs, but he
treats me okay. He continues to clown me about my shoes though.
And all his little rules, I discover, are just for me. He does whatever
the hell he wants.

   Checks start rolling in and blisters begin to erupt, but I still
don't buy a new pair. Before long I'm on my own. I make drops.
I'm courteous. I get to know faces and they get to know mine.

   I make a lot of deliveries to a flower shop on Wyckoff, close to
where the L and M trains rumble by overhead. I arrive early in
the morning, when buckets of fresh water are arranged here and
there, waiting to be filled. Mirrors multiply the potted plants for
sale, so going inside feels like stepping into a meadow, lush with
greenery. Aloe and snake, peace lilies and philodendrons. I know
what most of them are, but knowing stuff like that doesn't really
mean anything.

   One of the faces I get to know belongs to a woman who works
there, a face that makes me lean in toward it the next time. After
a while, my courtesy starts getting away from me, growing bit
by bit into something else, something I don't know how to control. The smiles linger. The looks lengthen, deepen. Dizzy from
the color and fragrance of the shop, I start pretending that the
deliveries are presents, masses of blooms just for her. I joke about
a secret admirer. The other woman there, the owner apparently,
older and white, with alarmingly small teeth and prominent gums,
clearly thinks it's corny. That's probably right. She smiles when she
signs but rolls her eyes. The one I pretend with though, she's cool,
she plays. But one day she changes the stakes of the game. She says

the least a man giving gifts can do is know a lady's name. I hesitate before asking, but she tells it to me anyhow. Zoelle.

She has baby locs, fuzzy sideburns, a gaze that won't flinch. The stormy hands of the eighth-grade girls who liked to play-fight with me and Troy in the parking lot after school—quick hands that sudden and seize the air—and I am waiting an especially long time for the delivery to be inspected on the Friday morning when those hands pluck a pink tea rose from a diamond-shaped dish on the counter and let it drop into my palm. The rose's stem, snapped, is just a couple of inches long.

Zoelle's eyes are on me. She laughs, cracks her knuckles with her thumbs. "All that flirting," she says, "and you actually have no idea what to do."

The pink of the rose is so pale it's almost white. I can't help but smile. "Don't think anyone ever gave me a flower before."

"Little kids like to yank off the petals," she says. She rests her elbows on the counter and points at the flower, starts using her inside voice: "But what you can do is act like it's a ticket."

The words seem to come before I choose to say them. "A ticket for what?"

She bites her bottom lip and then puckers her mouth, scrutinizes my worth. She asks if I've ever checked out the murals in Bushwick.

A feeling then of being swept up, engulfed. So deeply lost in the meadow you surrender all sense of not only where you are but also, briefly, who. Which means you'll do just about anything. When she suggests a plan for us, I say yes. She reminds me to bring my ticket.

Sunday. Time off work has become peculiar. It feels wrong not spending ten-plus hours a day in uniform, or in the truck, or

watching the other guys chop it up. The mirror shows I've already lost a few pounds in the August heat. Only one old T-shirt
shows off my chest and shoulders the way I want. The jeans I put
on sag too much off my ass, the style back when Troy and I were
boys.

On the kitchen counter, next to my hot plate, sits a shallow
ceramic bowl. The kind cats drink from. The pink rose lies in the
water, its stem angled like a tiny straw. Before I head out to meet
Zoelle, I pick it up with my finger and thumb. On the wet side the
petals hang loose, darkening a bit at their edges.

She stands cheerful and sweating with a tote bag on her shoulder, near one of the murals. Looks good as hell in her tight shorts
and tank top. The mural depicts two women, twins, with rainbow
arches for eyebrows, pursed red lips, and lettered dresses. One
dress repeats the phrase WHEN IT ALL GOES TO SHIT; on the other
COME BACK TO ART recurs. I give Zoelle the rose. She teases me
about its appearance, but says the ticket is still valid. As we walk,
she spins it by its stem. When she asks about me, I tell her a few
things. I left college, drifted for a while, went back later, but it still
didn't work out. She asks why. "Too expensive," I say. "Wasn't
what I expected. I wasn't any good." Not sure which of those is
most true. She waits for me to say more. Then she says working
UPS must be cool, the way it unlocks the city for you. I tell her it's
decent. It covers the rent, pays off the loans. Gives medical and
dental, vision.

She fills the quiet that follows. Tells me she likes how often the
murals change. She considered studying art or history at Brown
but her parents guilted her into an economics degree. She came
to New York, her dream, but hated her corporate job, so she quit
and worked for a while at a dive. If you think about it, she says,
tending bar isn't all that different from selling flowers, the way

people rush in because of joy or trouble and open up to you about their lives. Her grandparents, she explains, grew flowers and vegetables behind their little house, close to a lake in Ohio. She loved visiting them, digging in the ground, planting. Her favorite blossoms right now are French marigolds. She has an idea of starting a community garden. There's a vacant lot in her neighborhood she has an eye on. Her mother and father, no surprise, hate the idea, think it's another instance of her getting distracted. They give her bougie Negro speeches, she says. She's an only child, so they can focus their full attention on controlling her life. They're still married, her parents, though she isn't sure they love each other anymore. Or maybe, she says, it's just that love loses its color after a while.

The low roofs of old factories and warehouses and woodshops leave us little to no shade. My body begins to ripen, a slight armpitty odor threading up into my nostrils. The street art calls, and I retreat into it. There's some political commentary, about the violence of the government or the military or the police, but most of it is more whimsical in nature. Two skeletons soul-kiss, in defiance of death. A pirate-mystic wears a patch over his third eye. A cartoon sex worker, nude save for a floppy white hat, her skin two shades lighter than cobalt, her nipples the vivid pink of bubble gum. In one mural, with the likeness of Salvador Dalí, the illustration of a giant open hand extends several feet out from the bottom of the wall onto the sidewalk. For a while Zoelle and I stand together on the meat of the palm. Dipping her own hand, she lays the unraveling rose gently into her bag.

"What's your favorite so far?" she asks. "Let me guess. Slutty Smurfette."

I force a smile.

She laughs and calls me nasty, touches my shoulder.

The other people out on the tour thicken into a crowd, their sticky electric skins passing close. Zoelle tells me to say more about myself. She asks what I went back to school to study.

"Doesn't matter," I say. "What I tried to do, it wasn't me." Then, when she looks at me funny, I add, "Don't worry, I read and stuff. I'm not a dummy."

"Nobody called you a dummy."

"I'm just saying."

"Saying what?" she asks. "So far you haven't said much of anything."

"Just taking it all in," I tell her. There's exhaustion in my voice.

We keep walking but farther apart now, the gap between us widened by the plated armor of my silence.

After a while she perks up. She touches my forearm and says, "Hey, so what's your porn name?"

I give her a look.

"If you were a porn star—you know, *an adult film actor*—what would your name be?" She rubs her chin and narrows her eyes, exaggerating the poses of a thinker. "It has to be connected to your interests, but also cheesy as hell," she says, and then waits for a few beats. Everyone around us is talking, talking, talking. "Okay, it looks like I'm up first," she says. "I bet it's already taken, but mine would be something like May Flowers."

I fake a laugh to punctuate her joke. To end it. But she keeps going. She keeps reaching for me and I keep drawing back.

"Would you watch May Flowers get down? You would, wouldn't you?" Elevator eyes. "Dirty boy, I see you."

I shake my head and shrug.

"Come on, loosen up," she says. "It's just a game."

I tell her I can't think of anything.

"Here's what *I'm* thinking. You make special deliveries, and here's poor lonesome housewife May. She opens the door and there you are standing on the welcome mat, an enormous package in your hands. And then——"

"Look, just so you know, I'm not trying to drive a delivery truck forever or anything."

Zoelle stops midstride and adjusts the tote bag on her shoulder. "I didn't mean it like that," she says.

"You said interests."

"What *are* your interests?"

I shake my head and she watches me for a while. Without my uniform, without the counter of the flower shop between us and my truck parked and waiting on the corner, being with her feels reckless. For a while neither of us says a word. Not speaking seems like the reason we can keep walking together.

A bit later, we pass another mural that catches my eye: the wings of an angel stark against a field of sapphire blue. Zoelle notices me staring at it. As we stand there, a white girl poses between the wings for her friend. "You next," Zoelle says. "Go on, I'll take a picture."

The fact is, the mural bothers me. The human scale of it. My mind prefers to imagine angels differently, poised much larger, with fiery eyes and multiple wings. Like seraphim, closer to the horror and magnitude of a god.

When Zoelle repeats herself, I hear myself saying, "You know what I hated as a kid? I hated those cartoons where one of the characters dies and their spirit flickers up from the body, with a little halo and a harp and a long white gown." As kids, Troy and I would watch cartoons together on Saturday mornings. "It makes your eyes float off with the spirit and everything," I say. "Following it all the way up to heaven. But the actual fact of the matter is lying right there in front of you. The dead meat."

The pavement shimmers like the surface of water, hot enough to burn. I swipe my tongue across my upper lip, tasting salt, and look up at Zoelle. She makes a little grunt, a sound I've heard many times from my mother and my aunts. Then she hooks her thumbs into her belt loops, grinning in a rueful way that really hits me. It feels like she's offering me an out, a chance to say *Yes, this is how I am*, but she's still offering me a chance with her too.

"Sorry," I mumble. Then I find myself saying, "I think I'm just nervous, you know?"

She shifts her weight onto one jutting hip. "Is this about where I went to school? Or the fact that you dropped out? I don't care. I'm not out here to compare résumés. I just want to enjoy myself." Different people are standing in front of the wings now, two women who appear to be a couple. "This doesn't have to be difficult," she says, her gaze drifting away from the mural and directly into my eyes. "It's summer, we're both young, we both look good. Relax. I'm not trying to fall in love. Let's just keep it simple and have some fun."

Then we both laugh, marking a kind of agreement. She asks if I'm hungry, mentions a good pizza place not too far away. We walk for a bit. She smiles up at me and says I'm lucky she has a thing for the silent type. A little later, as we diagonally cross an intersection, I tell her I thought of a name.

"Finally," she says. "May's been waiting. So lay it on her. But it better be good."

"May Flowers," I say, hesitating, "meet Pierce Tulips."

Her head jerks back in response. "Oh my god, that is *disgust-*

ing," she says. "That is *awful*. It's perfect." And then she cracks up, nearly doubled over from her ringing laughter. When she catches her breath, she tells me she loves it. She says she knew I had it in me. Our bodies make contact again as she links her arm with mine. It feels good to be touched. "You know what," she says, "let's skip the pizza." She wants to show me the lot she's been looking at for the community garden. Then we can go to her place. She has beer. We can order in.

Jimmy and the other old heads compare injuries—sprained ankles, slipped discs, torn ligaments—and tell us new guys that soon enough time will come for our bodies. As if it isn't always in pursuit. They let us know which addresses ship sex toys, show us how to open and reseal the boxes. They goof around with the dildos and plugs. One of the them fits a strap-on over his shorts, jokes that he visits Jimmy's mother twice a week, illustrates how he does it to her. Everyone else, even Jimmy, laughs at the gross display. When I tell him it's not right, that it's people's private business, he tells me to lighten up.

Zoelle and I agree to keep things casual, but we see each other often over the next couple of weeks, mornings at the shop, where she gets playfully wide-eyed at the sight of my legs in the brown uniform shorts and makes fun of my shoes; or nights and weekends on the streets, taking the long walks she likes, exploring one neighborhood or another, and then she starts bringing me to the dive where she used to work, which acts as a way station, a place to drink past the uncomfortable lulls in conversation until we're ready to go, never to my place, always to hers, where I rub her sore feet and say I'm too shy to let her touch mine, where she massages my shoulders instead, and my back, where we undress and become other versions of ourselves and fuck. At the bar she tells me about the guy who keeps coming in looking for a special rose, his "baby give me one more chance" rose. She tells me about the woman who comes in to order flowers for her dying father and starts sobbing right there in the shop, and when Zoelle tries to comfort her, she interrupts and says, "No, you don't understand. I've never been happier. He's finally going to be gone. You must get this exactly right: I want the most festive arrangements you have." She tells me she did some research and found out the vacant lot she showed me that first day is publicly owned. She's started talking to neighbors and the local community board about putting together a proposal for the garden. "It's real," she says, excited, "it can really happen." Usually when she asks what I'm thinking, I don't say much of anything. Sometimes I don't answer at all.

The bartender, Zoelle's old coworker, a dark long-limbed woman with weary grinning eyes, pours us plenty of drinks we don't pay for, and the din of the shabby bar—the manic disclosures and lustful intimations, the percussive sounds of wood and glass, the piped-in music seeping into the fissures of silence— brings me back to the summer when I was fifteen and Troy and I worked as waiters for tips and under-the-table cash at the restaurant his father co-owned on City Island. It was a family place, where even the white people wanted you to make conversation and joke around, not just take their orders, serve their food, and disappear. The money we made then seemed like a fortune, a treasure we valued all the more for its element of secrecy, and we didn't have to spend any of it to taste scallops, oysters, and clam chowder for the first time. My uncle would get supplies from the pink-faced men at the bait and tackle store, and he taught us to fish for porgy, flounder, and bass. Troy and I took long walks

through what seemed like a maze of Victorian houses, and when
we got hungry for something other than seafood we went to Lola's
Delights for scoops of red velvet ice cream or milkshakes made
with freshly baked slices of pie. We would sneak onto party boats,
where we sometimes sipped the cheap champagne and always
tried to out-dance each other, pop-locking while the white people
cheered us on. My cousin was the better dancer, much better,
but not when he drank too much. He would stumble or lose his
rhythm, apparently oblivious that he was doing so, undisturbed
by his body's confused movements, smiling as the cheers turned
into mockery at his expense. It's a scary thing to witness, this
transformation of laughter, from an expression of joy you're help-
less against into a weapon deliberately honed and hurled. Whenever this happened, I would forfeit the battle and grip Troy in
a hug. I didn't want to see him making an ass of himself, and I
didn't want to enjoy an advantage over a fool. But Troy, oblivious as he was, and competitive, didn't like this one bit. Once,
as I hugged him, his muscles jumped and he flung me off. He
had made himself bigger, the way you're supposed to when you
encounter a bear in the wild. Then, with that mocking laughter
surrounding us, he started to dance again, with something like
arrogance on his face. When I decided I wouldn't dance with him
anymore, he said, "Come on, stop being such a bitch," repeating
it like the refrain of an angry song.

"Earth to Pierce. Hello, Earth to Pierce." Zoelle's swirling
her drink in my face. "Where'd you go?"

"Nowhere."

"You sure?"

"Nowhere at all."

"Well, May needs a little attention here."

I apologize. She stills her hand on my knee, asks if I'm ready to go.

One night, Zoelle calls and asks, with odd excitement in her voice, how I am, how work was. We haven't seen each other in a couple of days. I tell her about Jimmy's latest "trials," his disciplinary appointments with the managers and supervisors and union reps, one a couple of weeks ago for slaving his new helper and going off solo to enjoy roti during business hours, and another last week for wearing a Basquiat shirt, a nonregulation white T-shirt, while on the job. Before I go on, she interrupts and tells me she has a surprise. She's going to take me to see something special. A tour of the world's oldest subway tunnel. She says she loves places like that. Old places. I tell her I do too.

The person running the tours is a portly white guy in a baseball cap. He wears a plaid flannel shirt more suited for the beginning of winter. An orange safety vest that sits over the mounds of his chest like the top of a bikini. He explains over the noise of passing traffic that the Atlantic Avenue Tunnel was built back in the 1840s and then sealed up for over a century. Then he rediscovered it and began running tours. Zoelle and I, along with a dozen others, watch him work himself damp and musty as he places a number of traffic cones in the street and uses a steel hook to pry open and lift away the cover of a manhole.

"We're going down *there*?" I ask.

Zoelle looks at me. "It's a tunnel, genius."

The tour guide connects a portable generator to wiring that goes into the open manhole. Once he gets a ladder situated, he descends from the surface and the group follows. We step down and down and end up in a chilly space dimly illuminated by a series of light bulbs just above our heads. We have to stand more or less in a straight line. The walls pressing on either side of us are thickly packed with mounds of faded dirt. In his high-pitched voice the guide explains that he guessed the tunnel's location from old maps and newspaper articles. When he first came down, the dirt went all the way across, from wall to wall, leaving so little room at the top that he had to crawl on his belly, with an oxygen tank on his back in case there was no air, proceeding by slow inches in the pitch-dark. Later, he and other guys cleared out the dirt by hand to create the space we now stand in. It's tough to imagine it ever being any tighter than it is.

"You okay?" Zoelle asks. Her face is full of shadows and hollows.

I clutch two of her fingers and turn away.

"Isn't this crazy?" she says. "I love it."

One by one, we duck through a hole edged in orange spray paint, an opening blasted out of a concrete wall over twenty years ago by the guide. We emerge in a longer, somewhat wider area, the grim tunnel itself, with masses of tapered bedrock on either side and an extended stretch of arched brick above.

"This was the end of the line of the LIRR," the guide says. "Half a mile that way and you hit the East River. Sixty years before you get the subway system, you got this. And what this is, folks, is innovation." His voice deepens when he goes on to quote a poet, Walt Whitman: "*The old tunnel, that used to lie there under ground, a passage of Acheron-like solemnity and darkness, now all closed and filled up, and soon to be utterly forgotten, with all its reminiscences.*"

"Hey," Zoelle whispers to me, "what's wrong."

A few people in the group nod and murmur in appreciation, begin to follow the guide as he brings up the topic of Freemasons. They're getting farther away from us. I haven't moved. Sweat stings my eyes. I tell Zoelle I've seen enough.

"You're hurting me," she says.

I glance at her strange face. "This place is freaking me out."

"You're *hurting* me," she repeats. And then she snatches her fingers from my fist and hides them in the nook of her neck.

On the way to her place, I'm especially quiet. Zoelle keeps asking if I'm angry at her, and I keep shaking my head no. At the apartment, we drink beer, sitting on her bed without speaking. She breaks the silence by asking if I'm claustrophobic or something, but answers her own question, saying *of course not* and making a joke about how tiny her apartment is. She asks if we should stop going places together. She can just invite me over when she wants my company. That would be fine with her, she says. I shrug in response. She tries asking other questions, easy surface-level questions about what I'm feeling or thinking, what I want to do now. "I'm just trying to have a normal human conversation with you," she says. "That's all I'm ever trying to do." That's all. But to me it feels impossible. I'm sealed shut.

In some ways, this time is no different from any other time we go to her apartment. Alone together, in that private space, compacted between those four walls, it becomes excruciating. My silence, her careful attempts to draw me out. All we can manage, most times, even when we rub the aching parts of each other's bodies, is halting small talk, and the awkwardness of it resounds in our ears. But if we arrive drunk enough, or drink enough after we've arrived, we quicken past all that, or skip it entirely. In bed, naked, we both speak and we both listen. We learn a little more about each other. I learn, after the first few times, that she wants to roughen the sex. I learn, after she says it, that she likes a hand tightened around her throat. I learn, after she does it, that I like my face slapped. We've been silly, saying the names we made up among the murals. But mostly we say other names, names we impose on each other, names we insist on for ourselves. Names that sting and bruise. I learn her names, the ones that turn her on, names for someone who is there, in bed, only to be a body, only to be of use. She learns my names too, and I learn that there are more of them than I knew, names for someone who is filth, someone who is base, someone who isn't fit to exist, or who doesn't exist at all. We play our roles. We learn each other's secret names, and say them, but neither of us learns the reasons they exist. We don't say if there are any, beyond the kink itself, beyond the raw pleasure of play. Maybe, in her case, there aren't any reasons. I guess it's possible that there aren't any in mine.

But now, in bed, she gasps in a startling way, her eyes panic, and when I loosen my hand, I notice she's been rapidly *one-two-three* tapping my hip. This is the action we established, the signal to stop, and when I remove my hand from her throat, she also utters, between coughs and more gasps, the established word. When I ask what she needs, if she's in pain, she shakes her head, gestures toward the kitchen, for water. She's sitting up when I come back, drinks the entire glass at once. After some moments she asks, more calmly than I expect, what happened, if I didn't feel her taps on my hip, if I couldn't tell things were crossing the line. I sit beside her, and she takes my hand.

"I just got carried away," I say.

"What do you mean, you got carried away?"

"You asked me what happened. I got carried away."

Zoelle releases my hand. "That's not good enough," she says. "If we're gonna keep doing what we're doing, cool, maybe I'm still down, but this is the way it has to work. I need to feel safe. So I need you to talk to me, right now, about what happened."

A feeling of embarrassment falls over me. At first I think she's the one doing it, a casual lover making excessive demands and humiliating me, but that isn't it. What just happened between us is casting a light on everything that has happened between us, and it seems clear now. Despite my efforts not to, I've been constantly exposing myself, exposing my shame and cowardice to her at every turn.

"What are you doing?" she asks.

I rub my eyes and draw back wet fists. "Nothing," I say.

Zoelle stares at me, and then slowly shakes her head, her expression full of disappointment and confusion, as if I've taken something from her. She goes to the bathroom. The toilet flushes, and for a long time water runs in the sink. When she returns, she lies down facing away from me, completing the arc of her refusal. I lie down too, with my body against hers. It's getting darker one minute earlier every day, but sunlight still glows behind her blinds. She lets me put my arm around her. Then I begin to speak, I try to explain. But I can't start with any precision, I can't begin where she wants me to. I tell it in a way I never have before, all of it. The words pour out of me as I confess.

Back when my cousin Troy was alive, I tell her, before we put his body into the ground, back when he and I traveled from Mosholu Parkway east across the Bronx toward City Island, often, in the spring or summer or fall months, we would skip off the Bx29 bus just after it crossed Pelham Bridge into the park and together, walking on the edge, follow a trail with horses and their riders to a clearing obscured by trees, and there, difficult to find within the abundance of wood anemones, trout lilies, daylilies, blue violets, cutleaf toothwort, mugwort, garlic mustard, and knotweed, was a hidden place whose actual history and name Troy would never know: Bartow Station. Built of brick and stone, it was full of gaping holes, both doorless and roofless, abandoned, with no glass left in any of its arched windows. We climbed or stared into these holes and speculated about the fire that must have happened there. Looking up to where the chimney pointed at the mood of the sky, we grabbed the slender trunks of the trees that grew in the interior, if the open ruin could be said to have an interior. On every side the walls were brightly burned with graffiti, and to look closely at it we navigated a litter of scrapped metal, white plastic buckets, step-ladders, tipped wheelbarrows, and several lengths of blue lumber. When it was autumn and the skinny trees were stripped naked, each step we took crackled. Only the sound of our footfalls or our voices, or the horn of a train plunging across the tracks nearby, would disturb the quiet. Whenever the strong smell of fresh paint would penetrate the rot and leap into our noses, Troy would won-der aloud about the people who had been there the night before. He was drawn to the most legible declarations of who they were, the tags made in monochrome, and to the names cleanly thrown up using two or three colors and simple bubble lettering. One day, he pointed to a tag written in black letters, interlocking and angu-lar. If I'm remembering it right, the tag read *SCAM*. Troy loved these signatures, told me we should learn how to make them so we too could have our names up on walls. But I had no interest in an-nouncing myself in that way. I had no ambitions then of being an artist. The pieces I liked at the old station were mad with color, in-tricate, complicated. The arrows, spikes, curves, and overlapping layers made them difficult to read. I could stare at one for a very long time, fascinated, and come away with no clear sense of what it actually said or meant. When Troy and I stood next to each other, studying the walls in our respective postures, I imagined what we might have looked like to a passenger speeding by: not two differ-ent boys, but one caught mid-gesture, a brief illusion of motion.

When I stop talking, Zoelle stays quiet for a moment, her back still to me. "You said he died." Her voice low.

"He got hit," I tell her. "Tracks run close by the station and curve in both directions, so if a train comes . . ."

"My god," she whispers.

Troy and I decided to go to Bartow Station at night, I tell her, on the way back home from City Island, in hopes of seeing an artist or two there emblazoning their names. We'd been drinking to celebrate. He had turned seventeen the day before. I'd had enough, and he'd had plenty. I was the one who got us the booze. We hadn't brought enough light, so it was difficult to see, and we didn't go the way we normally went. But in time, I spotted the tracks. Told him I was sure we were getting close and began walking between the rails. When he hesitated, I grinned. I teased him. I told him a train was five million pounds of clanging steel. I told him we'd notice one coming a mile away. I cursed at him and told him to stop being such a bitch. I called him a bitch and I called him other names. Punk. Pussy. I called him weak. I rushed ahead and finally, to prove me wrong, he followed. Soon we were side by side, hiking up our jeans. The air was crisp. We traded insults in horrible freestyles as we walked, our choruses of drunk laughter oddly muffled by the corridor of trees. When it happened, I felt the light behind us, I heard the sudden blaring, the screeching. I turned and froze, but then a hard force on my back, a shove, sent me to the ground. I looked up, just in time to see Troy spin from being struck. The impact was like a sound inside of my own chest. I found my light and ran to where he had fallen. I crouched over him. He clung to the earth, grabbing it with his fingers and with the toes in his shoes. With his ear pressed down, he seemed to be listening to the earth too. I searched for pain, waited for him to cry out, but he didn't. His face, turned toward me, smiled. Then, under the smile, began the slow pooling of dark blood. But I stayed with him, I stayed until I couldn't, until his body began its arrhythmic jerking. He seized the earth again with his limbs and spasmed. The urge to hold him, to reassure him with my touch, jolted through me, but doing so was impossible. He already wasn't Troy anymore. I ran instead. I didn't run to the train though. I didn't even shout for help. I ran away, as hard and as fast as I could, until I reached Bartow Station. I collapsed onto its floor of leaf litter, staring at what I couldn't see, sheltering myself.

The next week, when I'm done driving for the day, Jimmy plops down next to me in the locker room. Leans over with his elbows on his thighs. "Tell me something good," he says.

I shake my head no.

He exhales loudly. Word is he had yet another trial that morning.

"You'll skate by," I say. "As usual."

"Not so sure about that."

"What you do this time?" I ask.

"Stole some shit. Defaced some fucking property. Wholly unprecedented crimes in the annals of the United Parcel Service. Sons of bitches. As if the bosses themselves aren't thieves and destroyers."

He goes on and on about double standards, about injustice. It gets under my skin. I don't give a damn about the bosses, I say. I tell him they don't even cross my mind.

Jimmy looks at me. "What," he says, "you're so free? You do whatever you damn well please? Fuck outta here. As if we aren't all bossed by something."

We stare at each other until I push air through my nose. He lowers his face to one hand. Holds this pose for a while. A show of pity might comfort him, or it might enrage him. It's hard to say.

"Listen to me," he says, sitting up, raising the block of his head back onto his shoulders. "Remember this. Shit rolls down-hill, always. You hear me, bro? You hear me? Remember that. Shit rolls downhill and then you're buried in it."

I'm right about Jimmy. He ends up getting another talking-to, but there are no real consequences. It is what it is.

I still make deliveries to the flower shop. Once in a while I see Zoelle there, or just a piece of her in the back, ducking behind a cooler to avoid me. But then after a couple weeks I don't see her at all. The owner doesn't smile when she signs anymore. And when I ask about Zoelle one morning she just glares at me and walks off.

Sometimes, even though it's out of the way of my route, I take the truck over to Zoelle's neighborhood to check out the vacant lot. I drive slowly past, expecting every time to see the beginnings of her garden, but it's always the same. Brown dirt, weeds, patches of dry grass. Nothing has changed. I make my drops. I go home.

When I wake up one morning it hits me: The job isn't half bad. The driving soothes, it casts a spell. The hours are long and my feet still hurt, but the days fill up with these harmless glimpses into other people's lives. And they manage, by a sort of alchemy, to add up to something that feels close to good. I like the daily practice of being polite, of exchanging pleasantries like flipped nickels. Kindness without consequence. I smile and the strangers of the city smile, and then, until next time, we absolutely forget about each other.

Still, that last day with Zoelle comes to me a lot. When I'm done talking, she flings my arm off of her. She makes herself big-ger, the way you're supposed to when you encounter a bear in the wild. She stands up from the bed and tells me I've told her an awful story, such a sad and awful story, possibly one of the worst she's ever heard, but she doesn't understand how it has anything to do with us. Don't I see I need help, she asks, professional help? My need for it shouldn't be her burden, and it won't be, not any-more. She says I'm just like the lake by her grandparents' house. It freezes every winter and people walk on the gorgeous shell of ice until it begins to crack. They fall in. Many of them never make it back out. She won't be one of those people. She says it's a thing about being a man, isn't it? To be so stingy that way, to deny even a sip of yourself, to deny and deny and deny until one day it all comes out as a violence, like water spewing forth from a hose. She tries a million ways of telling me about myself, but nothing gets through. "I never wanted much from you," she says wearily, "but it's not okay that you've never given me a thing." It's true. Even when I showed up with flowers it was make-believe. My mistake was acting as if I had anything at all to offer. "Are you apologiz-ing or are you letting yourself off the hook?" she asks. "It could have been so simple, but I can't trust you." "No," I tell her, "you can't." And then she says goodbye.

What I say to her now, many days as I drive my truck or lie on my mattress or lace up my old shoes, is this: I'm sorry I hurt you. Maybe I'll get that help you talked about. I think about it a lot. If I go ahead and do it, I guess I'll have you to thank, but honestly I doubt I'll do it anytime soon. I've also been considering what else you said, and I believe I know what is true: I'm not a lake. I'm just the small space I'm trapped in. And I hate it, I really do. I know it means that I'm afraid. Cowardly. But right now, the only other option I have is Bartow Station. This is a better kind of lonely than running back there on my own.

WITNESS

My sister threw open the door and it banged against the little console table she kept by the entrance. "Silas," she said breathlessly, before even removing her coat, "I have to tell you something." Which was enough to make me feel trapped, as though the words out of her mouth were expanding and filling up the space in her tiny apartment. I told her to calm down and apologized, and then I began making excuses for myself. I had assumed she would be angry at me because of the previous night, so I was primed for what she might say when she got home from work.

"Don't be so defensive," Bernice said. "I'm not talking about that." She tapped my legs so I would move them and then plopped down next to me on the love seat. The chill from outside clung to her body. I saved my reformatted CV, set my laptop on the floor, and listened.

The man who sang out of tune had been waiting for her again. He had started standing near the card shop on Amsterdam Avenue during her lunch hour two weeks earlier, and she had quickly noticed his repeated presence. As she passed him that afternoon, he faced her directly and gave her a meaningful look, which was more than he had ever done before. "But all he did after that was keep belting it out in that terrible voice," she told me. "A sentimental song, you know? The sweetness of making love in the morning." Even though he was thin and light-skinned and wore those big, clunky headphones—"Not my type *at all*," she said—Bernice did find him somewhat handsome. But since he didn't say anything, she just went inside the shop. She liked to go in there during her break because her job could be tough. She worked as a guidance counselor for high school kids, soaking up their troubles all day long, and the cards, however hackneyed or sentimental, gave her a daily boost she enjoyed. When she emerged a bit later, feeling affirmed, the man approached her. With the headphones clamped around his temples, his gloved fists tight around the straps of his backpack, he said he was sorry for bothering her, that he hoped she didn't mind but he had seen her walk by the other day and thought, well, she was beautiful. "Meanwhile," she told me, "with the kind of night I had, I'm sure I've never looked worse a day in my life." She didn't shake the hand he offered, but smiled at how flustered he was. His name, which he said was Dove, pleased her, and the way he scrunched his lips together and shifted them from side to side had what she described to me as a clarifying effect.

Bernice laughed now and said, "So, long story short, I said yes."

"What do you mean you said yes?"

"I gave him my *actual* name and my *actual* number," she said. "He's a DJ, and he has a gig this weekend. Maybe I'll go see him do his thing."

I couldn't tell if she was being serious.

"You think I'm crazy."

"I don't," I said reflexively, but only somewhat honestly. I knew she found our mother's warnings to avoid men on the street excessive. She'd told me once that doing so would be like forbidding the use of a shower because water could get hot and scald. Bernice didn't want to be seen as weak, and she always trusted her own instincts. I didn't have much faith in them, though. In my mind she could be reckless.

The previous night, she had texted and called me in a panic, but I wasn't available for her. I was out with a woman when my phone lit up, so for a long time I ignored Bernice's texts, her calls, and her voice mails, too. The truth was, I found my sister exhausting, the way she could crowd you out of your life with the enormity of her own. The entanglement I was trying to have with that woman, I told myself, was too urgent to be interrupted. I didn't find out what had happened until the morning, when I finally listened to her messages and read her texts. By then she was already on her way to work.

Unable to reach me last night, she had requested a car to drive her to the emergency room. She sat in the dingy waiting area for a long time before she was able to meet with a doctor, and she told him what she told me on the first voice mail: "I don't know what it is, but I just feel off. I can't think straight, and my body, it doesn't feel right." She had texted me again afterward, saying that her blood pressure was elevated, but in the doctor's opinion her issues overall seemed minor, most likely stress-related. Just learn how to relax. That was all she needed to do.

"So," I said now, "you're feeling okay?" As the heat hissed steadily into the room, I looked down at the love seat, where I'd been sleeping for weeks during my impossible job search. Perhaps foolishly, I was hell-bent on being in New York, but it seemed like every other Americanist in the country was, too. Bernice had offered to let me stay with her until I got my bearings and found something.

"I already told you. The doctor says I'm fine."

"So you're fine."

"That's what the doctor said."

"That's good," I said.

"But they shooed me away, Silas," Bernice said, her voice growing large. "You should have seen it. It all happened so fast, I didn't even get a chance to explain." When she saw the smirk on my face, she glared. "What's so funny?"

"You're doing really well with the whole relaxing thing," I said. "Terrific job. Truly top-notch."

She nudged my shoulder with hers. "Well, I'll be doing plenty of relaxing with my new friend *Dove*, if he plays his cards right."

"That's awful," I said. "That's just too much. You're always saying too much."

"Doesn't matter how much you talk if people don't listen," she said.

I picked at the edge of my borrowed pillow. The love seat faced the door to the apartment and next to it, above the table, hung a framed photograph taken by our late father, of our mother and us when she was a young woman. In it, Bernice is three, cranky from an ear infection, and I am a frowning infant in her lap. Sitting beside us on a stiff-looking blue sofa, wearing a pale summer dress, our mother smiles with her teeth. "'Well, let me ask you this,'" I said suddenly now, in a brassy imitation of her. "'Was that doctor you saw a *white* doctor?'"

"Oh god," my sister said, "of course he was." She began shaking her head and we both laughed. "I should have remembered what she always says. What was it again?"

"You remember."

"'But when it comes to those white doctors,'" Bernice cried, now imitating our mother too, "'always, *always*, exaggerate the pain.'"

Bernice did go to see Dove DJ, and he must have been adept at it, because that weekend sparked a whirlwind romance. Despite the inconvenience of my presence, Dove was a frequent visitor, often after his gigs. Things hadn't worked out with the woman I was interested in, so I was usually there, curled on the love seat, and he would wake me up when he came in, a bit clumsy, unsure in his lankiness as he made his way through the dark apartment. Crates of Dove's records began accumulating around me. When I asked Bernice if she would consider slowing things down, she said, "I'm doing exactly what I want to do, exactly the way I want to do it." Then she smiled and added, "Exactly how I always have." For her, the choice to begin anything significant was a powerful exertion, one the universe couldn't ignore, proof of the force of her will. She felt that if you really wanted to and if you knew how, you could control your life.

Within two months, Bernice and Dove had willed an engagement into existence. The speed of this made our mother furious. When I spoke to her on the phone, she told me Bernice was being an idiot, and she refused to come to New York for their marriage at the city clerk's office. I was their only witness. We went through the government's metal detectors and sat together in the crowded waiting room until we were called in for the quick ceremony. Bernice wore a tea-length dress, simple but elegant, the white of it stark against her skin. Dove had on baggy slacks, dark shoes, and a large cream-colored guayabera. With his clothes as loose as they were, he looked ridiculous, and he was as giddy as a child, with all the happiness the occasion called for but none of the solemnity. He seemed possessed of no seriousness, completely unlike the sort of person you should commit your life to. When he extended his arms so he could hold my sister's hands, I waited for him to bungle something. He didn't appear to be reliable at all.

Bernice improvised the presence of our mother by bringing the framed photograph from the apartment. Despite our inclusion in it, the image belongs absolutely to our mother. All three of us are brown, but her skin is particularly dark, full of tiny glints, as though enriched by a day walking in the sun. Her eyes are tired, but happily so, the way people appear sated and spent in the wake of a long, demanding meal. She looks so beautiful and strong that you would be tempted to think her children, in that moment, are beautiful and strong, too. This, our mother's sovereignty, is the source of the photograph's power, and the reason why it's my sister's favorite.

Dove, who had been living with his father, didn't make much money, and the newlyweds' combined income wouldn't have gotten them a better place than the one Bernice already had—rent was still reasonable in that part of Crown Heights. So her apartment soon became their apartment. For two people it was very small. For three it was nearly hopeless. When we ate together, they sat on the love seat and I was relegated to the floor. There were always conflicts about the bathroom. The arrangement began to wear on us more and more. I complained that at night I could hear them, to use Dove's phrase, *making love*. He complained about the photo of us and our mother, so he took it down and replaced it with one of him and Bernice. She complained that he had done this and switched them back, declaring that no one she lived with was grateful for her. After that she kept more company with the books she began bringing home from the library.

The person who lived upstairs was a friendly man who worked as a high school basketball coach. Bernice liked him, though he had a habit of watching games with the volume on his TV turned all the way up. He also walked through his apartment with astonishing frequency, and his steps were very heavy. His stomping constantly threatened the photo of our mother on the wall, shaking it askew. Usually it was Bernice who ran over to straighten it and make sure it didn't slip completely from its nail. But in the three months since the marriage, she'd become more irritated and depressed than I'd ever seen her, and she seemed more interested now in causes than in their effects. So late one night, as the upstairs neighbor stomped and his TV roared, all she did was raise her head from the arm of the love seat, where she had been reading, and sneer at the ceiling.

"This is getting ridiculous," Bernice said. "What time is it now?"

I took the photo down and laid it on the console table, next to a thin, empty vase. I explained that it was exactly six minutes later than the last time she had asked. I pointed at the fully functioning, prominently displayed clock. It was 4:18 a.m.

"Tell that motherfucker I can't stand him anymore," she said. "Tell him next time I see him, he should just gumboot dance directly on my chest."

Was she talking about the coach or Dove? Neither man had a connection to South Africa, as far as I knew, but my sister's mind had become increasingly global in range. The books surrounding her on the love seat and the floor included library copies of fiction and poetry in translation, various travel writings and studies of cultural practices, histories of colonialism and insurrection throughout the African diaspora. She collected as much information as she could, as furiously as she could, about the lives and trials, real and imagined, of Black people everywhere. Willy-nilly, she regurgitated facts and ideas at me. It was an undisciplined affront to my years of graduate training, especially annoying since she refused to explain exactly what she was doing. But it was clear that whatever else it was, this new habit was a way to resist being crushed by the altered circumstances of her life.

When she wasn't absorbed in a book, or overtaken by a depressive sleep—in one way or another conjuring dream-routes across the planet—Bernice was forced to deal with local matters. She was running out of sick days at work, and her performance there seemed to be declining fast. She mentioned that parents of the students she counseled had started to complain that she was giving out strange advice. Much of it was about her philosophy of love, which at this point, she told me, was "also a philosophy of hate." At the apartment, she seemed sad and anxious when Dove was out late DJ'ing, but she also fell into despair and rage when he was at home. Not once did I say *I told you so*. It seemed she had come to understand, on her own, that we always overestimate how much we can govern our lives.

Dove finally got home that night a little before five. He unlocked the door and shuffled in ass first, bent over two milk crates of LPs. He was one of those DJs who boasted about playing vinyl, but the undignified way he entered the apartment punctured his self-righteousness, as did the sheepishness that came over his features when he turned around and saw the complications on my sister's face.

"Oh, you're still up?" he said now, to both of us. He looked frightened as he pulled his sagging jeans to his waist.

"Silas sleeps *here*," my sister said. "And where am I? Here. Silas can't sleep here if *I'm* here."

"Why do you sound angry?"

"I'm not angry, I'm sick."

Dove rolled his eyes at me, but I gave no sign that I agreed with him. "Well," he said, "why aren't you in bed, then?"

Bernice collapsed onto her side and faced the back of the love seat. Her hair was slicked into a sad curly bun, and her head rested on an open book, a history of compulsory sterilization in Kenya.

Dove began to take a step forward but then retracted it. He often moved this way, as if the floor were booby-trapped. He jerked his head toward the front door and said to me, "Come on, professor, let's go get some grub. I'm paying."

Bernice moaned without turning. "There's food here," she said. "What is it about having a little bit of money in your pocket that immediately makes you want to spend it? Are you a child?"

He glanced at me. "I'm a man," he replied. "The man of *this* house."

"Man. Child. What's the difference?"

Dove didn't argue. He approached my sister with trepidation, moved some of the books aside, and crouched by the love seat, but he seemed unsure of what to say. Except for Bernice's whistling breath, everything was quiet. Even the coach and his television were idle. Dove cleared his throat and told my sister he would bring her back something good. "Some soup to help you feel better."

"Soup again?" she replied. "You think soup fixes everything. At the farthest reaches of your imagination, way out there in the wilderness, the grandest discovery an explorer could make would be a bowl of soup."

"Oh, come on, sweet girl."

"You stink of liquor," she said. "Liquor and sweat and desperation. Please, I'm begging you, just go away."

Ejected from the apartment, Dove sprinted down the stairs.

I followed him outside. The sun would be up soon on another warm spring morning. There was a twenty-four-hour diner he remembered. It was pretty far from the apartment, but he insisted that we walk.

"Back in the day," he explained, grinning, "me and my boys would eat at this place after partying all damn night. Man, we were just kids then. I miss those dudes. They're the jokers who gave me the name Dove," he said, and laughed good-naturedly. "Because I'm so light."

"Oh, is that why?" I asked, but he didn't detect the sarcasm.

He shook his head, full of nostalgia. He seemed to find solace in calling forth and repeating the past. "That's when music was good, you know?" Then he began to pontificate on what he called the golden age of hip-hop. He even lectured about producers and the art of sampling. "Old-school is where it's at, man. Why do you think I spin records?"

"I haven't really thought about it," I told him.

"With digital files, the music gets compressed. Details get lost. The depth, the textures: gone. It's actually sad. Nothing's the way it used to be."

I asked what happened to his friends.

"They got married. Had kids. Or they moved. They moved on."

He changed the topic, asking about my job search. I had several new applications out and was now hoping to piece together enough adjunct positions to make a decent living.

"And find a place of your own?" he asked.

"Bernice says I can stay as long as I need to," I told him.

He just hummed in response. Then he asked if the sort of thing I was trying to do wasn't a ridiculous hustle in New York. I said it was. I asked if trying to pay the bills as a DJ in New

York wasn't a hustle too. He nodded. After that we didn't talk. Our interest in each other had been exhausted, and neither of us wanted to talk about Bernice. Dove started singing to himself in his horrible voice.

Maybe he also sensed she was moving on, around and abroad, or further and further back into accounts of the past, escaping with her books to places and times that seemed closed to anyone but herself. From the way she looked as she conducted her arcane scholarship, it seemed easeful to pass the days like that. At least until her husband or brother came home, breaking her loneliness and her peace.

When Dove and I arrived at the diner we were met by construction barriers, a perimeter of chain-link fencing backed with lengths of green screen. The building that had housed the diner was gone, replaced by the gleaming bones of a condominium. A sign showed an image of what it would be eventually, a sky-piercing complex sheathed in glass. Applications for buyers were already being accepted. Dove stared at the sign, headphones snug at his temples, his lips scrunched together. I tried to glimpse what my sister had ever seen in him. Could he have been anyone, any person whose gestures and manner she might have chosen to recognize and accept, or was there something more substantial about him? The way his untucked shirt and jeans hung from his body made him look even more puerile than usual. Maybe it was something related to this, Dove's frivolity, that made her think he would be easy, that she could fit him wherever she pleased. He turned to me, jolted by some notion, and said he knew of another place not too far away, an "old-school" doughnut spot that had great coffee. Was the new plan to bring my sister a doughnut? The idea of it made me angry. I told him I was tired from the walk, that I needed to go home and try to sleep. Dove seemed relieved. "What you *need* to do," he teased, "is hurry up and find your ass a job." Then he bumped my fist hard with his and we went our separate ways.

Everything I saw on the way back to the apartment became the object of my anger. The cracks in the sidewalks, the dust on the parked cars, the slowness of the occasional pedestrian—it all seemed jammed full of stupidity. The city struck me as an impossible place to live. What was I even doing here? I walked on, pausing whenever I passed an open bodega. I told myself I was thinking of what I could buy for my sister, something that would please or help her. But I didn't have much money and, honestly, I was just giving myself excuses to delay. I didn't want to be with Dove, but I didn't want to be in the apartment either. Bernice was just another kind of burden.

When I came in, Bernice yelled from the bedroom, "Oh Jesus, what kind of soup is it this time?" A month had passed since my walk with Dove, and though it was a sunny afternoon outside, the apartment's main window, which faced an air shaft, made it seem like evening. From the bedroom came sweetly fragrant wisps of musk that added to the gloom. The bedroom was filled with even more smoke. Sticks of incense had been lit, well over a dozen, and scented candles burned. In the middle of this cloying cloud, the bed was strewn with books and other objects, and Bernice's head and torso were elevated on a pile of pillows. She squinted at me in the doorway and I squinted back at her, disturbed by the scene.

"It's just me," I said.

"It's just me," she replied, mocking me, and then stabbed her cloud with a sharp cough of laughter. She watched with a pleased grimace as the wound sealed itself. "Was baby brother out trying to make a lady friend again?" she asked.

"I'm broke and I live on my sister's couch," I said. "Once that becomes obvious, no one wants to be my friend."

"Ghosts," she said. "Ghosting you." Then she studied me again, still just outside the room. "It smells so good in here now, but you can't stand it, can you? I know you can't. That's all right. Don't want you in here anyway. Just stay there and let me look at you. I can see your true nature now . . . I want to see his too. Where is he?"

"I don't know," I said. "I'm assuming he'll be back later."

"That's good," she said, and then she seemed to shrug. "It's messed up too."

In addition to her books and the incense, she had recently started collecting a significant number of translucent crystals, which glimmered within the smoke. I asked her what they were.

"Quartz," she said. "They're healing stones. I ordered them online."

"What do they do?" I asked.

"They're healing stones, Silas. What do you *think*?" Bernice had complained of headaches two weeks ago, and had gone back to the doctor, but was told again that she was fine, and that she needed to work harder to relax. She had taken a leave of absence from work.

"Maybe you really are sick," I said. I wanted her to know I was starting to believe it.

"No shit, detective. Shall I confess to you my pain? Shall I confess my other crimes?" She groaned and rubbed her eyes with the heels of her hands.

I peered in, trying to see her clearly, unsure of what to say.

Everything I could think of felt wrong. "Go to the doctor again," I said. "Please. I'll go with you this time."

"No."

"Tell me why you don't want to."

She laughed dryly. "Silas, I've tried. They just keep sending me home. Why would I go where people don't know how to treat me? That's just more helplessness."

"We can try to get you a Black doctor," I said. But in truth, I had little sense then that this could make a difference. I hardly went to the doctor myself.

"Okay, sure thing, *Mom*," she said, amusing herself. "Listen, do you know what I read yesterday—no, what am I saying, I just read it—do you know?"

"Bernice—"

"Get this. When slavery was abolished, there were all these little children just walking around, confused, completely separated from their kin. How's that for a picture of freedom. Can you imagine? How scared they were? The danger they were in? Well, do you know what happened next? Other Black folks, *strangers*, took them in. Families. Adults who were on their own. Sometimes people who were hardly adults themselves. Saw these wandering children and adopted them, just like that."

"Well, it was more complicated than you're saying," I began, even though African American history wasn't my area of expertise. "If you study any of the oral accounts—"

"Strangers did this, Silas! Not so long ago . . . And it happened here!"

She said *here* as if shocked to find something of use anywhere on the planet. Then she watched for my response, which was to say and do absolutely nothing. I remained on the edge of her cloud while the coach stomped around above us. Then there was

a sound like the spitting of a lit candle. Bernice's body went rigid
on the mattress and started jerking. I couldn't move—I didn't
know what to do. Her back arched as she continued convulsing,
and the spitting sound, I realized, was coming from her mouth
as she labored to breathe. She wouldn't stop her rigid shaking.
I approached the bed finally, and saw that her eyes were rolled
back into her head. It was the sight of the reddened saliva at her
lips and the stain growing in the crotch of her shorts that jolted
me into action. I took out my phone, called 911, and was told what
to do. I began by removing the books and crystals from the bed,
and I stayed with her until the paramedics arrived.

Bernice went through triage, a long wait, an examination, another
long wait, and then, after being admitted, a CT scan. By the time
Dove showed up at the hospital, hours later, every emotion and
reserve of energy seemed to have been boiled out of her. He zipped
past her wheezing roommate and stopped short. "It's gonna be
okay," he cried out uselessly. "Don't worry, it's gonna be okay!"
    Bernice's head rolled slowly on the pillow until she faced him.
She gave a wasted smile and tapped her ear. His eyes widened.
Up flew his hands to remove his headphones. We could all hear
his loud music scratching the air.
    "Hey, Mr. DJ," my sister said quietly. She pointed at her mon-
itor and added, "Can you find a song with a pulse that matches
mine? Find it for me, play it for me."
    I watched Dove from the seat near the foot of the bed. His
eyes, full of affection, communicated that he thought she was being sincere. He tiptoed up to her, took hold of one of her hands,
and said, "Oh, sweet girl . . ." Then he repeated it with a hint of
unruly pleasure. Maybe he was falling in love with her all over
again. If so, and if her condition allowed her a choice, she seemed

to be indulging him. He held both of her hands in his and, moving his lips wordlessly, looked as though he was renewing his vows.

"The results of the CT scan are negative," I said.

Dove nodded. "Good. Wait, that's good, right?"

"When I asked about getting a Black doctor they didn't take me seriously," I added.

My sister turned to me. She must have heard the hollowness of my words. I heard it too, as I had earlier as the hospital staff spoke to me, the same conspicuous tone of lip service. Bernice wouldn't take her eyes off of me, and Dove wouldn't take his eyes off of her.

"I just read that racist patients have no problems, absolutely none, when they demand white doctors," I said, holding my phone out toward them. "There was this Nazi out in Michigan, he got every Black nurse in a ward reassigned so their 'filthy jigaboo' fingers wouldn't touch his newborn alabaster child."

Neither of them paid attention to what I was saying. They were still holding hands, whispering to each other.

"What took you so long?" I asked Dove angrily. "I called you. I texted too." The irony of me accusing anyone of being remiss wasn't lost on me, so my words came out with added bitterness.

"I was on the train," he said bluntly, as if that explained everything. Then he let go of Bernice's hands and took off his backpack. "I went and got you something, baby." He reached in and gave her something small and white: a flat, folded paper bag.

My sister rustled the bag. "A card?" she asked.

"Two cards!" Dove said, beaming.

She examined them. One was a get-well greeting with a cartoon dog on it, the other an anniversary greeting with an illustration, the heads of two red roses. "But it's not our anniversary," she murmured.

"I know that," he said defensively. "I picked it for what it says inside. It's how I feel."

Bernice read it aloud: "'The years may pass and pass, but our love shall never grow old. Knowing you're mine makes me feel so alive. Each day with you shines like gold.'"

After she was done reciting that canned poetry, she smiled weakly. Dove took the paper bag from her linens, smoothed its wrinkles and folds, and then pointed at it. "Check this out, though. Look where I got them from."

Bernice recognized the logo, from the card shop she liked to visit, outside of which they had spoken for the first time.

"So what do you think?" he asked.

She scowled and closed her eyes. "It hurts."

"What?"

"My head," she said. "The medicine they gave me. It's not working. They didn't give me enough."

Dove rushed to press the call button. He was frantic when a nurse didn't come right away. I said I could ask at the nurses' station, but when I stood he blocked my path, insisting he would do it. I really did want to go—to do something for my sister, and to escape that room—but apparently it had to be him. He ran out into the hallway to let someone know my sister needed more for her pain.

After that, Dove would come to her hospital room, hold her hand, and sing. She was quiet around him, but when I was alone with her, she would talk, intent on expressing herself despite the trouble she was starting to have with her speech. I listened. I came to understand that this was the way she remembered our childhood, the way she always wanted it to be between us. I went as far into this fabrication as I could, until it, as well as the notion that she wasn't angry at me for not believing her, started to feel real. When she became too tired to talk, I would read to her from her library books.

Our mother arrived in the city to lend Bernice strength. Whenever she was at the hospital, Dove made sure he wasn't there. He knew she didn't approve of their marriage. She would sit in the chair by the foot of the bed, which seemed to calm my sister, but she would rise whenever a doctor or nurse came in, challenging every word they had to say. When the doctor told us one day that Bernice would be able to go home soon, our mother asked how on earth he could think such a thing. When he said the tests were clear, she said, "Well, how many more tests you got?" When he said Bernice's pain was under control, she asked him how he could possibly know.

Despite our mother's protestations, Bernice was discharged. A few days later she suffered a massive stroke. Back at the hospital, she passed away. Our mother and I were there in the room. I would have imagined my sister's last breath as a tremendous thing, but it wasn't; it was no different from any other. The moment that breath was released, however, her face straightened, settled, went smooth. Our mother felt that Bernice had transformed. "She's my little baby again," she said. "She looks just like she did as a baby."

Her voice was soft when she said this, but afterward it became hard and enormous, like a slab of iron, and she hurled it at every doctor and nurse she saw. She was my sister's guardian, fiercely so, calling them murderers and demanding that they admit they had killed Bernice. She even made it difficult for the body to be attended to.

Dove arrived at the hospital during a respite in our mother's tirade, but the sight of him, ugly with crying, roused her again, and to an even greater degree. She started screaming her accusations at him. He was shocked, stricken; he had probably expected the three of us, in grief, to have a family embrace. I told him to go away, to go downstairs and wait in the cafeteria. He took a moment to compose himself and then complied, but his leaving had no effect on our mother's rage. It got so bad I had to restrain her. I held her in my arms and told her she had to calm down. She turned her head so that our noses almost touched, her eyes suddenly lucid, and wider than I'd ever seen them. "You did this too," she said, "you're one of them, you're a murderer." She kept saying it, with unblinking composure, until it became a kind of chant. After a long time, her voice shrank into a murmur. Then all she did was breathe in and out, heavily, and allow herself to go limp in my arms.

Our mother stayed with me in the Crown Heights apartment as we conducted the costly business of settling Bernice's affairs. She slept in the bedroom—Dove had gone back to his father's place in Harlem—and as usual I slept on the love seat.

Dove didn't come to the funeral. Some of Bernice's old co-workers came, as did many of the students she had advised. The coach was there too. I was surprised to see that many people there for her, but their presence, which confirmed she wasn't as isolated as I thought, made me feel worse. When it was my turn to take the lectern and speak about my sister, I couldn't. This wasn't because I hadn't prepared a speech for her. As I sat there in the front pew, words flowed easily into my mind, just as I had expected. It wasn't a problem of being unable to think of what to say. But the words that came were the bloated kind one used to satisfy the unknowable and therefore impossible expectations of

others, words that shined a light so dazzling it washed out every
distinctive feature. Our mother, sitting to my left, turned to me.
Her expression pleaded with me at first, and then demanded I
rise, but I was unable to get up from my seat.

When we got home, she put on her eye mask and earplugs
and went directly to bed. So she was spared the mess and noise
of my sorrow. That night, as the coach lurched around upstairs,
I lay awake sobbing. I kept thinking how unbearable the drama
of her loss was, and how unbearable my role in it felt too. Her
medical treatment could have been better—it simply should have
been better—but why had I expected that it would be? A better
version of me would have pushed them to do more. Something
as routine as an MRI might have saved Bernice's life. Despite
everything I knew, I couldn't believe that there could be so many
obstacles. I couldn't believe how difficult it could be to take care
of somebody else.

I grabbed my laptop and opened it. As the blue screen glowed
in the darkness of the apartment, a memory came to mind, of
Bernice and me as children. We were in our parents' bedroom,
wearing our mother's clothes, our small feet in her big shoes, our
limbs hidden in the sleeves of her blouses, her headscarves draped
loosely around our necks. We stood side by side in front of their
mirror, looking at ourselves, our mouths winged and reddened
from sucking on cherry ice pops. And then she began to narrate
tall tales about us, about who we were and what we had done
and the business we would conduct brilliantly in the future. I
wondered about that. Had it actually happened, or was I just
imagining another story she had told me in the hospital? It didn't
matter. I hit a key on the laptop to awaken the screen again.
I opened a blank document and typed: *My sister Bernice is dead*. I
wrote it as a simple matter of fact, as a way to begin accepting it,

but then I kept typing. The document became something like a eulogy, but a very honest and private one. No flash, no oratory. It was just for me.

Not too long ago, after our mother had left the city and I had finally managed to find steady work, I reached out to Dove. Almost all of his records were still in the apartment, crates in every room, so he must have stopped working gigs. With Bernice's books returned to the library and her quartz lined neatly on the console table, it was Dove's stuff alone that gave the apartment its oppressive character. He said he would rent a van and come to the apartment to get his records. We decided on the arrangements and it felt like a larger, unspoken agreement had been made between us.

The sound of his singing got louder as he came up the stairs and approached the door. He knocked, and when I opened it he stood there haggard and stooped, and his headphones hung like an anchor from his neck. An unflattering beard grew like patches of moss along his pallid cheeks and jaw. I got two beers from the refrigerator and, for no reason he or I could have articulated, we clinked our bottles together. We sat on the love seat and he glanced at the quartz. Then he looked up at the framed photograph of Bernice, our mother, and me, back on its nail.

"I always hated that damn picture," he said. "Bernice is so ugly in it, just a sad-ass, ugly-ass kid. Me and her took plenty of pictures together, nice ones I framed, but she never put none of them up. Never posted any online. Nothing." He tilted his head back and took a noisy sip from his beer. "Don't tell me you're gonna stay here."

"No," I said, "I couldn't do that. But I have to for now."

He pointed the bottle up at the ceiling. "How's the coach?"

"Gone."

"Gone?"

"Gone," I said. "Why didn't you come to her service?"

Dove turned toward the air shaft. "I just couldn't, okay?" He took a long drink of beer. "Hey, I have to tell you something, professor—no disrespect, all right?" he said. "I'm just telling you in case you run into us on the street or something. I started seeing someone new. I know it's real soon, but it's not like I was looking. I swear to God I wasn't. Truth be told, she came after me. And she's great, she really is. A girl you can't say no to. She's the kind of girl who puts your pictures on the wall." He took his phone from his pocket as if to show me something, but then thought better of it. "She likes who I am, is what I'm saying. She's not ashamed of me, you know."

I was quickly losing any sympathy I felt for him.

"Man," he said, staring up at the wall again, "I really fucking hate that photo."

"It was her favorite," I said.

"It makes sense, I guess, the way you two turned out. Must have been hard growing up with a mother like that. I mean, look at her. You know, I still have nightmares about that shit she said to me, at the hospital." He shook his head. His eyes were wet.

I could have explained to Dove that our mother had been screaming her charges of murder to nearly everyone she saw that day, that in her rage and grief he was just another person she could blame. But I didn't tell him. Nor did I tell him how she had leveled her accusations at me. I didn't want to give him the comfort of thinking he and I were the same.

"*I* killed Bernice? *Me*? I loved her," he was saying now. "All I ever did was love her."

"But how does it feel," I asked, "to know she never loved you back?"

Dove's jaw tightened. "She married me."

I nodded. "But she was already sick then—you understand that, right? What happened to her was already happening. A sick woman married you, but she didn't love you." I was holding my beer so tightly I could have shattered the glass. I set it down on the floor. "She told me she *never* did," I said, which wasn't true, but punishing him was easier than punishing myself. And for the moment, at least, it felt good. "And here you are," I added, "thinking a girl putting your picture in a frame means anything at all."

Dove stood and sniffed, drank the rest of his beer, and set the bottle down on the floor. He stepped away from me and went over to where the crates of his records, grimed with dust, were stacked against a wall.

It was clear at once, from how he moved, that my words had broken him, in a way that might never be repaired. He crouched on the balls of his feet and slowly began to flip through his records. I watched as he moved silently around the little apartment. Before he hauled out the crates, his fingers touched every single sleeve of his vinyl, making a methodical inventory. He had to be sure, you see, that nothing else he claimed or cared for had been taken away.

ACKNOWLEDGMENTS

My gratitude to Stanford University, the Lannan Foundation, the University of Iowa, and the American Academy in Rome, whose support made it possible for me to draft, revise, and finish the stories that compose this collection.

Thank you to Jin Auh, for your clarity, energy, advocacy, and discernment, and for always knowing how and when to proceed. Additional thanks to Luke Ingram, and to Alexandra Christie, Elizabeth Pratt, and Abram Scharf.

Thank you to Jenna Johnson, for your confidence in me, for your enduring enthusiasm, and for your keen, thoughtful editing. Additional thanks to Lianna Culp, Carrie Hsieh, and the entire team at Farrar, Straus and Giroux. Special thanks to Na Kim, for your beautiful, perceptive artistry.

Thank you to the magazine editors who had forthright belief in these stories, especially Brigid Hughes at *A Public Space*.

Thank you to my fellow fiction writers at the Wallace Stegner Program: Jacob Albert, Brendan Bowles, Neha Chaudhary-Kamdar, Yoon Choi, Lydia Conklin, Devyn Defoe, Matthew Denton-Edmundson, Darri Farr, Kate Folk, Sterling HolyWhite-

Mountain, F.T. Kola, Gothataone Moeng, Michael Sears, Rose Whitmore. Thank you to my excellent teachers there, particularly to Chang-rae Lee and Elizabeth Tallent, for your genuine and unambiguous kindness.

Thank you to the following writers, all brilliant witnesses, whose work continually provides inspiration and instruction, and to whose call I sometimes dare to imagine these stories were crafted in response: James Baldwin, Gina Berriault, Gwendolyn Brooks, Mavis Gallant, Natalia Ginzburg, Shirley Hazzard, Edward P. Jones, Yiyun Li, James Alan McPherson, Alice Munro, Ann Petry, Jean Stafford, William Trevor. Thank you to the artists, scholars, and everyday people who tell ghost stories, who recognize the presence and power of what haunts us.

Thank you to Lan Samantha Chang, for your leadership, wisdom, and care. Thank you to Corey Campbell, Charles D'Ambrosio, Garth Greenwell, Donika Kelly, and Margot Livesey, for the lifeline of your good company in Iowa City during the otherwise lonesome days of the pandemic. Thank you to Marilynne Robinson for your generous hospitality. Thank you to Bennett Sims for thinking of me. Thank you to those I don't even know to thank by name, who have supported me or my work from behind the scenes.

My heartfelt gratitude to my family, my colleagues, my students, my readers, and my friends.

A Note About the Author

Jamel Brinkley is the author of *A Lucky Man*, which won the Ernest J. Gaines Award for Literary Excellence and was a finalist for the National Book Award, the PEN/Robert W. Bingham Prize, the Story Prize, the John Leonard Prize, and the Hurston/Wright Legacy Award. He has also been awarded the Rome Prize, an O. Henry Award, a Wallace Stegner Fellowship, and a Lannan Foundation Fellowship. His work has appeared in *The Paris Review*, *A Public Space*, *Ploughshares*, and *The Best American Short Stories*. He was raised in the Bronx and Brooklyn and currently teaches at the Iowa Writers' Workshop.